Calabasas Wife War

RAE WEISER

DEDICATION

For Jason, Dylan and Cooper,
always and forever.

AUTHOR'S NOTE

This is a work of fiction. Names, characters and incidents either are the product of the author's imagination or are used fictitiously. Any resemblance to actual persons, living or dead, or events, is entirely coincidental unless intentional. However, the author would like to state that she has met many women who live in Calabasas, California, who act just like the characters in this book.

The author would also like to apologize to the City of Calabasas. While the author is aware that not all Calabasas residents are rich, materialistic and good-looking, she was forced to embellish these myths because she read a literary agent's blog that said to get a publishing deal, do not write about real life because real life is boring.

CANDY'S SCREWED UP

CHAPTER ONE

It was only ten past eleven when the day turned to crap. I slammed the door of my Mercedes CLK on my right index finger in the parking lot of the Calabasas Tennis and Swim Center and crushed my nail.

"Shit! Shit! Shit!" I screamed as I pulled off the mangled acrylic tip.

"Mommy, she said shit, shit, shit." A little boy walking by in an inflated one piece swimsuit, packing floaties in the lining, said.

"Jason, we don't say that word." The mom told her son while giving me a dirty look.

"Shit. Shit. Shit." He said again and again.

"I'm sorry." I yelled out while shaking my aching finger. It hurt. The tip of my nail was crushed and jagged. I just knew it would irritate me until I could get it fixed, but I didn't have time to get to the nail salon. I was already late for my pre-game meeting with Mindy at the pool.

We were playing doubles at noon against Stacy and Katie, two housewives we pretended to like, but considered our enemies. They won our last match even though Stacy's eyes were still swollen from her puffy eye surgery and Katie's teeth were in pain from over-

1

bleaching, because I kept hitting long. I didn't mean to, it was just an off day for me on the court. Mindy was furious that we lost. She warned me that if we didn't win the rematch, she'd kill me. She was joking, of course, but Mindy isn't the kind of friend you want to disappoint.

Holding my Dior bag that's twice as wide as my hips thanks to palates, I hurried through the clubhouse and came out the glass doors to the pool. On the other side, I spotted Mindy posing in her Christian Audigier Royal Panther in Black bikini on a chaise. I spotted it first on the rack at Neiman Marcus, but after she threw a fit in the dressing room, I agreed that she could buy it even though I thought it looked better on me.

Mindy waved at me. I hurried over.

A young lifeguard sitting high on the lifeguard tower checked me out as I passed by with eyes hidden behind Ray Ban shades. He ran his fingers through his feathered blonde hair and unhooked his pucca shell necklace that was stuck on his right nipple. He was young, but still, he was hot. He had the look of a surfer, tan feet in Billabong flip-flops, red Quicksilver board shorts, bronze skin, hair free chest, wide shoulders and a six pack of abs, but I don't think he ever went surfing. Malibu beach was only a twenty minute drive from Calabasas through the Las Virgines Canyon, but he was always at the club.

The pool was busy. Kids bounced in and out of the water in the free swim area screaming nonsense. A cluster of Hispanic nannies swarmed under an umbrella afraid to step out of the shade. Close by, two old men stood by the lap lanes in wet Speedos that clung to their floppy packages like Saran Wrap. They were always at the pool dressed like this. Putting themselves on display seemed to be how they got off in retirement. I didn't want to be the one to break it to them that they were obscene in a Speedo, but seriously somebody needed to. Their old bodies were melting like lit candlesticks.

"Candy, why are you always late?" Mindy said as I approached.

"I slammed my finger in my car door and broke my nail."

"Don't snap at me." Mindy said.

"I'm not snapping." I set down my bag and put my towel on the lounge chair. "It's just... look, there's blood." I held out my finger.

"Barely any. You're over-reacting."

"I'm not. It hurt."

There was blood on the surface of my nail bed. It just wasn't enough for Mindy.

A water drenched girl in a pink poke-a-dot bikini ran beside Mindy's chair, sprinkling water on Mindy's foot.

The lifeguard yelled, "Walk," into his megaphone.

"Little girl." Mindy said in her deepest alto tone that made her sound so scary.

The girl froze. Her drenched pigtails were stuck together and looked like upside down horns.

Mindy lowered her sunglasses and fixed her green eyes on the shivering girl. They were the exact color of the eyes of a black cat that roamed the alley behind the apartment building I lived in when I was eight years old. It meowed all night in a wicked high-pitched tone that sounded like it was coming to get me.

"Wipe that water off my foot." Mindy told the girl.

"NANNY!" The girl screamed, then ran into the arms of her Hispanic nanny hiding in the shade.

"Mindy, oh my God, you scared her."

"I know." She said with a slight smile as she wiped the water off her leg. I noticed she painted her nails charcoal to match her swimsuit. Mindy always liked to match.

I took off my bathing suit cover and rubbed sunscreen on the back of my thighs. I felt the eyes of the young lifeguard on me. I looked up and caught him checking out my ass. It wasn't his fault. I was wearing a Brazilian cut bottom that teased like a G-string. No teenage boy in the middle of a hormone surge could resist. Even though I was just over forty-years-old, I was in the best shape of my life. You could bounce a quarter off my ass.

"Damn it! It's burning." I shook my finger and wiped it with my towel.

"What's wrong now?"

"The sunscreen… it's burning… it got all over my broken nail! I don't know if I can play with this. We need to reschedule."

"We're not canceling."

I sat down on the edge of the chair with my back to Mindy, hoping she didn't notice that my voice cracked on the word reschedule.

"Are you crying over a broken nail?"

Mindy's upper lip raised, like how an angry dog raises his gums to show his teeth before he bites, as she waited for me to answer.

"No!"

I was about to cry. My emotional melt-down started three days before. The slightest thing would set me off and I wasn't sure why.

"You are! Oh, my God, this can't be happening to me. Not today. We have a game in less than thirty minutes."

I couldn't help it. Tears started flowing out of my eyes.

"What's wrong?"

"You'll think it's stupid. Just forget it!" I snapped back.

"Don't snap!" She was right to be annoyed with me. This time I really did bite her head off.

"I can't help it…. I'm… I'm… never mind!"

Mindy's face softened and oh, my God, she seemed compassionate. Then she spoke in this really, really sweet voice and placed her hand on my arm. "Candy, I'm your best friend. You can tell me anything."

I sat back and hid my tear drenched eyes under my Marc Jacobs shades.

"I think... I think... just forget it."

"What? You think what? Just tell me. You will eventually anyway."

"I think I'm really shallow." I confessed with as much guilt as a murderer confesses their crime.

Mindy looked away dramatically and put her Prada sunglasses back on. Any ounce of compassion she had for that brief moment disappeared.

"Oh, please, Candy, if you're shallow then I'm shallow because we're exactly alike and I'm not shallow."

I turned to Mindy and was blinded by sunlight reflecting off her three carat solitaire diamond necklace. It sat between her large breasts. You couldn't miss it.

"Your diamond is blinding me. Put it away."

Mindy tucked the rock into her cleavage.

"My boobs still hurt four months after getting them."

They hurt because they were too big. She was feeling old after turning forty-three and thought bigger knockers would give her a lift. I respected her for getting double D's. Staying attractive in our forties wasn't easy. Torturing ourselves with diet, exercise and cosmetic procedures was a must if we wanted to keep our milf status.

"How do we know we're not shallow?" I asked.

Mindy pressed around the outer rims of her breasts and sucked in air threw clinched teeth as if touching them was painful. It could be taken two ways, as a woman in pain or a woman on the edge of sexual completion.

"We know because every time someone asks us for money, we give it to them." Mindy said as she turned over on her stomach as if tanning her back, but we were

5

both coated in Chanel UV Essentiel Protective UV Care Anti-Pollution SPF50 PA+.

We got our tans at Zen Tanning Studio where their mission is to caress your skin with soft tones to enliven your color. We wanted the look of a tan, but the wrinkles, God forbid. We'd already been to eight Botox parties since January. I worried that injecting too much botulism into my face would one day backfire. You know, when you read years later about something everyone thought was safe causing cancer.

Mindy wasn't concerned. She told me any risk was worth it if it made you look younger. Besides, she didn't like to smile too much so having a paralyzed face didn't bother her. She once told me rarely smiling made women fear her and men think she's nasty in bed. She was right about the first thing. Three moms in our neighborhood confessed to me that they were friends with Mindy only to make sure they never got on her bad side. I told them that Mindy's attitude is just an act and once they really got to know her, they'd really like her. As for her being nasty in bed, that was more than I wanted to know.

"Last night on the Discovery Channel, I saw a biography on Angelina Jolie. They showed a clip of her on the Today Show wearing a bandana on her head and no make-up, well it looked like she wasn't wearing make-up, and she still looked gorgeous."

"What in the hell are you talking about?" Mindy asked.

"Let me finish. She was in Namibia talking about all the suffering children in Africa. I'm forty-one already Mindy, forty frickin' one damned years old already and I've never done anything for suffering children."

"Angelina only did that stuff so all those countries will let her adopt one of their children." Mindy said. "It's so obvious."

I smacked her arm. "I'm serious. I'm beyond halfway to dead Mindy and I'm... I'm...." I started crying again. "I'm nothing."

I was going through something. I was looking for meaning in life. This wasn't like me. I usually only looked for brand names.

"That's not true, Candy. " Mindy said like I was an annoying child who bothered her. "You're... you're... something."

"Yeah, you can't even think of anything."

"Knock it off. You're being ridiculous. We've got a match in twenty minutes. This isn't the time to cry or worry about being shallow. It's time to think about smashing the ball down Stacy and Katie's throats."

Mindy was competitive, not sensitive. She liked to win so when we had a match, nothing else mattered.

"I can't stand those two." She raised her head so the diamond came out of her cleavage and swung down into her face. "They're going down." She said and pointed with her right index finger towards the ground like she planned to send them to hell. "Stacy's backhand is pretty good. Katie's sucks. We get the ball to her as much as possible, we're gonna win."

I wiped my eyes with the corner of my towel. "I can't help it. I'm half way through my life. Isn't there supposed to be something more?"

"Than what?"

"Than this?" I gestured to the pool where swimmers were doing laps, kids were swimming in the kiddy section and the hunky high school lifeguard watched over them in between sneaking glances at us.

Mindy turned over onto her back. Her breasts poked up to the sky. If they shot bullets, they could have taken out a few birds, maybe even a few planes.

"We've made it, Candy. This is it. We're married. We live in The Oaks, the most expensive gated community in Calabasas which is the Beverly Hills of the San Fernando Valley. We each have a child and a dog, and most important, lots of money. We not only have what everyone wants, but we are who everyone wants to be."

"How do you know?" I asked. "How do you know there's not a better life out there somewhere? Am I having mid-life crises?"

"No, you're not." Mindy said and pinched together the wings of a bee that landed on her belly button and flung it to her right.

"That was a bee you just picked up."

"Yeah. So?"

In Mindy's world, grabbing a bee with her hands was as normal as batting away a fly.

"Mindy, I'm serious. Something's wrong. I cry at a moments notice. I drove by Nordstroms and saw their half-yearly sale sign and didn't even think about going inside."

"You're not having a mid-life crisis. You're bored. You should have an affair." Mindy said.

"I don't cheat. I shop."

"Have sex with that cute lifeguard?"

Mindy pointed to the hot young lifeguard who was having a hard time keeping his eyes off me. Then I realized he was the boy who played the prince last year in the school play of Rapunzel that my daughter was in at Calabasas High School. It was a modern take on the Grimm Fairy tale. The Prince was a skateboarder and Rapunzel wasn't trapped in a tower, she willingly refused to come down from the second story of a rent controlled apartment building the city wanted to demolish. The moral of the story was that even poor people need a place to stay, even if it's gross.

"Mindy, I think he was in drama with Kelly last year. He's a senior. Seducing a seventeen year old is how you think I should get out of my depression? You're my best friend. You should be telling me I'm whacked out and that I should see a shrink and get some Prozac, not screw an underage kid!"

"Shrinks are quacks. Pills might not be a bad idea,

not Prozac, maybe Zoloft or Valium, but I'm telling you, that lifeguard's always looking at you. You could have him." She said with a half smirk, her way of laughing.

"But I don't want him! Maybe I am bored, but I'm not going after jailbait to fix it!" I said angrily, and then found myself laughing. "Why am I friends with you?"

"Because, I'm interesting." Mindy half smirked, again, put her head against the chaise and breathed in deep like a satisfied woman. Her breasts raised and fell as she inhaled and exhaled, as if her lungs.

Mindy was interesting. That wasn't a lie. She had a magnetism that made me stick around even though sometimes I knew she wasn't good for me. She reminded me of this friend I had in second grade named Paula. She was a Baptist preacher's daughter who always dared me to go into the boy's bathroom. Even though I got caught eight times and was the first second grader in the history of Cole Elementary to be permanently expelled and to earn the nickname Weenie Girl, it was worth it. I had fun. Until I met Paula, second grade was so boring.

My friendship with Mindy started seven years earlier at the park inside our gated community three days after we moved into our big house. I was dropping my daughter off with Maria, our Ecuadorian nanny I found the day before through a classified ad in the PennySaver. I was on my way to get three diamond gems replaced on my neon pink acrylic nails that had fallen off. I had my manicurist spell out my name in diamonds so each finger, starting with my pinky, had a letter… C.A.N.D.Y. It was part of my costume when I was a stripper that I just couldn't let go because I'd gotten into a habit of holding up my hand when someone asked me my name.

Mindy was at the jungle gym with her perfect figure yelling at some kid who just threw sand in her daughter's eyes. Her long brown hair swooshed side to side on her back like a windshield wiper even when she wasn't moving. She looked at me with her hunter green colored eyes that were framed by her perfectly waxed eyebrows and I was floored. Before she even spoke to me, I knew she had some kind of charisma that I didn't. She looked me up and down, settling on my bright pink diamond studded nails and her perfectly waxed eyebrows raised again. I got a bad feeling in my gut.

I had that same feeling when I was nineteen and I applied for a day job at Nordstrom's in Junior Fashions. The department manager was only in her early twenties, but I knew I wasn't going to get the job by the way she looked at me while reading my resume. My button-up was too tight in the chest and my D-Cup cleavage was showing through the holes between the buttons. The look on her face told me she thought I was white trash, so when she told me the pay was $6.95 an hour, I told her I was making $300 a night stripping. I picked up my Louie Vuitton purse I bought from Hot Tottie, a stripper who needed cash for an eight-ball, and said, "Drop twenty pounds and come see me over at the Bang Bang. I'll get you up on a pole so you can make you some real cash." And held in my tears as I strutted off.

Mindy looked away from my diamond studded neon pink acrylic nails and went back to handling a problem. Her daughter, Cindy, was crying and trying to wipe the sand out of her eyes. Elva, Mindy's nanny she flew up from Tijuana after finding her ad on the internet, was flushing Cindy's eyes out with water while Mindy debated if she should call 911. Mindy was on a jog and just happened to run by the park right when her daughter had the sand thrown in her eyes by another little girl. It was a good thing, because Elva didn't speak much English and didn't think it was necessary to call in for help. "No necesita." She kept saying to Mindy.

"You tell that little girl's nanny in Spanish to tell that little girl in English that I will be calling her mother!" Mindy told Elva. "I know which house she lives in."

Elva started talking to Maria in Spanish, but the girl who threw the sand said something to them in Spanish and all three of them laughed. Mindy became very angry.

"What did she say?" She asked Elva.

"I said, I heard you, weirdo." The girl said, and then stuck her tongue at Mindy.

"I know where you live. I know who your parents are and believe me little girl, this is not over." I heard Mindy say as I approached the scene.

"Hi, everyone. I'm Candy Katz."

Mindy turned to me again and I got sort of nervous because she was so mad at that little girl that she looked like she might take my head off. I didn't hold up my hand so she could see my name. With the missing diamonds on the D it read C.A.N.L.Y. and who wants to be called that.

"We just moved in down the street."

"Oh, my new neighbor with the handsome husband." Mindy said and sort of smiled. "I'm Mindy Klein. I live three houses down from you."

After that, Mindy and I became instant best friends. Since I was new to the neighborhood, Mindy became my lifeline to the social scene. She had a cocktail party to introduce me and my handsome husband, Tom, to the neighbors. She went through my wardrobe and told me which clothes I could no longer wear and then took me shopping. She forbid me from wearing neon pink nail polish with fake diamonds on my acrylic tips and burned all my tube tops. It was like having a stylist for free.

And as for that girl at the park, I never saw her again. Rumor has it that Mindy went to her house for a sit down with her parents later that night. No one knows for sure what Mindy said, but one week later her family put their house on the market and four weeks later moved out of The Oaks. It's kind of why some women in the neighborhood joke about not wanting to be on Mindy's bad side. They say she has some sort of Voodoo powers which Mindy and I just laughed about, because it was so not true.

But Mindy and me, we got a long great because we had so much in common. Both our homes were the Manors Plan 4, a Tuscan Villa in the prestigious Estates of the Oaks of Calabasas. Elegance from the outside in is what the handsome realtor told me and my husband, Tom, in the sales office as our daughter stole lollipops out of the candy basket. He said it had a gorgeous entertainer's yard complete with pool, spa, built-in barbeque, a grassy area, beautiful views and all the amenities you would expect, quality on a grand scale.

Tom didn't care about his spiel. He told the realtor he wanted to know the square footage, not his sales pitch. The agent said sixty five hundred square feet, five bedrooms and six point five baths. Even though we only had one child and were not planning on having anymore, we bought it. Tom had suddenly come into a lot of money and wanted a big house to show off. He'd been working a little for his father who owned a mortgage brokerage, but most of the money Tom had was handed to him by his dad. Tom was a bit of a playboy when we first met. He liked to hang out in strip clubs and party all night, which was lucky for me or else I never would have met him.

But once we had Kelly his father yelled at him all the time that he needed to get it together so he could take care of his stripper, which was me, and his kid, who was our daughter Kelly. That's how he always referred to us. Luckily, he passed away before Kelly got too old to get her feelings hurt by her grandpa. On his death bed he told Tom, "The company is yours. This is your one shot, Tom. Don't fuck it up." That's how Tom got his company and his high paying salary.

Luckily Tom and Mindy's husband Barry hit it off, even though Barry was in his late fifties and had a personality dryer than lizard skin. Soon after we moved into The Oaks, the four of us were having dinner together every weekend. Barry and Mindy were an odd couple. He was bald and overweight, but Mindy was so proud she hooked him because he had money.

"Candy, marrying wealthy men is my career. It's how I survive." She told me when we were shopping for a diamond tennis bracelet for her. "Sure, there's a little work involved. Some obligatory blow jobs here and there, but for the most part I hardly ever see Barry. He's always at work making money and I'm always busy spending it. It's a win-win situation."

I was trying to settle down from my freak out when everyone was ordered out of the pool. The lifeguards were herding out the swimmers from the water to do a chemical treatment. Too many kids were having accidents intentionally and the chemical levels needed to be adjusted. I watched the jailbait lifeguard casually strut up and down the deck asking people to get out of the pool.

"I'm not having sex with the lifeguard, Mindy. I don't have jailbait in mind." I didn't know exactly what I had in mind, but something was wrong with the universe. My chi was out of balance or something like that was off. "You and I don't cheat." I reminded her.

Mindy gawked at other men in a way a cat looks at a rat, but she didn't sleep around. I was sure of this because I knew everything about Mindy Klein and she knew everything about me.

It's horrible, I know, but if she did find some young guy on the side, it wouldn't bother me because Barry was about as attractive as a trash can. What's worse, he suffered from indigestion and was always gassy. How she had sex with that man was beyond me, but they did every Tuesday and Thursday night, right after he came home from work. He had a schedule he liked her to keep. Twice a week was all his heart could handle and twice a week was as much as Mindy could take.

"But if he was eighteen?" Mindy said about the

underage lifeguard, as if making it legal would make it all right.

"Not even if he was eighteen."

"Eighteen is legal."

"But immoral."

"Not necessarily. Depends on who you ask."

"Ask his parents then." I told her as I looked over at the high school boy we were discussing. He was talking to another lifeguard and both were checking out our breasts.

"They're checking out our tits." Mindy said, then smiled as she pushed up her breasts and shifted so they shook side to side. "Just shaking the pacifiers so they have something to think about tonight when they're rubbing their shafts under the sheet."

"Jesus, Mindy! You're terrible!"

"I know." She said with a sneer. "At least I keep it spicy."

And even though I was in the middle of a crisis, I started laughing again. Mindy could always do that to me. Life was never boring when Mindy was around. She had a way of shaking things up. It was like being on a drunken binge where anything goes without the alcohol. Never a day went by that she didn't say something inappropriate or do something inappropriate. I thought she was hilarious. She didn't worry about what she said or what she did to other people. Never once had she mentioned starving children. She was utterly free of caring about anyone other than herself.

"Nothing's worse than boredom except poverty." Mindy said.

"Here, here." I raised up my bottle of Evian water to toast and took a swig.

Poverty sucks and I knew this first hand. I grew up literally without a dime in my pocket. My mom was so cash poor that every time I searched the bottom of her purse for change, I didn't find any. We were a welfare family and even though I tried to forget those days, I was still haunted by one trip we made to an industrial building where we waited outside at the bottom of a conveyor belt for a box of food to come. It had just stopped raining and there was a hole on the side of my Wallabee shoe. Water had seeped inside so as I walked back to the car carrying a box of poor people food, my socks got soaked and water swoosh between my toes. Then a car full of teenagers swerved so their car tires went into the gutter and scummy water sprayed all over me. I set the soggy box of food down, sat down on top of it and broke into tears. Then, if you can believe my luck, it started raining.

"Candy Katz, get your butt off our food and get in the car!" My mom yelled at me from down the sidewalk. "You can cry about it on the way home! God's pissin' on us again!"

God's pissin' is what my mom always said when it rained.

"No!" I yelled back at her for the first time in my life, and did not move. It was the defining moment of my life. The cardboard box caved as it got soggy. Something crunchy inside was being smashed, probably potato chips or corn flakes. I looked up at the heavens. "God, you better make sure I ain't poor when I'm old." I told the man upstairs.

Six months later I got my first Malibu Barbie Doll. My mom bought it at a second hand store and some kid colored her face with a brown marker. I scrubbed her with Ajax cleanser and an SOS pad. The brown faded so she looked like a Latin Malibu Barbie who had emigrated from Brazil and dyed her hair blonde. I was only seven years old, but the minute I saw her I knew the way out for me. If I was thin, blonde and big breasted, I'd find my Malibu Ken who would take care of me.

I had séances to make Barbie come alive so I could talk to her about how she stayed so thin and had such big boobs. I wanted desperately to switch bodies with her. I made up spells, created potions out of snippets of her hair and prayed that I'd turn out to be just like Malibu Barbie. I just knew that if I had her figure, gorgeous blonde hair and perky breasts that I'd hook a man with money. I'd be happy. After many years of stripping and two breast augmentations, I found my Malibu Ken in Tom. Not only was Tom handsome and came from a wealthy family, but I was completely head over heels in love with him. It took many years and three hundred and forty-two lap dances to find him, but finally my dream had come true.

"I'm not interested in an under-aged lifeguard. I'm happily married." I reminded Mindy. "Tom is handsome, faithful and we're still in love after almost twenty years together."

"Right." Mindy said. "I forgot." She was smiling, I think. I couldn't be sure because she looked away.

"What?"

"Nothing." Mindy looked at her watch.

"You don't think me and Tom are in love?"

"I didn't say that."

"The look on your face did."

"Candy, stop being difficult. We have to go change. "

"Mindy, can't we tell them I broke a nail and reschedule?"

"Seriously, Candy? Unless we want to suffer humiliation at the next neighborhood cocktail party, we have to make sure those bitches go down today." She sat up, looked me straight in the eyes and snapped her fingers in my face. "Pull it together. I need your head in the game." Mindy had turned wicked again.

"All right. I'll do it." I said like a woman who agrees to have sex with her husband when she really doesn't want too. Giving in was easier. Mindy would just chew at me until she got her way and I wasn't in the mood for it.

I packed up my magazines in my Dior bag, stood up and wrapped my skirt around my waist for my walk into the locker room. The skirt wasn't necessary, really. So sheer you could see through it, it was a clothing accessory I liked to wear because little skirts are just so damn cute.

I turned around to put on my Swarovski Sweet Treats Hollywood wedge flip-flops when my toe got caught by the chair leg and I fell backwards. Right when I thought my behind was about to hit the cement, someone caught me. I looked up and starring down at me was the sexy, muscular and legally off limits lifeguard!

"I've got you." He said.

Jailbait! Bars! Handcuffs! But wow, with the blue sky framing his blonde hair and his mocha eyes staring into mine, I was mesmerized and couldn't speak.

The lifeguard lifted me upright, quick and with the strength of a full grown man because he had biceps the size of Popeye's and an eight pack of lean meat for abdominals that waved like rippling water as he flexed. In a second, he had me flipped back up as erect as my plastic Malibu Barbie doll and there was nothing I could do about it.

"Thanks" I said, flustered while brushing my sheer skirt flat and my long blonde hair out of my face.

He let go of my waist and held out his hand out for me to shake. "Brad." He said. The sly smile on his face told me this kid was trying to pick me up.

"Brad." I repeated as I shook his hand and stared at him speechless like a school girl with a crush. And then, oh my God, a chill ran up my spine! "Thank you, Brad." I said like a mother of a seventeen year old girl should. "I'm Mrs.," I emphasized Mrs. so he would know I'm married, "Candy Katz."

"Yeah. I know who you are."

"You do?"

"You're Kelly's mom."

"Oh, yes, yes. Kelly is my daughter and I'm her

17

mom. That's right."

It had been many years since I'd felt this way around the opposite sex. But this wasn't about wanting to jump in the sack with this kid because I was losing my mind over a mid-life crisis. This feeling was because I was sure I was going to hell for even considering what he'd be like in the bed.

"We're in drama together." He said like a high school kid, while moving his fingers through his hair and looking like a hot James Dean with muscles.

Mindy was bending over to gather up her stuff and had her bikini wearing butt pushed way up high. It was so embarrassing. She should have bent at the leg, but knowing Mindy she intentionally did this to tease Brad. We looked at her butt.

"That's Mindy Klein."

"I've seen you both around." Brad said.

Mindy looked up. "I'm sure you have." Mindy said with a half scowl, half smile because she got an extra dose of Botox two days before. "Looks like you've met your prince charming, Candy." Mindy added just to annoy me. I got the urge to slap her.

"Bite your tongue, Mindy." I demanded and looked back at Brad, who didn't seem to be going anywhere so we stood there together for an uncomfortable moment. "Okay, so um, Mindy, time to go!" I added hoping to get him to move off, but this kid still wasn't budging and I needed him to go away because having an under-aged teen make me feel so nervous was just so wrong! "Well, um, we've gotta go. We've got a match."

"Come watch, Brad. It's gonna be brutal." Mindy said when she stood upright.

"Cool. Sounds harsh. I'll check it." Brad said.

He'll check it!

I gulped.

No! No! No!

This can't be happening to me today!

I gave Mindy a dirty look.

"Oh, no, you shouldn't, really, there's nothing to watch, nothing to check, just me and Mindy playing doubles with two other moms. It's nothing to see, really, just, it's sort of stupid. We're not even that good. It's not even a real match. Half the time we lose track of the score."

"Candy, it is too!" Mindy said when she stood up. "We're going to smash the ball down their throats over and over.

"Cool. I'm game." He said.

Cool! I'm game? Was that a double meaning?

This day was not going at all like I planned. I was at a crucial stage of my life. I had screwed up chi, an outlandish desire to help suffering children and now I was being played on in my vulnerable state by a handsome, and I mean really handsome high school boy I was sure was going to wank-off that night thinking about me. If only I could get back to thinking about simple things like how I look in my True Religion jeans, I'd be back to normal.

"Yeah, well, we're gonna be late," I said. "Thanks again for catching me, Brad."

"Anytime." He said and winked before he walked away.

You know how some women toss their hair back to be sexy and show a guy that they're interested. This kid winked like that, in a way that told me he was available if I was willing. He moved his hands through his hair, then looked back at me and smiled. For just a minute, I wondered what he would look like without board shorts. God or the universe or the force, whoever or whatever was out there was going to strike me down for sure.

"Mindy, why did you tell him to come watch?"

Mindy finally had her Juicy Couture Pammy Top Zip velour tote over her shoulder so we headed towards the club.

"Oh relax."

"Anytime? I mean, God, Mindy, why didn't he just kiss me? What is wrong with kids these days? I mean, really. Anytime?"

"Now listen, get the ball to Katie. She sucks and I want to win." Mindy was in game mode. The incident with Brad could have been ten years ago.

"Do you know what just happened?" I asked as we walked into the club.

"Yeah, a hot young lifeguard just saved you from getting a bruised tailbone. That would have affected your game more than a broken nail. Did you bring your white Nike tennis outfit with the pink border on the skirt and the pink and white shoes?" She asked.

"Yes."

"Good. I like us to look like a team."

We made our way past the weight lifting room, the cardio room, the yoga studio and the germ filled kids club to the ladies locker room where Stacy and Katie were heading out.

"Hello, ladies. Ready for a great game?" Mindy asked Stacy and Katie sweetly, as if they were her best friends.

"Sure are." Stacy said.

"You two are going down." I said in a humorous way and we all laughed except for Katie, who looked down at my feet. I was worried that something was wrong with the French pedicure I got the day before. Sometimes they don't get the lines straight with the white tips and that can be quite embarrassing, but my pedicure looked fine to me.

"Word got out about our rematch. We've got a crowd." Stacy said.

"A crowd? How fun!" Mindy said while looking quite fierce. Even when she was excited, she looked like a stoned-faced dominatrix.

A crowd!

I didn't feel like playing in front of a crowd. It was an off day for me. My nail was broken, my yin and yang were twisted up and I was just groped by a seventeen year old who took my breath away. Now I had to play tennis in front of a crowd full of competitive rich women who would be analyzing not only my athletic ability, but my outfit as well.

"See you on the court?" Stacy said as she turned to walk through the doors, flinging her braided pony tail so it whipped by barely an inch from Mindy's face. I almost laughed, but my attention was drawn to Katie, who gave me the weirdest look.

"Did you see that? She tried to hit me in the face with her pony tail." Mindy whispered once the locker room door shut.

"Oh, come on. She just turned her head." I said, as I entered the combination on my locker.

Mindy looked around the locker room to see if anyone else was there and might hear what she was saying. "She is such a bitch. I'm gonna smash a ball into her face out on the court."

"Okay, now you're the one who needs to relax." I told her as I opened my locker and got a whiff of Channel No. 5 perfume. Inside I saw a note on pink stationary folded in half that had "Candy - For Your Eyes Only" written on the top.

"Just a game? No, it's not. I'm in the middle of a war here. Do you know what Stacy said behind my back?" Mindy said as she came closer. I shut my locker door so she wouldn't see the note.

"No."

Mindy sniffed the air. "Do you smell that? Channel No. 5. I don't know why Katie always wears that scent. It's perfume for old ladies."

"So what'd Stacy say?" I asked as I changed into my tennis clothes.

"She said I married Barry for his money."

21

"You did."

"That's not my point."

"What is your point?"

"She shouldn't be talking about me behind my back. That is the point." Mindy explained as she took off her bikini top and stood in front of me with her double D's exposed. "Are they straight?"

"Mindy, I don't need to see those again Every time we're in here you show me your tits." I said as I gestured to her breast.

"Because you tell me the truth. Are they still even, because I looked last night and I thought the right was slightly higher?"

Yikes! I felt bad. I had been lying. I'd never want to be the one to tell her the left nipple was lower than the right so I lied again. "I'm not looking at your tits again, Mindy. Ask your husband." I told her and lucky for me, she put on her sports bra.

"They're a bit much for Barry. He starts panting and I'm afraid he's going to have a heart attack."

I put on my Nike tennis outfit, then went to the mirror and wrapped my hair into a pony tail that I pulled through the back of my cap. My broken acrylic nail hooked on some hair and I couldn't get it free. "Damn, nail." I said as I ripped a chunk of my blonde hair out and I almost started crying again. Being this sensitive just wasn't normal.

"I want blood out there on the court today." Mindy said to me like a drill sergeant while on her way into a restroom stall. "And no more crying. It's getting ridiculous already."

"I'm not crying." I yelled as I hurriedly opened my locker.

"You are too! Over a broken nail!" Mindy yelled from the bathroom stall.

I pulled out the note, sniffed it to smell the Channel No. 5 perfume because even though Mindy thought it was for old women, I loved the way it smelled. I opened the note. Inside it had one sentence.

MINDY IS FUCKING TOM.

"HOLY SHIT!" I screamed.

Mindy flushed the toilet and hobbled out of the stall pulling up her underwear while her tennis skirt still flipped up onto her belly. If I wasn't so shocked by the letter, I would have laughed because she looked so funny.

"What is wrong with you today?" She yelled at me.

My mouth was open so far I could have shoved my fist in it. I didn't know if I should ask if she was sleeping with my husband. I had no proof. I had an anonymous note most likely from Katie and Mindy was my best friend. I trusted her.

"Spider. Huge spider." I said, while trying to catch my breath.

"So just kill it."

"Can't." I said and started hyper-ventilating.

"Why not?" She said, frustrated. "Oh, where did it go? I'll squash it." Mindy looked around the floor for the spider

"It's okay. It's gone now." I was panting and had my right hand over my heart as if ready to say the Pledge of Allegiance.

"What's that?" Mindy said, pointing to the note I still held in my hand.

"Oh, ah, grocery list. I have to go to the store later." I told her and tossed the note into the locker, slammed it shut and spun the dial on the combination lock so she couldn't get to it.

"Oh, God, just have your maid do it. I never grocery shop."

If there was anyone I didn't want to be at war with, it was with Mindy. But I decided right then that if she was sleeping with my husband, I'd kill her.

Mindy looked at herself in the mirror, checking to

23

make sure not one part of her outfit was out of line, and then looked me over. "Candy, your skirt is stuck." She told me and unhooked my skirt from the built-in underwear attached to it.

I hadn't moved. I wasn't sure what to do or what to say.

"Let's go." She said, and tugged on my arm. "Snap out of it. It was just a stupid spider."

We grabbed our Prince rackets, our bottles of Evian water and headed out.

Early June in the San Fernando Valley can be a bit overcast. We call it June gloom, but this day was unusually hot. Stacy and Katie were volleying on the main court, already sweating as they hit warm up shots in front of an usually large crowd. My hands started to sweat. It was a hundred degrees out and on the court that felt like a hundred and ten.

"Idiots. They should be reserving their strength. They're gonna overheat." Mindy said to me as we placed our bottles of Evian water on the bench and took off our racket covers.

I glanced out at the crowd and there, amongst a thick crop of Calabasas moms and a few men so rich they didn't have to be at work, sat Brad leaning back against the bleacher behind him. He nodded his head to me. I looked away, mortified.

Mindy strolled onto the court cool as a cat. "Game time, ladies." Mindy yelled out sweetly to Stacie and Katie who had huddled on the other side to discuss their game strategy. Not a hint of Mindy's ferocious need to win showed. She was a master at deception.

Mindy and Stacy took their spots at the back court. Katie and I were at the net. I hunched over, held my racked at ready position and bent at the knees, ready to do an interception. I looked across the net at Katie.

"You wrote the note, didn't you?" I whispered.

"Oh, my God, how did you know?"

"It smelled like Channel No. 5, Katie, and you're

24

the only one I know under seventy-five who wears Channel No. 5."

"I think you should know that your BFF is sleeping with your husband." She admitted.

"Zero. Zero. Love. Love." Mindy yelled behind me and served, slicing the ball by Stacy before she could even see it.

"It's a lie. It can't be true. You're trying to throw me off to win the game?" I whispered as I smacked the ball, slamming it on the court in front of her. Katie missed the return, but Stacy sent it to Mindy on the back court.

"It's not a lie. I know someone who knows someone who saw them." Katie said, while hunched over and bouncing side to side.

"I don't believe it."

"It's true." Katie insisted.

Stacy returned the ball. It skimmed the net and dropped right in front of me. I missed an easy return. We lost a point.

"Time out!" Mindy yelled and ran up to me at the net. "Candy," she said while looking at me straight in the eyes and pointing two fingers back and forth between her eyes and mine. It was the gesture that meant war. "Focus."

Focus! I'll show you focus you two-timing bitch!

"Remember, this is war." Mindy whispered in my ear, and then patted me on the back like a coach does to a player before hustling back to the serve line.

I turned to Katie at the net. "Why should I trust you?" I said while prancing side to side. You have to prance in tennis, which is why I like the sport. It's so girly and the short skirts, so adorable.

I hit an overhead smash. I jumped high and caught a ball that would normally be out of my reach. I was angry so my adrenaline gave me the extra boost I needed. The ball drilled onto the court, then bounced up fast, hitting Stacy in the head.

"Ouch!" She screamed as she dropped her racket and held her forehead.

The crowd gasped.

Mindy ran up to me and whispered, "Good one," on her way to check on Stacy. I got an urge to smack her in the face, but figured I should check on Stacy first because she was bent forward and holding her forehead.

The three of us rushed over to Stacy.

"I'm so sorry."

"Let me see?" Mindy said.

Stacy lowered her hand. She had a red mark on her forehead the size of a tennis ball.

"It's a pretty big mark. Do you want to forfeit the match?" Mindy asked, almost drooling at the thought.

"Forfeit? Never! I'm fine. Let's go." Stacy growled to Mindy. "There's no blood. I can handle it."

This match between them was definitely war.

"She's fine!" Katie yelled out to the crowd.

"What are you two talking about at the net?" Mindy asked me as we headed back to our side of the court.

"Katie knows someone who is having an affair with someone's husband." I told Mindy, just to see her reaction. She wasn't fazed.

"Juicy." She said and licked her lips. "Tell me all about it after the match." She tapped me on the arm. "Remember, focus." She jogged back to the serve line.

I wanted to vomit. Seriously, who says juicy when they hear about a wife being cheated on?

I looked up in the stands. Brad leaned forward and kept his eyes on me. I didn't even have to look up in the stands to know he was watching me. I could feel it. Near him, eight women on the edge of their seats huddled in a mass, all Stacy and Katie's friends, gave me the evil eye.

"Sorry." I said to the women. "It was an accident." Sweat dripped between my fake C cups. They used to be double D's like Mindy's before I had them reduced. I was getting back-aches.

"Ready." Stacy yelled out as she bounced side to side on her tip-toes with her racket in position.

We played out Mindy's serve and then Stacy's, with each team winning one game. I don't know how I was able to hit the ball at all. My mind kept racing on and on about Mindy and Tom. I couldn't decide if I believed that my BFF was sleeping with my husband. It was like all those stories I'd heard about people having an out of body experience or were abducted by aliens. I just wasn't sure if it could be true.

Mindy was at the net. It was my turn to serve. I walked to the back of the court, seething in a way I hadn't since a stray dog that roamed our apartment building bit off my Malibu Barbie's head when I was twelve. If Mindy was sleeping with my husband, and Katie knew, then Stacy knew, and all those women in the stands knew. You know how gossip is. It spreads fast from person to person. It's like the Faberge shampoo TV commercial from the 1970's. If I tell two friends, and they tell two friends, and so on, and so on. I was searching for meaning that morning, and thought an excursion to Africa with a few pounds of food for the starving children was the answer, not learning that my best friend was ruining my marriage and that every wife in Calabasas probably knew. This was a disaster!

I grabbed two balls, tucked one in my ball pocket under the flap of my extra-mini Nike tennis skirt.

"What's the score?" I asked.

The women in the bleachers laughed.

Mindy looked back at me. "One. One. Love. Love. Candy, get it together." Mindy said as she gave me a dirty look.

I felt a twinge in my neck. My shoulders tensed and I could feel inside that I was ready to snap. Since getting that note, my mid-life crisis had moved from minor to major and my emotional state, unpredictable.

I set my stance. Mindy bounced side to side at the net, which annoyed the hell out of me. I'd had enough of her smart mouth, her condescending attitude, oh, and the fact that she might be fucking my husband. I tossed the ball up, aimed at her size two behind and slammed my racket down on the ball as hard as I could. Bingo, the ball pegged Mindy right in her butt!

"Candy!" Mindy yelled out as she turned around to face me. Coming right at her was my racket that slipped out of my sweaty hand.

"Watch out!" I screamed and held my hands to my mouth. It pegged her right between the eyes and made a crack sound so loud you would think it had broken in two at impact. Mindy passed out and fell onto the court.

"Call 911!" Someone yelled.

"We need a paramedic!" Someone else added.

The crowd rushed to Mindy, swarming her size two body like she was the queen bee. Cringing, I moved towards her slowly. "Is she still breathing?" I timidly asked. The sea of D cups leaning over her parted, allowing me access to my BFF that I just inadvertently, well intentionally actually, tried to kill. "It was an accident." I said, but I could tell they really didn't believe me this time.

I looked down at Mindy lying in such a perfect pose and thought how does she do it? No matter the circumstance, she still finds a way to look good. She had a bump the size of a tennis ball between her eyes and her nose was swelling. Any other woman would look like a hag, but Mindy still looked gorgeous in her vixen sort of way.

Her eyes blinked! She was waking up. The crowd backed away, afraid. "Hey, Mindy." I said. "You okay?"

Her eyes opened wide and then squinted into their usual scowl. "You." She said.

"It was an accident!" I squeaked.

"You bitch!" She yelled and charged at me faster than a black panther.

Mindy tackled me to the ground. The women screamed and backed away from us in unison like a flock of birds. Mindy and I wrestled on the ground, first me on top, then Mindy, then me, along with a few bitch slaps, yelps and hits until someone pulled me off her. I looked back. It was Brad again, my underage knight in surfer wear.

"Ladies. Ladies. Come on. Break it up." Brad said, like we were children and he was the adult. He pulled me into a bear hug to keep me from swinging at Mindy who was down on the ground pulling strands of her hair out of her mouth.

"That's it! You, you idiot!" Mindy yelled.

"Idiot! I'd rather be an idiot than a back-stabber! I yelled back. "Let go of me." I said to Brad.

"Only if you promise not to hit her." He said.

"Brad!" I screamed.

He released me from his grip the second time that day. I was mortified worse than when I was kicked off the middle school cheerleading squad for wearing a G-string under my uniform. Our team kept losing because they couldn't keep their eye on the ball. It took the coach three games to figure out why their eyes were on my tush. Once he did, he demanded our squad leader give me the boot. It's best for the team, she told me. It wasn't until she had me do the Spartan cheer, "Spartans, Spartans, ra, ra, ra," that I agreed to take a hike for the team.

The other women helped Mindy up. My broken acrylic nail had scratched her across the cheek and she was bleeding. That, along with her mini-head between her eyes, made Mindy look like she was in a horror film. If my heart wasn't racing and my underwear weren't wedged up, I would have laughed at her. It was right then that I decided my friendship with Mindy, the two-timing backstabbing whore was officially over, when a voice came over a loud speaker.

"We have an urgent phone call for Mindy Klein in the lobby." The loudspeaker voice said.

Mindy was looking down and readjusting her boobs to make sure her nipples were in alignment inside her sport bra. She paused when she heard the message. "Did she say urgent call for Mindy Klein?"

The crowd of Calabasas women shook their heads yes.

"Oh, my God." Mindy said.

A cell phone rang. We looked around for the mystery phone. Then our eyes landed on Mindy's boobs. They were ringing. Mindy reached in between her breasts and pulled out her phone. "Hello." She listened for an agonizing couple of minutes, gasping, sighing and saying, "Oh, no," over and over. Then she dropped the phone. It shattered into pieces that rolled different directions all over the court.

"Mindy, what's wrong?" I asked.

"Barry was eating a salami sandwich for lunch and it got stuck in his throat." She started crying.

"He choked?" I asked.

"No. He panicked and had a heart attack!"

Mindy thought her double D's would give Barry a heart attack. Instead, it was a sandwich with more fat content than we'd eat in a year.

"Mindy, I'm so sorry." I told her because I did feel terrible. Barry was unattractive and boring, but he was a nice enough guy. It was just so weird to have someone I'd knew be gone as fast as a finger snap.

She looked at me with tears rolling down her face. "Candy…" she said as she reached out to me. What else could I do? I had to hug her, especially with all the Calabasas moms watching. How would it make me look if I didn't?

As I held Mindy in my arms and we cried together

over losing Barry, it just wasn't the right time to accuse her of sleeping with Tom. Her husband just croaked on a salami sandwich so the end of our friendship would have to wait.

"Candy?"

"What?"

"I think I'm going to pass out again."

And just like that, Mindy slumped forward. Her eyes rolled back and she fainted. I tried my best to hold on to her, really I did, but somehow she slipped through my arms and fell to the ground.

MINDY'S SCREWED OVER

CHAPTER TWO

After her fainting spell, Brad and some guy who looked like a Kennedy in his white polo shirt with the collar up, carried Mindy to the stands after she insisted she was too dizzy to walk. She laid down on a bleacher as if she was posing for Playboy. She put one leg up, arched her back, aiming her breast to the sky, and let her hair fall towards the ground.

Mindy's hair was only shoulder length, but none of the Calabasas moms knew this. She'd been getting extensions in a Beverly Hills salon by Dickey, her hairstylist. When she first started going to him, he used hair offered to the Gods by poor Indian women at Hindu temples for all his clients. After seeing a report about it on 60 Minutes, Dickey decided to boycott Indian hair. Mindy went postal. If he didn't use Indian hair which is the most flexible and felt the best, she told him she would sue him. After that, Dickey bought Indian hair only for her and cried the entire time he applied the extensions. Mindy didn't care that she forced her stylist to go against his beliefs. She only cared that her hair looked good and it did.

Only eight minutes had passed since Mindy was pulverized by my racket when the paramedics arrived and rushed to her carrying large medical bags. One of them looked like the Brawny Paper Towels guy. You'd think, with his rugged outdoorsy look, that he'd cut trees for a living.

"What's your name?" The brawny paramedic asked Mindy while examining her swollen forehead.

"Mindy."

"Mindy, do you know what day it is?"

"What kind of question is that?"

"Just procedure. Have you had any dizziness?'

"Yes."

"You, hold this ice pack to her forehead." He said to me while he grabbed other medical equipment from his medical bag. I took the ice pack and pressed it on Mindy's bump.

"Ouch!" Mindy yelled at me. "I'll hold it." She said and pushed my hand away. Maybe I did push down a little harder than I needed too.

The medic checked her eyes with a flashlight and then checked her pulse.

"Do you have any pain?"

"Yes, you idiot. On my face. That's why you're here."

I kind of felt bad. The brawny medic didn't deserve to be called a name.

"Any feelings of nausea?"

"Listen, I don't feel good. I've got a bump on my head. Stop asking me all these questions. It's really bugging me!"

"You need to get checked out in a hospital. There's a lot of swelling." The brawny paramedic said.

"Mindy, he thinks you should go to the hospital. It's a good idea." I said.

"Barry's at Cedars-Sinai. Medic!" Mindy yelled out. The medic was only one foot away talking with his partner. He jumped at the sound of her nail-scratching voice. "Take me to Cedars."

"We only transport to West Hills Hospital."

"Medic!" She yelled again.

"Lady, you should take it easy with that bump. Don't yell. It increases the blood flow to the injury. "

"My husband just died and he's at Cedars. I have a head injury, thanks to my best friend, here." I cringed, again. "Take me to Cedars so I can see my husband and get my head fixed at the same time or else I'll put a curse on you!"

The brawny medic's lower lip quivered. He was afraid of her. "I'm sorry about your husband, but it would take about an hour and a half to get through the traffic on the 101 and 405 freeways." He answered.

"Then get me a helicopter. If you don't, and I die from an untreated head wound, your career as a paramedic will be over. I have all these people as my witnesses and that guy over there..." Mindy pointed to the Kennedy look alike she'd never met before. "He's a lawyer and he'll sue your ass if you don't do what I'm telling you." She whispered fiercely.

The next thing I knew, court attendants quickly took down the net and in five minutes a medical helicopter landed in center court, right where we played our rematch.

I was loaded up with Mindy and within minutes we were flying high over the San Fernando Valley, zooming over the congested 101 Freeway toward Beverly Hills. The pilot insisted I wear a headset to protect my ears from the loud noise. I was worried that it was full of germs from other people, but the paramedic assured me that they sanitize the headsets with an antibacterial wipe between customers.

Quietly, I sat by Mindy and held her hand, wondering if it had ever inappropriately touched my husband. "Mindy, you're going to be fine." I yelled, but I lied. If that huge mass ever went down all the way, I'd be amazed.

I looked down at the line of cars going about five

miles per hour. Los Angeles has a subway and a metro rail, but neither gets you far. The subway cost a gazillion dollars to build and after spending all that money and losing a few businesses to sink holes construction caused, it only connects a few parts of the town and doesn't come near Calabasas. I've never seen the metro rail. I heard it runs somewhere in the north valley, but I never go more than a mile north of Ventura Blvd.

I've always thought the idea of public transportation in L.A. is stupid anyway. Having a car in Los Angeles is a requirement. Our basics included food, shelter, clothing and a car, which is kind of silly when I think about hungry children wishing for one meal a day, and poor Indian women donating their hair for pennies so Mindy Klein in Calabasas, California, can look beautiful. But, you know, this is L.A.

Mindy had a panic attack in the helicopter after she insisted on looking at herself in a mirror. The bump looked worse than the birthmark on Mikhail Gorbachev's forehead and the long scratch across her cheek from my broken acrylic nail didn't help. Add in her wild eyes and tangled hair, and she looked like the Joker with a hangover. She gasped for air like a fish out of water. She complained of chest pains and a rapid heartbeat and insisted she was having a heart attack. The medic checked her vitals and assured her that it was just a panic attack. Mindy didn't want to put on the oxygen mask, but gave in after he insisted that it would calm her down. Now she had a scratch on her cheek, a bruised bump between her eyes, an ice pack, and an oxygen mask over her face. If I didn't know it was her, I never would have recognized her.

Ten minutes later, the helicopter landed on the rooftop helipad of the hospital. Marked with a huge yellow and red circle, the target was impossible to miss. The medics rolled Mindy's gurney out onto the landing and I followed, walking low as if doing squats. I'm sure I looked ridiculous, but I was afraid the helicopter blades spinning above us were going to chop off my head.

I looked out at the Los Angeles skyline as I followed the gurney walking with bent knees. Not that it mattered then, considering that Barry was dead and Mindy was injured, but the top of the hospital had a pretty good view. I could see the downtown skyline to the East, the ocean and Santa Monica to the West, the Hollywood Hills to the North, but I wasn't sure what was to the South except for L.A.X airport and a horrible brown haze in the air. No one I knew spent time south of Los Angeles. If we took a day trip, it usually was north to Santa Barbara or Montecito where Oprah chose to build her mansion.

They loaded me and Mindy on her gurney onto a high speed elevator that zoomed down to the emergency room in seconds. When the doors opened, Mindy was swarmed by a trauma team that evaluated her condition. The removed the oxygen mask from her face. In charge of the team was the most handsome doctor I've ever seen, way beyond McDreamy cute. On a one to ten, this doc was a twelve, and because he was a real doctor, that made him even cuter. The helicopter medic filled the trauma team in on Mindy's vitals and the injury to her head. Once the trauma team realized Mindy didn't need to be put in the resuscitation room, the team members all seemed disappointed that they didn't have an official trauma case and walked off, which left just the handsome doctor.

"You two play on a team?" The doctor asked me. Our matching tennis outfits suggested that we did.

"Sort of, but it's not an official league." I said. "It's complicated."

He smiled at me as he stood over Mindy. It seemed, even though he was there to examine Mindy that she hardly existed. "Let's see the damage." He said as he took the ice pack off Mindy's forehead. He glanced down at her face, then looked up at me again and said, "She's got a nice bump, there, don't you think?"

"It's a pretty big one." I confirmed.

"Excuse me, doctor, but could you stop flirting with my friend. I'm injured. I've got a serious problem on my face." Mindy reminded him and pointed to her forehead.

"Feisty one, isn't she?" He said to me and I almost laughed, but held it in because even though Mindy might be sleeping with my husband, this wasn't confirmed, and her husband was somewhere in that hospital dead as the pig his salami sandwich was made out of. I wanted to be sensitive to her situation.

"She's having a hard day." I said, as a way to make Mindy feel better, because she really was having a hard day.

"It does look pretty bad." The doctor confirmed. "I can see why you're in a grouchy mood." He said to Mindy.

"Oh, God, you've made me deformed." Mindy said to me. "How could you do this to me?"

"It was an accident." I hollered out, without realizing I was yelling so loud. I was getting tired of having to defend myself so many times in one day. While my subconscious may have intentionally allowed my racket to slip from my sweaty palm and smack her in the face, my conscience had no part in it. Well, at least I hope it didn't. I'd hate to think I was that kind of person.

The doctor chuckled. "You did this?" He said to me as he looked at Mindy's pupils with a flashlight. "Nice work." He added as he checked her reflexes on her elbows and her knees in such a routine way I wasn't even sure he knew he was doing it, like when you arrive home in your car and you can't remember driving there.

"I served. It was hot. My palm was sweaty and the racket slipped."

"Some serve you've got." He said to me and laughed.

Mindy was about to blow. Her eyelids lowered and she scowled, but it didn't look the same since she had an enormous bump between her eyes. "Doctor, can we get on with it. My husband is somewhere in this hospital. He choked on a salami sandwich… and…" Poor Mindy couldn't finish her sentence because she actually had to pause her complaining to cry.

"Your husband wouldn't be Barry Georgina Klein, would he?" The doctor said.

"Georgina?" I asked Mindy.

"Named after his mother. It's a middle name. It's doesn't matter. No one ever uses their middle name." Mindy told me.

"Do you know where the morgue is?" I asked the doctor.

"Third floor, but he's not there yet." He said.

"Then where is he?" Mindy asked.

The doctor pointed to the curtained-off bed next to us.

"Oh, my God!" Mindy and I both yelled.

"We're waiting for a space to open up." The doctor said.

"In the morgue? There's a backup in the morgue?" I asked.

"Oh, yeah, it's our most popular unit." He said.

He informed Mindy that her injuries were superficial, which she had a hard time believing. He assured her that even small bumps to the head can cause a lot of swelling because the forehead and scalp have an abundant blood supply. This often causes bleeding under the skin, but it only stays in that one area. It's called a hematoma. He said hematoma like a school teacher. With ice and time, she'll be good as new. But he did warn her never to play tennis with me again. What a comedian.

The doc left to get a pain prescription for Mindy and her release papers, leaving us alone and next to dead

Barry. We debated what to do. Mindy and I stood at the curtain that hid Barry.

"You go in." She said. "I can't do it."

"I'm not going in."

"Please, Candy. Barry always liked you best."

"Mindy, he's your husband."

"But you're my best friend." She said in that way that made me feel that taking care of her was my responsibility. "And you just nearly killed me on the court."

"All right. All right." I told her, while wondering how long Mindy was going to use the bump on her head against me.

"Just see if he looks like he died in pain." Mindy said.

I poked my head in between two curtains. There was Barry in his business suit and his Oliver Peoples eyeglasses. His transition lenses had darkened from the spotlight shining down on him. He had a huge smile on his face, which was so unusual because Barry never smiled. He looked like a dead happy Blues Brother.

I brought my head out of the curtains. "He looks happy."

"Happy? He never looks happy." Mindy said as if she didn't believe it. She poked her head in between the two curtains for a second and came back out. "He died smiling. Maybe he saw God at the end." She started crying. "Maybe there is an afterlife."

"Excuse me, are you Barry's wife?" We heard a sweet voice say behind us.

We turned and saw a gorgeous girl still in her twenties, wearing a waitress uniform so tight around her chest that two of the buttons had popped. Her nametag from Nate'n Al's Famous Deli said Nina. She had opted for D cups from her surgeon, but being so young and fresh, they looked so much better on her than Mindy. She was crying and wiping tears away from her eyes.

"I'm Nina." She said. "Barry was one of my regular customers."

"At the restaurant?" I asked, because I really wasn't sure if she meant there or in a hotel room.

"Uh, huh. I gave him mouth to mouth, but it wasn't enough. He died in my arms." She said and started crying real hard again.

So that's why Barry was smiling, I thought, and was pretty sure Mindy was thinking the same thing.

Mindy grabbed hold of Nina's shoulders. I wasn't sure if she was going to head-butt Nina or hug her. "You!" Mindy said to the girl. I couldn't decipher her tone and wondered how this was going to turn out. "You!" Mindy said to Nina again.

"Um, that hurts a little." Nina said as she looked down at Mindy's charcoal black acrylic nails piercing into her skin.

"Don't do anything crazy. She tried to save Barry's life." I reminded Mindy.

"You angel!" Mindy said and brought the beautiful girl in to a close embrace. Well, as close as two women with double D's can get.

I grabbed the curtain hiding Barry and wiped my forehead. I was so afraid that Mindy was going to claw the eyes out of this red-haired waitress that within seconds I'd worked up more of a sweat than I had out on the tennis court. Nina had no idea how lucky she just was. I knew Mindy pretty well, and I'm pretty sure for a minute there, Mindy was about to say words to her that would have made Nina run out of the hospital screaming as if she was on fire. Mindy could be that vicious when she was mad.

Mindy and Nina held each other as they walked to the waiting room where Nina told her all about Barry's last moments.

"Every Tuesday and Thursday Barry came in and ordered the Salami Slam Sandwich. He always requested my station and always gave me a hundred dollar tip. I came to rely on this money for my budget, you know."

I found this bit of information interesting because Tuesday and Thursday night was Mindy's special time with Barry. Now we were learning that he spent his lunch every Tuesday and Thursday getting a Salami Slam from Nina and staring at her double D's, and if I was thinking this, I was pretty sure Mindy was too.

I called Tom, my potential ex-husband, at work and told him about Barry. He was upset, but immediately he started asking questions about Mindy. I told him she was doing fine, but that I needed him to pick us up at Cedars or else send a town car, and that I would fill him in later on why we took a helicopter to the hospital. He said he would arrange for a limo immediately, because Mindy would need room to lie down.

"Why are you so concerned about Mindy?" I asked him.

"Candy, you're being so insensitive, which is so unlike you. Barry and Mindy are like family. Anything I can do to help Mindy in this trying time, I will."

Yeah, like taking off her G-string to get to her G-spot, I wanted to say, but held my tongue.

Tom said he would have Shibuya, the best sushi restaurant in Calabasas, deliver a sushi feast to our house so dinner would be there when we returned because Mindy would need protein to cope. By the time I got off the phone, I felt like a schmuck. How could I ever doubt my husband? How could I ever doubt my best friend?

"Tom's sending a limo to pick us up." I told Mindy.

"He's so sweet." Mindy said. "Where do you live, Nina? We'll drop you off."

"Really. That would be great. Hollywood and Vine." Nina said.

"Hollywood and Vine? People live there?" Mindy asked while holding an ice pack on her swollen brow.

"Neighborhood's cheap. I'm an actress. We'll I

haven't really done any acting yet. Just a few porn films, but that's not real acting, I just have to be myself." Nina said.

If anyone could have blown the life back in to Barry, you think it would be a porn star. It really must have been his time to go.

"Barry loved my movies. I gave them to him for free, because he was such a good tipper. Hard to find loyal customers like him." Nina said.

"Nina, my husband was a successful lawyer at the firm, Reed, Reed and Reed." The tears stopped pouring out of Nina's eyes. "But I'm sure you knew this, right?" Mindy said.

"He may have mentioned it a few times." Nina said.

I didn't know what was going on. Then Mindy leaned in close to Nina's face. "How much to keep you quiet?" Mindy asked.

"Two thousand." Nina said.

"Please. A grand." Mindy came back.

"Fifteen hundred and you've got a deal." Nina said.

"Done."

Mindy pulled out a wad of cash she counted and handed over to the bimbo just as our limo pulled up outside the emergency room doors.

"Our limo is here. We're not going to be able to give you a ride home. I'm sure you understand." Mindy said to Nina and walked out of the glass doors to the sidewalk in a huff. Well, with as much huff as a woman can when she's holding an ice pack on her forehead.

I followed her like a dog follows their master. "Mindy, my God, that woman was waiting for you the whole time to blackmail you." I said. "I did not see that coming." Mindy caught on to so much that passed me by. She had more street sense than a homeless woman.

The limo driver opened the door for Mindy. She stopped before getting inside, and turned to me. "That's why no one should ever fuck with me. I'm an expert at this crap."

We got in the limo and I was stunned from coming face to face with wicked Mindy. That was the woman I'd be doing battle with if she was sleeping with my husband. Mindy put her feet up and laid her head back. The ice pack was sweating so it dripped water on her cheeks like Mindy, if she truly loved her husband, should be dripping tears out of her eyes, but as soon as we were away from Nina and the hospital staff, her tears dried up.

"Don't speak for a moment, Candy. I need to think." Mindy said.

"Okay." I told her and folded my legs up crisscross applesauce on the seat like a preschooler on a circle time carpet. Things didn't feel right. For one thing, whenever Mindy took time out to think, it wasn't good. It meant she was thinking about how to mess with someone's life, but luckily that person was never me. Being a close personal friend of Mindy's, I never had to worry about her wrath like some of the other Calabasas mom's she'd stung in the past. I was exempt because I was her BFF.

We drove in silence. I looked out at pristine Beverly Hills homes, taking in the landscaping and luxurious architectural designs and in the middle of this picturesque scene, I saw a homeless lady pushing a grocery cart full of disgusting stuff that was so dirty, every item was brown. But the worst part was that she wasn't wearing any shoes.

"Pull over by that homeless lady." I demanded of the limo driver.

Mindy sat up, annoyed. "I told you not to talk. I'm in crisis here."

The limo pulled over next to the homeless woman. I rolled down the window. "Excuse me, but where are your shoes?" I asked her and she started yelling at me.

"Look here, you cracker girl, in your limo and your fancy clothes." The homeless woman said.

I looked down at my skimpy athletic tennis outfit. "Oh, this isn't fancy. It's athletic wear." I told her and I'll be damned, but she rushed at our limo waving a dirty old cane like a crazy woman, and then opened the door. She stuck her head into the limo. Mindy and I screamed, not because of her hairstyle, but because she smelled like fertilizer. We both held our noses shut.

"You can't kick me out of this neighborhood, you cracker girls. I got a right to walk these streets, just like you." The homeless woman said.

"We're not hookers." I told her.

The limo driver got out of the car, rushed around and pulled the homeless lady out of the limo.

"Get your hands off me, you slave working, cracker limo driver." She yelled and then socked him hard in the stomach. He keeled over and went down on his knees while holding his stomach.

"I just want to give you shoes." I told her. "What size do you wear?"

"Oh, I'm a size eight, cracker girl." The homeless woman said.

"Mindy, give me your shoes." I tried to pull one off her foot. "I wear a seven. They won't fit her."

"Are you crazy? I am not giving her my shoes!" Mindy screamed.

"You have fifty pairs of tennis shoes at home." I demanded. "Give her your shoes." I grabbed hold of her foot and slipped one tennis shoe off. I tossed it to the homeless woman. She caught it like a football receiver and she had it on her foot in seconds.

"Nice." The homeless woman said to the limo driver about the shoe who stood up and limped back to the driver's seat. I think I saw him wipe tears out of his eyes in the rear view mirror, but I figured it would embarrass him if I asked him if he was crying.

"Candy, she's got my shoe." Mindy said.

"Well, you're not going to want it back now." I grabbed the other pink and white Nike Tennis Women's Air Max Breathe Cage II off her other foot. We purchased the tennis shoes to match our outfit. They're the same shoes worn by Lindsey Davenport.

I got out of the limo, kneeled before the homeless woman and held out the other shoe. It was rather disgusting because her foot was desperately in need of a pedicure, well, more like five to ten pedicures since one would barely touch the surface dirt she had on her soles. I tried not to seem grossed out, because I didn't want to hurt her feelings, but I couldn't help cringing when her foot was in my face. She slipped the shoe on and I tied it for her.

"There. A perfect fit." I said.

"I feel just like Cinderella." The homeless woman joked or at least I think she was joking. When she spun around a few times and tried to do a pirouette and fell, I wasn't sure.

"You should." I said. "You deserve respect just like us rich people, even though you don't have a pot to piss in." I told her.

"Yeah, I do, cracker girl." She said, and grabbed a pot out of her grocery cart.

"You do. Excellent!" I told her and went to go back in the limo.

"Cracker girl, Cinderella could use some green." The homeless woman said and I couldn't help thinking how much younger she would look if she had her teeth whitened. It really does take years off your life.

"I don't smoke marijuana." I told her. "I'm against drugs."

"I mean cash, Cracker Girl. You finish high school?" She said.

"GED." I told her, which was a lie. I always said

that because not having my high school diploma made me feel stupid. I learned years ago, if you tell someone you graduated high school, they always ask which year and which school, but if you tell them you got your GED, no one asks a thing. It's a given that GED's can come from anywhere and at any time.

I went in the limo and dug a few hundreds out of my wallet. "Mindy give me some money." I said to her and she looked like she wanted to kill me.

"I don't have any. I gave all my cash to the porn star that blew my husband, remember?"

"You rich folk have a way, that's for sure." The homeless lady said and she burst into a loud, high pitch laugh and showed her yellow teeth. I wanted to tell her she looked sort of ugly when she laughed, but decided not to because at least she was happy.

"It's not what you think." I told the homeless woman as I handed her two hundred dollar bills. "Now, go on and do something good with your life."

And she just laughed and laughed as she pushed her cart down the sidewalk. Up against her dirty brown trench coat, that she was wearing in June I might ad, Mindy's sparkling clean white and pink tennis shoes glowed as if they were neon.

"I hate you today." Mindy said when I got in the limo.

"But look, we gave her shoes. Don't you feel good helping the less fortunate?"

"No." Mindy said, but I didn't care that she was mad at me for taking her tennis shoes. I was on a high I hadn't experienced since I took the stage as a pole dancer in my late teens.

I rolled down the window as we drove by the homeless woman. "Bye." I said as I waved. She flipped me off, but I understood why she was so defensive. It must have been embarrassing for her to have to piss in a pot and wear Mindy's hand-me-down shoes.

Pleased with myself, I sat back and smiled for the

first time that day. I was hoping for a relaxing ride home, but then Mindy pulled the ice pack off her forehead. She took my hands in hers and tears poured out of her eyes.

"Candy, you're my best friend. I need you now more than ever."

"Sure, Mindy, whatever you need. I'm there for you."

"Really?"

"Totally."

She grabbed me into a tight hug. "I need you to tell Cindy that her father is dead." She said.

I pulled back. "What? Mindy, I can't tell her that."

"I can't either."

"But you're her mother."

"I know, but see how sweet you were to that homeless lady. You have a way of talking to people I just don't have."

She was right about that, I had to admit. In the area of sensitivity, I did excel far beyond Mindy Klein. I never knew she admired that part of me. She always seemed so annoyed whenever I took time out to ask the guard at the Oaks security gate if he was having a good day or when I moved an injured bird off the tennis court during a match.

"Mindy, it's your responsibility. This is one of those crucial moments in Cindy's childhood that she's never going to forget. You have to tell her."

"I'm a widow. I can't cope with all this. Candy, I need you to tell her and I need you to plan Barry's funeral. You throw the most amazing cocktail parties where the food is perfect and the table decorations are gorgeous. I'm not good at party planning like you."

She was right again. I did have a way of throwing events together that ran seamlessly and were talked about for months.

"A funeral is not a cocktail party."

"Sure it is. There's picking the venue, printing the invitations, the food, the appetizers, and the open bar. It's the same thing."

"But the guest of honor is dead." I told her, which was kind of insensitive, because then she started crying really, really hard and sort of yelped like a dog does when they're in heat and haven't been neutered. It was horrible.

"Okay, okay, I'll do it. I'll do it all, just stop that sound." I yelled while holding my hands up to my ears. This day was a train wreck from the beginning. Now I was pegged not only to be the funeral coordinator, but I was the designated to be the Messenger of Death.

"You're the best, Candy. I don't know what I'd do without you." Mindy said, and dramatically fell back against the seat, closed her eyes, put the ice pack over her forehead and put her sock-covered feet on my lap. They smelled, but I didn't think it was the time to point that out.

Traffic wasn't too bad heading back into the Valley, so the limo pulled up to the guard gate less than an hour later. Carl, the Oaks security guard, stopped the limo and looked over the driver as if this was a military checkpoint.

I rolled the window down and whispered. "It's okay, Carl, it's just me and Mindy." I talked quietly because I didn't want to startle Mindy who was still resting.

Carl walked back to my window. "I heard about Mr. Klein." He said. "It's a shame. He was a good man."

It was weird for Carl to say Barry was a good man because he didn't really know Barry. Barry never gave him the time of day. He only waved to him as he drove through the gate. But the weirdest part about hearing Carl say that Barry was a good man was that I knew Barry really well and still wasn't sure if Barry was a good man. Easy-going, heavy-drinker, over-weight, moneymaker, these were two word combinations that fit Barry Georgina Klein much better than good man.

"Yes, he was." I whispered to Carl, because you know, what else was I going to say.

"How's Mrs. Klein doing?" Carl said.

I pointed to Mindy on the other seat. He didn't realize she was in the limo with me and when he saw her scratched and bruised face, he jumped back. "She looks like she's been in a war. Look at that bump on her head."

"I know. I need to get her home."

I didn't want to be rude and hurry him along, but I was tired and hungry and had no desire to have a long conversation with Carl. He always chatted with me for a long time because no one else talked to him. They just waved, but I always stopped and asked him how his day was. The other residents had the attitude that Carl was a service worker and since they paid his salary with their home-owners association dues, they didn't need treat him as their equal.

Carl raised the gate and we drove on, passing the community park where I met Mindy. I saw three Hispanic nannies with three Caucasian infants playing there and I couldn't help thinking of how wonderful it was that we were wealthy enough to hire nannies to spend time with our children. As Calabasas mom's, we have so much to do, hair and nails, playing tennis, resting at the pool, going shopping, telling our maids how to clean our house and working out, that it's difficult to spend every day with our children. To be a good full time mom in Calabasas you need a full-time nanny.

I looked at Mindy, who was still knocked out. She fell asleep soon after I agreed to handle all the funeral arrangements. At first I worried that the hematoma was worse than the doctor thought and that she had internal brain bleeding because she slept so deeply, but when she snorted and woke herself up for a minute, I decided the strain of the day must have knocked her out.

Our limo drove around a bend and up ahead I saw neighbors waiting on the sidewalk in front of my house.

"One of you women famous or something?" The limo driver asked.

"We're not famous, but we're popular." I told him. "Mindy. Wake up. Look at all these people waiting for you." I said to her while shaking her smelly sock-covered feet that had been on my lap for the entire drive home.

"People?" She said and sat up. "Oh, they must have heard about Barry."

The limo pulled up in front of my home and next to the group of neighborhood women eagerly waiting our arrival.

Mindy looked at herself in the mirror and adjusted her boobs. "How do I look?" She asked me.

I wasn't sure what I should say. In all the years I'd known Mindy, she'd never looked worse. "You look great. You can hardly tell you got hit in the face." I told her.

The limo came to a stop, and even though there were about twenty women available to open our door, the crowd waited for the limo driver to do it.

"Here goes." Mindy said to me.

Mindy got out of the limo as if she was an Oscar winning actress and these women were her adoring fans. The women gasped when they saw her and the group took a few steps back. Mindy began crying and they rushed to her and put their arms around her. It was a high pitched group with lots of "oh, my God's" being said and "I can't believe it" and "you look really good considering Candy hit you with her racket" and "Sorry about Barry" and "He was a good man."

They were lying. Mindy looked awful, but it was an unspoken requirement that we women tell each other we look good even when we look like shit. And, while Barry wasn't a bad man, he really wasn't a good man, but

I guess when a person's dead, people are required to say they were good even if they weren't.

I got out of the limo after Mindy and felt such relief when I saw Tom amongst the group of women, standing with his arms wide open to hug me. I needed a hug from my hubby. It had been a long and brutal day, but just as I was about to walk into my husband's arms, Mindy rushed over to him and leaned her head into his chest and cried. He held her and patted her on the back.

"Tom?" I said.

I wanted to tell Mindy to get away from my husband, but the neighborhood women were out and I didn't want to cause a scene.

Tom put his index finger up, a gesture to tell me one minute. "She's distraught, Candy." Tom said.

Mindy was putting on the performance of her life. This was the same woman who was just sleeping in the limo, totally at peace after seeing her dead husband.

"Come inside, everyone, I have sushi platters." Tom said to the neighborhood women. The group followed Tom, who held his arm around Mindy as they walked into the house. "What happened to your shoes?" Tom asked her.

"Candy stole them off my feet to give to a really mean homeless lady." She said, and the group of women gasped in unison, looked back at me and sneered.

My stomach churned. I needed protein. I had only eaten a yogurt parfait all day.

"Ah, lady, that'll be $300 dollars." The limo driver handed me a slip to sign. And I should get a big tip for taking that punch." He added.

"Didn't my husband arrange for the payment?"

"Uh, no. That him? The guy holding the other woman?" The Limo Driver asked.

We looked over at Mindy and Tom. They stopped in front of a puddle of water the sprinklers created on the sidewalk. Tom told Mindy he didn't want her socks to get wet and then lifted her in his arms and carried her over the threshold of our house, just like he did to me on the first day we moved in.

"Yep, that's him." I said and handed over my credit card. "How big do you think your tip should be?"

"One hundred."

"Make it two."

It didn't matter to me anyway. I didn't pay my Visa bill. In fact, I'd never even seen my Visa bill. Tom had it sent to our accountant and every month, like magic, the balance was paid in full.

"You sure, lady?" The Limo Driver asked.

I could tell he was excited. Two hundred was probably the biggest tip he'd gotten all month.

I watched Tom and Mindy go into the house, turned back to the limo driver and said, "Make it three hundred."

MINDY SCREWS CANDY

CHAPTER THREE

Inside my house, ten neighborhood women milled about dipping sushi rolls into tiny cups of soy sauce mixed with wasabi on my Kate Spade "June Lane" dinnerware. I just had it delivered and was hoping to use it for a special occasion, not for a horrible time like this. I bought it at Macy's. They described the design as a whimsical pattern of dragonflies and ladybugs, sure to give any dinner party a magical experience. Now every time I'll use it, I'll think of Mindy in my husband's arms and the smile on Barry's dead face.

Tom and Mindy stood in the kitchen, eating sashimi tuna. He kept rubbing her shoulder and she kept talking about how horrible it was to be on the hospital bed next to Barry. All I kept thinking was how odd it was that she was able to eat raw tuna, spicy no less, on the day her husband croaked on a salami sandwich. I think I'd opt for a glass of water, maybe a shot of hard liquor and saltine crackers, but I'm not Mindy Klein. She was in a class of her own.

"Tom, I need to talk to you upstairs." I said, and walked off in a huff, expecting him to follow, but when I made it up five stairs, I glanced back and he wasn't behind me. "Tom!" I yelled out just as he came around

53

the corner.

"Why are you yelling, Candy? I had to help Mindy to a chair. She doesn't feel good and that knot you put on her forehead looks like it could have been fatal." He said.

"It was an accident." I told him and then stomped up the stairs, gesturing for him to follow.

We went inside our master suite. Seven hundred and fifty square feet with a view of our entertainer's yard and the Santa Monica Mountains, I had it decorated in an Indian Moulin Rouge design after seeing the movie starring Nicole Kidman. The walls were a vibrant shade of fuchsia with a large damask style pattern. The four poster bed was placed in the corner of the room. I had it custom made with gold posts. Each one was stapled with sari material to create curtains and a canopy for the bed. The gold bedspread was made out of Damask fabric and it was accented with throw cushions in black, gold and fuchsia. But the best part of the room was the swing hanging from the ceiling that was decorated with gold ribbon and tassels. I absolutely loved it, and Tom was fine with having a fuchsia room, so long as I hopped on the swing naked for him a few times a week. After all, we were married and needed to keep it spicy. His big joke was that our bedroom was Candy Cane Lane, which was my stage name back when I was a stripper so I thought it was adorable.

I slammed the doors shut and turned to Tom. "Are you…" I said, and suddenly my anger turned to tears. "Are you having an affair with Mindy?" I asked.

Tom smiled and opened his arms to me sweetly. "Oh, come here, Candy Cane." He said with a laugh.

"Are you?" I asked again while melting into his arms.

"Of course not." He patted me on the back. "Why would you ever think that?"

"Katie told me a friend of a friend of a friend of hers saw you two together."

"Ridiculous. I would never cheat on you. You're my Candy Cane. There's no one sweeter than you." He kissed me real deep and full of passion.

Finally, for the first time that day, all was right with the world. Yeah, Barry was dead, but you know, you can't have it all at the same time, right.

"Oh, Tom." I said. "I was so worried and didn't know what I was going to do without you. I kept wondering how I would explain to Kelly that her father was sleeping with my best friend. It's something out of a soap opera, you know, like Days of Our Lives."

We walked down the stairs arm and arm to the group of Botox'd and big-breasted moms eating raw fish on the first floor. If I added up the cost of procedures done on the women surrounding Mindy, I'd say a half a million in medical bills were invested in their bodies. They all listened as she went on and on about how my racket knocked her unconscious on the court and then the horror of being right next to Barry in the Cedars-Sinai Emergency Room. She neglected to tell them about Nina, however, and how Barry saw her every Tuesday and Thursday for a Salami Slam, the same nights he gave Mindy his salami slam at home.

"Candy." Mindy said when she saw me. I went over to the matron of honor at the raw fish reception my husband threw together for her. "It's five o'clock. Cindy comes home now. Can you see if her car's in the driveway?" She asked.

I glanced out our living room window and saw Cindy's Smart Car in the driveway. Mindy's house was three houses down and across the street. Mindy was absolutely mortified when Cindy insisted Barry buy her this car instead of a stylish Mercedes 250 or a BMW 335i. Cindy wanted to be responsible about the environment, to which Mindy told her the environment didn't care if she was a dork, but her mother did. To save face, Mindy would go on and on to our friends about how unmaterialistic her daughter was and how she cared more about preserving our natural resources than appearances.

Secure in my marriage again and completely positive that Katie was a big fat liar, I walked over to Mindy's house to give her daughter the dreaded news about her father. This was a job for a super friend, something I decided to be again for Mindy who was suffering from a terrible loss.

I walked up the driveway and saw the 100% Bitch sticker Cindy put on the window of her tiny Smart Car and started laughing. I'm terrible, I know, but my daughter told me Cindy put the sticker on her car after she read The Secret. Cindy is a lesbian and told my daughter she wants to attract women who are 100% bitches into her life because those are her type. I got it together as I headed for the front door, but then I heard this awful screaming coming from inside the house and I wondered if there was a burglar inside torturing Cindy. I tried to open the door. It was locked. I pounded and rang the doorbell.

Cindy opened the door, holding another girl's hand.

"Cindy, are you all right?" I asked.

"We were proclaiming our lesbianism. It's scream therapy. It helps us cope with the oppression we encounter in our everyday lives."

I looked at their outfits (flannel plaid button up shirts, Levi jeans cut off just below the knee, military combat boots, hair shorter than my husbands) and was pretty sure it was their fashion sense that set them apart from the world, not their attraction to the same sex.

"Cindy, I have to talk to you about something important." I told her as I took her one free hand and led her and her lesbian lover to the couch. "Sit down." I told them. They didn't let go of each other, so I had to deliver the news of her father's death with her 100% Bitch lover sitting next to her. "I'm sorry to tell you this, but today your father passed away."

"You mean Barry?" She said.

"Yes. He had a heart attack. It was very sudden." I told her and waited for the tears to flow. "I'm so sorry, sweetie. I know you loved your father."

"Barry's not my dad."

"He's not?" I said.

"No. I got a sperm dad, and I think I might have gotten a sperm with a twisted tail or something freaky like that because my mom is such a horn dog for men and I'm a lesbian. Go figure."

I always liked Cindy. She had a way with words and never held back. I admired her honesty.

"Wow. In all the years I've known your mom, she never told me. I thought we knew everything about each other." I said.

Cindy started laughing. "My mom's got a lot of secrets. Comes from a family of gypsies, and you know how gypsies are." Cindy said, and she and her 100% Bitch lesbian lover laughed. I wasn't sure what the joke was because I didn't know much about gypsies, and still couldn't get over how deceived I felt by Mindy.

"Barry thought he was my dad, but he was infertile. My mom hooked him by making him think he got her prego. Her whole life is bullshit, but I love her, you know, 'cause she's my mom. But, poor Barry. Man, what a drag." She added, but I wasn't sure she meant it.

Then Cindy started screaming really loud and her 100% Bitch girlfriend joined in. After a few minutes of this, they stopped.

"Scream therapy?" I said.

"Yeah. To take away the pain of Barry's death." She told me.

Delivering the news took ten minutes. I returned home to find Maria, our live-in housekeeper we paid seventy-five dollars a week, gathering up my magical Kate Spade butterfly plates the neighborhood women left all over my house. I didn't feel bad about paying her so little because she got to live in our luxurious home, eat all our food, and shop at Gelsons, the finest grocery store in the valley with my Visa and I'm sure she bought things for herself that weren't on my list.

"These plates can't go in the dishwasher." I told Maria. "Carefully hand wash and dry them."

"See, Mama." She said. She always called me Mama since I rescued her from Tijuana eleven years before, even though she was fifteen years older than me. I think she had unresolved issue with her mom from childhood.

"Where's Tom?" I asked and she pointed outside.

Tom and Mindy sat in the back yard by the pool, looking at the sunset. It reminded me of a final scene you'd see in a movie with romantic music where the couple kisses and the picture fades to black. Tom had assured me he wasn't cheating and when he gave me that awesome kiss, I knew he wasn't lying so I wasn't worried about Mindy anymore. I was 100% sure my husband was 100% faithful.

Then, just when I thought the day couldn't get any weirder, my daughter Kelly came home with Brad, my knight in surfer wear, just as I slipped a raw piece of tuna sashimi in my mouth. I started gagging at the sight of him.

"Mom, what's wrong? You're face is turning red." Kelly said as she and Brad rushed over to me.

I tried to speak, but couldn't. I didn't want to spit out food in the kitchen sink with the hot lifeguard there, so I chewed quickly so I could swallow it fast.

Brad rushed over and grabbed me from behind. "She's choking!" He yelled, and performed the Heimlich maneuver with such expertise that the tuna sashimi flew out of my mouth, slapped onto the door of our stainless steel refrigerator, and slid down to the floor.

"I'm not choking." I said while gagging. "Too much wasabi!" I said while fanning my mouth. Maria gave me a glass of water. I chugged it down, but then realized it was from the tap so I spit it out into the sick.

58

"Maria, I never drink tap water." I said. "Get me a bottle of Evian, quick."

She rushed over to the slimmed refrigerator door, opened it and got me Evian water. I rinsed my mouth out with it three times while starring at my husband and my best friend watching the sunset by our pool through the window over our kitchen sink.

"This is so embarrassing." Kelly said. "Everyone's talking about you trying to kill Mindy with your racket on the day her husband died and now you're hurling sushi out of your mouth."

I hate to admit this, but sometimes my fabulous daughter reminded me of Mindy. It's probably my fault, though. I picked a nanny from Tijuana with more attitude than a poodle to raise her. I bought Kelly her first car when she was seven, you know, one of those battery operated jeeps, and didn't take it away even when she kept running over our Golden Retriever's tail. And when Kelly demanded her allowance of fifty dollars a week be increased to one hundred on her tenth birthday, I agreed. She was our only child. We could afford to spoil her, so we did. I grew up poor, so there was no way my daughter was not going to have what all the other kids had.

"What are you doing here?" I asked Brad while coughing.

"Mom! How rude!" Kelly snapped at me. "He just saved your life. OMG!"

"I didn't mean it like that." I said.

"We're working on a scene together." Kelly said. "This is Brad, the lifeguard from the club and he's in drama with me." She added as if I should know all about Brad, but this was the first time Brad and my daughter, to my knowledge, had ever spoken. And now, after the day I had with Brad, he was standing in my kitchen. I found this odd.

"Your mom and I met today." He said. "She almost fell in the pool and I caught her. Then I had to pull her off of Mrs. Klein when she was beating her up." He added.

Man, this kid was really good, and now he was infiltrating my daughter's life. My mom radar was on alert.

"So, you heard about Barry?" I asked Kelly.

"Yeah, he croaked right after you tried to kill Mindy with your racket. Mom, the whole town's talking about it."

I looked over at Brad. I was pretty sure he was the one who told her, not the entire town.

"Mindy's in the backyard with Dad. You should go say something to her." I told my sassy daughter.

"Oh, all right. Brad, this will just take a minute." Kelly said and went out to the back patio.

When the patio doors shut behind my daughter, I turned to Brad. "Are you trying to date my daughter?"

"I'd prefer to date you." Brad said and winked.

Maria, who I always suspected spoke more English than she ever let on, was cleaning up the tuna I spit onto the refrigerator and started coughing real loud.

Stumped, I couldn't speak for a minute. "Brad, not only am I out of your league, I am happily married and you're underage. You're jailbait, buddy."

He smiled and ran his fingers through his hair, as if he could care less about what I just said. "Not in two months. Turning eighteen." Brad said, as if eighteen was going to give him the right to do whatever he wanted. I almost told him his eighteenth birthday was no big deal compared to his twenty-first because he could drink and go to bars unless he had a really good I.D, but I held it in.

"You watch yourself young man or I'll call your parents." I added as an additional threat, but he just smiled and winked again.

Kelly came back inside. "Brad, let's go to my room." She said.

"Keep the door open." I said.

"Mom, would you stop being so weird. I'm like, seventeen. OMG, you're so embarrassing."

I always thought I was cool, but according to my daughter I was not fit to be around anyone even remotely in her world.

Still in my mini-tennis skirt, athletic bra top and white and pink tennis shoes, I thought I looked adorable, but Tom didn't look up at me as I walked towards him and Mindy in the backyard. Hearing insecurity in my subconscious again, I told myself that I was irresistible and that my husband loves me.

"Mindy, it's time to take you home. Cindy's waiting for you." I said.

"How'd she take it?" Mindy asked.

"I'd say pretty good."

"Did she cry?"

"Uh, no, she screamed."

"Oh, God, that damn scream therapy. I can't wait until she's out of this stage."

Cindy's screaming didn't stop. For the next two days, I planned Barry's funeral while hearing Cindy scream off and on. It turns out she did love Barry more than she thought, and as she told me, having death touch her family was just so freaky that she had to scream. Mindy wasn't much support for her daughter. She went to her bed and didn't get out of it unless she had to change her Victoria Secret nightie or go to the bathroom. She could afford more expensive lingerie, but she liked the sexy edge the Victoria Secret collections had. They were a little nasty, but still not as nasty as Fredericks of Hollywood.

It was quite a scene. Every hour a mom from the neighborhood or the club or the nail salon or our book club or Zen Spa paraded platters of food into the house or stopped by with something for Mindy to help her relax. One brought spa candles from Pottery Barn and lit fifty of them all over her room. Another slipped

Mindy a bottle of valium that I quickly hid from her. One woman plugged in a humidifier with a Splash Rain Forest Scent in Mindy's room to prevent her skin from drying out during this trying time. Most women brought a bottle of wine, which was good since Mindy drank wine continuously over the next forty-eight hours while watching TV in bed.

As for all Tom's blabbering on about being there for Mindy, he went back to the golf course the next morning and worked until nine at night the next day. In times of crisis, Tom has a way of disappearing that is so subtle, it takes you a minute to realize you're on your own. Tom even had his secretary insist, every time I called up with a question, that he was in a meeting. I told his secretary that B.S. is alive and well. She didn't laugh and I had to explain that it was a joke. Then she got mad at me for accusing her of lying. I told her she misunderstood because I wasn't accusing her of lying, I was accusing Tom. She started crying and threatened to quit. Her breathing got real loud and I had to spend an hour with her on the phone listening to her talk about how horrible her life is. That morning, her fiancé left her for his best friend and this was a huge shock because she had no idea he liked men. I told her I was sorry for upsetting her. I told her I was sorry that her fiancé left her. I told her I was sorry for anything and everything that was wrong in her life, in between being put on hold about twenty times so she could answer the incoming calls.

Mindy signed a book of blank checks and told me to write a check for whatever I needed. She had no opinions at all about color or a theme for the food, so all the details for poor Barry were up to me, even down to which suit and tie he would wear. The only information she had was that Barry had a spot reserved in Mount Sinai Memorial Park, which made it easy for me because I just had to call up the Manager of Funeral Services and tell him that Barry Georgina Klein was coming in. He handled everything after I brought him a check for five thousand dollars. Turns out Barry was behind on his payment for his spot and they were about to give it to someone else. Not that it's a good thing that Barry died, but at least he went before he lost his plot.

Barry was Jewish so I had to work fast. I had a two day window to prepare. Barry died on a Tuesday and the funeral was on Friday, not a lot of time to put together such a big event alone, but I had no other choice. My best friend was in crisis and was still estranged from her family of gypsies. Mindy hadn't spoken to her mother for fifteen years. I never knew why. Their feud started before our friendship began, so it meant that the only person Mindy had to rely on was me.

I arranged for Jerry's Deli to deliver lunchmeat platters and had all the moms instruct their nanny's to make a dish for the reception that was to be at Mindy's house after the service. I convinced Maria, by giving her a $100 dollar bill, to help Elva clean all of Barry's things out of Mindy's house. Mindy demanded they be gone by the time she returned from the funeral. She planned to start fresh right then and didn't want to see one item of Barry's in the house. Elva and Maria boxed up his Gucci suits and shipped them to their relatives in Ecuador and Mexico

It was all going as planned, until five a.m. Friday morning when I got a call from Mindy who insisted I get over to her house right away. She was crying and I could hear Cindy doing her scream therapy in the background. I threw on my Uggs and my long Chenille Robe I bought on Oprah's online store that has her "O" logo, and ran across the street to Mindy's house. I rushed up the stairs to her bedroom.

"Mindy! What is it?" I said.

"I need to go to Zen Spa right now." Mindy said. "I need my hair and makeup done for the funeral."

I felt that twinge in my neck again, that same feeling I had the day I pulverized her with my racket.

"Mindy, you can't go to the spa the day of your husband's funeral." I told her.

"Why not?" She said.

"It's tacky." I said, and she gasped louder than when I told her I was concerned about starving children in Africa.

"I might be many things, but I am not tacky." She said and started crying which set off Cindy into another bout of scream therapy in her room down the hall. "Look at me. Look at my face. I can't go to Barry's funeral looking like this. I need cover-up."

The bump I gave her between her eyes had gone down, but it looked worse because it bruised into horrible colors of blue, red and yellow. Even the scratch on her cheek looked worse because a scab had developed. It looked like someone took a black Sharpie across her cheek.

"All right. All right. I'll call an emergency session with Nancy.' I told her. "But, no guarantees." I added.

Nancy, our spa guru, had given us her secret number only for emergency sessions, but she informed us that we were granted only three in our lifetime, so we should be sure that it was a real emergency.

"This is an emergency. It doesn't get any more desperate than this." Mindy said while pointing to her forehead.

Mindy handed me a white business card that had a phone number printed on it so small, we had to use a magnifying glass to read it. I dialed the number.

"What's your emergency?" The voice said.

"Hair and make-up for Mindy Klein." I said.

"Oh, and a rub." Mindy added. "I'm really tense."

I rolled my eyes. "And a rub. She's tense." I said to the covert voice.

"What's the occasion?" The voice said.

"Her husband's funeral." I told the voice.

"One moment." The voice said.

Mindy kept tapping me on the arm. "What's she saying? Can they get me in?"

"I'm on hold." I told her. "Stop hitting my arm." I added.

"Be at the back door in fifteen minutes." The voice said. "Wear a hat and knock three times and only three times."

I hung up the phone. "You're in." I said to Mindy who sat back exhausted.

"Oh, thank God." She said.

"But we only have fifteen minutes to get there." I said.

Mindy rushed into her closet, grabbed a black dress and shoes, threw on a robe and was ready in three minutes. Truly this was a first. Mindy was never ready in three minutes.

We ran to my car and I drove her down the hill to the back door of Zen Spa in record time. We knocked three times. The door creaked open an inch.

"Your name?" A voice said.

"Mindy Klein." Mindy said under a hat that was so huge, the brim flopped over her face, covering her to her nose.

"Lift up your hat." The voice said. Mindy raised the brim and the voice gasped.

"It's not that bad." I said.

"Yes, it is." The voice said. An arm reached out and grabbed hold of Mindy's wrist. "I'll need six hours with her." The voice said.

"You've got four." I said. "The funeral's at noon."

The arm pulled Mindy inside quickly. "I'll have to hurry." The voice said, and just like that, Mindy disappeared into Zen Spa.

Nancy takes these emergency sessions way to seriously, I thought, as I looked down and saw a lady bug crawling on a leaf in the flower bed. I walked over to it, careful not to step on any plants, which was kind of hard because Uggs are not the daintiest shoes. I knelt down, put my finger out and it crawled on me.

"Oh, you're so sweet." I said to the lady bug. "Now I'm going to have good luck today."

I heard a weird sound, a sort of buzzing that I couldn't place. I looked around and didn't see anything, but whatever it was startled the ladybug. It flew away and as I watched it, I was hit in the face with a stream of water spewing out of a sprinkler, then another and another. I was being hit on all sides and just when I thought it couldn't get any worse, I saw a warning sign that said, "Reclaimed water. Do not drink."

Reclaimed water!

That's water they've strained the poop and pee out of. I wanted to die.

My Oprah Chenille robe was soaked, but I couldn't take it off, because I was wearing my birthday suit underneath it. I ran to my car and drove home thinking about the germs on my body. I ran a stop sign, intentionally I might add, because when you have reclaimed water on you, you want to get to a shower fast. A police car rushed up behind me with lights blaring. I pulled over.

The officer walked up to my window and tapped on it gently. "Your license." He said.

"I don't have it with me." I told him after rolling down the window.

"Name?"

"Candy Katz."

"Is that your real name?"

"It's Candace. Candy was my stage name."

"You an actress? Work in the theatre?"

"Something like that." I said.

"Oh, I get it. You're one of those girls." He said.

"I am not one of those girls." I insisted.

"Why are you wet?" He said.

"Oh, uh, I got caught in the sprinklers." I told him.

"Where are you coming from?" He asked.

"I can't tell you." I said.

Nancy had sworn us to secrecy about her emergency sessions. She told me if I ever let it get out, she would deny me services at the Zen Spa. I knew the cop could put me in jail if I didn't answer his questions thoroughly, but I wasn't giving up Zen Spa for the rest of my life.

"Get out of the car, Miss." He said.

I got out of the car and he slapped handcuffs on me.

"What are you doing?" I asked.

"Taking you in." He said, and sniffed at me and then looked away as if I smelt bad.

"On what grounds?" I asked.

"I believe you are under the influence of an illegal substance." He said.

"I am not. I just have a robe soaked with reclaimed water on." I insisted.

"Not making sense, no identification." He mumbled as he wrote an electronic ticket with his stylist. Then he looked at me. "Possible flasher." He added on his notepad.

I looked down. My robe had come open an inch down to my naval. He could tell I wasn't wearing anything underneath it.

"Officer, you've got it all wrong." I insisted.

He closed my robe and double knotted the tie since I was in handcuffs and couldn't do it. "No indecent exposure on my watch, lady."

And just like that, I was taken to jail. As I rode in the back seat of the cop car wearing my wet Chenille Oprah robe and having reclaimed water seep into my pours, I couldn't help but think about Mindy on the massage table getting a rub. This was so not fair.

Tom got me out of the Lost Hills Sheriff Station by

eight a.m., with only a charge of running a stop sign. He explained how I had been tirelessly helping a good friend who was just widowed and that with all the pressure I'd been under, I wasn't myself. Free finally, I only had a few hours to clean up, get Mindy's house ready for the reception and pick up Mindy from Zen Spa.

When I got home, I rushed into the shower. Tom was feeling frisky and in order to get him away from me, I told him I had been doused with reclaimed water and so until I was sanitized and purified, he should keep his hands off me or he might catch something. Tom had a minor case of hypochondria, so whenever I wanted to be left alone, I told him I was feeling sick, but the reclaimed water excuse really worked.

Quickly I did my hair and make-up and put on my Robert Rodriquez Bow Strap Double Knit Dress and my black Christian Louboutin Drapiday shoes with the red soles I got at Barney's, because it's always nice to have a hint of color, and drove to Zen Spa to pick up Mindy.

I knocked three times on the back door, listening and watching the sprinklers to make sure they didn't catch me again.

"We need a credit card." The voice said.

"Mindy has a credit card." I said.

"Declined." The voice said.

"Did you try it again?" I asked.

"Five times." The voice said. "We take Visa, Master Card, Amex, Diners, and debit cards. We can't release her until payment's been made in full."

Reluctantly, I handed over my credit card. The door shut, and after two minutes, Mindy appeared looking beautiful and vibrant in her Chanel little black dress and her Manolo Blanick black leather pumps.

"Wow. Where'd the goose bump go?" I asked. Nancy had done such a great job of covering it up, that you couldn't tell I whacked her with my racket.

"You're late." She said to me.

"I had a rough morning." I told her and almost went on about my stint in jail, but decided to take the high road and keep in mind that this day was about her.

"Here's your card." Mindy handed me the card and receipt as we walked to my Mercedes.

I looked at the receipt. "Two thousand and five hundred?" I blurted out without thinking.

"I'll pay you back. I don't know why my card's not working." Mindy said as we got in my car. "Do I have to go today?" She added. "I really don't want to go. Funerals just aren't my thing."

"Mindy, no one ever wants to go to a funeral, especially their own." I said. "We'll be in and out in no time, then after a little while at the reception, you can sneak upstairs with the excuse that you're too distraught to carry on."

"It's not an excuse. I am too distraught. At least I got a two hour rub. That helped." She said and all I kept thinking was that Mindy got a two hour massage while I got hosed with reclaimed water and stuck in a jail cell wet. At least I wasn't brought up on charges of indecent exposure. I don't know how I would have explained that one to the neighbors.

We returned home where Tom had a limo waiting to take us to the funeral home. Cindy refused to drive in such a gas guzzling, environmentally disgusting car and needed to be alone in her Smart Car with her 100% Bitch girlfriend so they could scream whenever they wanted. Kelly told me she was driving with her BF, so Mindy, Tom, and I drove to the cemetery with Elva and Maria. Tom was worried about a deal at work that was going south and Mindy was worried that the makeup over her bruise would wipe off. I was the only one concerned if Rabbi Bronstein was going to show and if the deli platters would make it to Mindy's house before all the people arrived. I was expecting a big crowd. Not because Barry had such a large family and a lot of friends, but because Barry was part of our Calabasas community and when there's drama, people flock to it. After all, if you're not at the hottest party or the latest funeral, you're no one.

When we arrived in the vestibule, the Mortuary Manager called me over to the side. "I'm sorry to tell you this now, but the check you gave me for $5,000 bounced. Do you have a credit card or a check from another account you could give me or we may have to post-pone the funeral."

"You would do that?" I asked.

"We have in the past. It's not something we're proud of, but we're a business, not a charity service." He said.

I took Mindy to the side. "Mindy the check I gave them for Barry's funeral bounced."

"It bounced?" She said. "What is going on?" She snuck a peek out at the crowd, searching for someone and then waved at me to come closer. "Mindy, see the bald skinny man sitting in the third row, right in the middle. That's Barry's accountant. Get him over here."

I went out into the crowd of over two hundred people. Sixty percent of them were Calabasas moms dressed for the event. Diamonds were out, Botox had been injected and more women had their hair professionally straightened in that audience than I've ever seen. I was saying my hellos on my way to the accountant when I saw Kelly walk in arm and arm with Brad. I rushed over to her.

"Kelly. I thought you were coming with Brianna." I said.

"I said my BF." Kelly snapped. "God, why don't you ever listen to me?"

"I listen. I thought you meant best friend." I said.

"No, Mom, boy friend." She said with as much attitude as a seventeen year old can.

"Hey, Mrs. Katz." Brad said to me and winked.

Not that I would ever compete with my daughter,

but I was pretty sure Brad was honing in on my daughter so he could get access to me, but I couldn't deal with it then. I had a funeral on hold, a bounced check and a bald accountant to drag by his ears to Mindy so she could eat him alive.

"Oh, there's Cindy and her girlfriend." I said. "Kelly I need you to do me a favor. Take her to the curtained off room to the right for family and immediate friends."

"But, Mom."

"Kelly Carla Katz, I've got a lot going on. Do me this one favor." I said.

"Uh, oh, all right, but only since you're forcing me." Kelly said.

I moved on to retrieve the accountant, stepping on a few toes on the way. He was in the middle of the isle so I had no choice. His bald head glistened under the lights and I could see my reflection in it. I checked my teeth for lipstick before tapping his shinny skull.

"Mindy Klein needs to see you.' I whispered in his ear.

He looked scared and gulped. Reluctantly, he followed me. Mindy was in the restroom reserved for family of the deceased. The accountant wouldn't go in to speak with her without me. He insisted that he needed a witness in case Mindy physically harmed him.

We entered the bathroom and found Mindy relaxing on a lounge chair, chewing an acrylic nail.

"Where's all our money?" Mindy asked him.

"You're broke." He said. "Barry was trying to keep it a secret from you. He thought he would lose you."

"Broke?" Mindy said as she stood up and walked close to him. "Since when?"

"Since Barry had to pay up on some bad gambling debts. He's been the hole for years. In fact, he owes me $3500. I was going to wait until the funeral was over to ask you for it, but since we're talking now…" He added.

Mindy turned really red, like scary red as she processed the fact that she was broke. She stabbed her heel into the top of his foot, pressing down on it until he started crying.

"I will not pay you a dime, you scum sucking maggot." She said.

"Please. It's not my fault. Ouch! Ouch!" He said.

Mindy's started clawing at his head. I've never seen anyone so scared in all my life. He had sweat coming through his armpits on his sport coat, a cheap one I might add.

"Mindy! Stop it." I yelled.

The accountant rushed out of the bathroom with scratches all over his bald head.

"You'll be hearing from my lawyer!" He yelled.

"Oh, God. I'm broke! I'm broke! That mother fucking Barry!" Mindy said and then she screamed real loud for a really long time.

This was turning out to be the worst event I'd ever planned. Mindy refused to come out of the bathroom. In her words, Barry was a liar, a cheater, a salami sandwich eater, which is probably what gave him the heart attack, and now he wasn't even good with money. He had ruined her and she was not coming out of the bathroom for his service.

After all I've done for him, she kept saying and I kept thinking, what have you done for him? She never made him breakfast, lunch or dinner. She never did his laundry. She never called him at work just to say hello, only to tell him she needed more money. And yes, if I'm honest, all that described me with Tom, but at least I asked Tom how his day went. I rubbed his shoulders. I'd get him a shot of Stolley when he came home from work. I'd even swim naked in our pool just to give him a good time when he had a bad day, even if it embarrassed Kelly, because marriage is about doing the little things and Mindy never did the little things for

Barry.

I poked my head out at the crowd. They were getting antsy and I think they heard Mindy screaming in the bathroom, but the Funeral Manager was holding us hostage until he got his money.

I pulled Tom off to the side and convinced him to put the $5,000 on a credit card and went in front of the crowd to explain.

"Excuse me." I said, tapping on the microphone. Feedback pierced through the room. All the guests held their ears. "We'll be starting in just a minute."

Then we learned the Rabbi was holding us hostage for a five hundred dollar payment. He had been given a heads up by the funeral manager that Mindy's checks were no good, and he didn't take credit cards. Luckily, Tom had five one hundred dollar bills in his wallet so the service was back on.

The rabbi gave a generic eulogy that would fit any middle-aged successful man, because he'd never met Barry. And then when he asked friends and family to come up and speak about Barry, no one volunteered. Mindy was still in the bathroom and Cindy was trying not to scream by holding one hand over her mouth and her other hand on her GF's hip. Elva didn't speak English and Tom had a fear of public speaking. It was up to me to make Barry's send off a memorable one.

"I've got a few things to say." I said and took over the stage from the rabbi. I looked out at the people there for the show and not one person was crying. "What can I say about Barry?" I said. "Oh, Barry, Barry, Barry. I just loved the guy."

And then I realized, I had absolutely nothing to say about Barry. I'd eaten dinner with the man more times than I could count and I'd been on five vacations with him and still, I had nothing to say about Barry except that he was always gassy and smelled like salami.

"I can't believe this." I said to a sea of faces, most rolling their eyes, some chewing their nails, others yawning.

"Say it all ready." A heckler shouted.

"I can't believe Barry fooled you all into thinking he was just a lawyer."

Suddenly I had their attention.

"No, no, no, that was just his day job. Barry secretly worked to provide food for starving children in Africa. When people thought he was traveling for business, Barry was in the Africa handing out canned food to villagers. He worked with the Red Cross, the Salvation Army, the United Nations and Save the Children. You know that commercial you all see late at night that shows you a picture of a starving child and then tells you that just a penny a day could feed him. We'll Barry didn't just donate a penny a day. He donated five pennies a day for the last fifteen years. That means he probably saved like 50,000 thousand kids from starving to death, who would all be here today, but they didn't have money for airfare."

The crowd was silent.

"He even knew Bono." I added, and now I had them. "Barry didn't care if you wore Gucci or Chanel or Manolo Blanick. Barry wasn't about brand names. Barry Klein was about the heart. Barry was more than just a lawyer. He was a good man. In fact, Barry was a super man." I said in a sort of way a preacher delivers a Sunday Sermon. "Thank you."

The audience jumped to their feet, clapping and crying. I was so proud. I told a few white lies, but I got Barry a standing ovation for his send off so I figured it was worth it.

At Mindy's house, the platters weren't there because Mindy's credit card didn't go through. I demanded the delivery boy return immediately. Tom paid for the food and gave the driver a huge tip for his inconvenience. Mindy had no idea about any of this, nor did she care. She went into her room as soon as we came back and slammed the door. I heard muffled cuss words coming out of her room and hoped the guests downstairs couldn't make out that she was calling Barry a fucking asshole.

I went downstairs and told the guests that she was too distraught to come down. Calabasas women and men milled about eating food and drinking from Barry's high-end stash of liquor. I walked around making sure the guests were well taken care of. There was a buzz amongst the guests about how much Barry had done to help starving children and how amazing it was that he kept it all to himself. I was proud that I was able to make people think better of Barry on his last day and realized I wanted people to talk about me the way they were talking about Barry. I'd given Barry the eulogy I'd like to have, but to be that sort of person I'd actually have to start doing things in my life a little differently. Shopping, getting my nails done, having regular spray tans and playing tennis would have to be cut back. I was ready to make a difference and couldn't wait to tell Tom about my plan.

"Maria, have you seen Tom?" I asked my maid who I had to pay an extra fifty to get her to work the party. She was really raking in money and clothes since Barry's passing.

"No se, Mama." Maria said while washing a platter in the kitchen sink. Elva didn't like that she was at the main station at the kitchen and kept gesturing for Maria to move over.

I searched the living room and back patio for Tom and saw Kelly and Brad kissing in a corner.

"Young lady, this is not a time for that. It's called a reception, not a make-out session." I said to my insensitive daughter.

She and Brad giggled like school kids because they were still in high school and that sly Brad looked me up and down like I was a steak he wanted to eat.

"Where's your father?" I asked Kelly.

"I don't know. I'm not his babysitter." My

daughter said and it was all I could do to avoid making a comment.

I left my daughter with Brad, probably not the best decision, but this was not the day I had the time or the energy to deal with my daughter's new BF who I was absolutely positive was going to be a cheating husband in his future.

I started up the stairs to check on Mindy, and saw Stacy and Katie huddled in the corner of the living room, whispering and watching me. I needed to have a sit down with Katie about the rumor she was spreading about Mindy sleeping with my husband, but I didn't have time yet. It had been a harrowing 72 hours. I didn't know how I was ever going to recover. Not only was I exhausted, Tom and I were out ten grand we'd probably never see again.

I continued up the stairs feeling so bad about Mindy, who was hiding in her room, freaking out about her horrible financial situation. Not only did Barry gamble their money away, he also borrowed against his life insurance and had mortgaged the house so many times through Tom's company, there wasn't any equity left.

I knocked on the double door to her master suit before walking in. The room was dark. The blackout drapes were closed.

"Mindy? I came to check on you." I said, but I didn't see her in her bed.

"Oh, uh Candy, I'm fine. Stay there, I'll be right out." She said, and then whispered, "I thought you locked the door?"

I walked farther inside and turned towards her master bath and there was Tom with his pants down to his ankles, standing in his tightie-whities with his button-up shirt unbuttoned.

"Tom? What are you doing in here?"

Mindy scooted out of the closet, adjusting her double D's inside her little black Chanel dress that was on backwards. During their make-out session, the makeup Nancy applied at the emergency spa session had smudged off. Mindy looked like Michael Gorbachev's daughter again.

I could not breathe, literally. Nothing came in and nothing went out my nose.

"I ah, oh come on Candy Cane, Mindy was so upset. She needed me. It was nothing Candy. Come here, sweetie." Tom said.

He actually thought I would run into his arms and forgive him. He probably was thinking he could have both of us now that Barry was out of the way.

"Candy…" Mindy said.

"Don't say another word." I said to Mindy.

And then ran out of the bedroom, down the stairs, through a thick group of guests, and I may have knocked over an older lady, I'm still not sure, because I was so upset. I ran out of the house and down the street to my Tuscan Villa. I ran up the steps to our second floor, went through the double door to my master suit and let out a scream that made Mindy's fit in the funeral parlor john seem like a mouse squeak.

"OH, MY GOD!"

CANDY'S SCREWED

CHAPTER FOUR

You know, it's a really strange feeling when you find out your husband's cheating on you with your best friend. Suddenly, the two people closest to me after my daughter, who hardly talked to me since she turned fourteen, were gone.

Barry was the lucky one of us. At least he died thinking his wife was faithful. I now had to carry on for both of us and deal with our deceptive spouses, but the only thing I was able to do was stay in bed. Four days had passed since I saw them together and I was still in the dress I wore to the funeral. I told Kelly I had the flu, but when I didn't change my clothes or come out of my room, I think she suspected something else. I didn't have the heart to tell her that her father was a total and complete loser, so I told her nothing.

My life was a soap opera after all, a pathetic soap opera full of clichés and backstabbers. I grew up watching General Hospital. Luke and Laura's wedding was one of the highlights of my teenage years, but I never wanted my life to be a soap opera. I wanted money, a fancy car and a good-looking husband, but I never wanted him to sleep with my best friend. Then add in Brad, the high school senior honing in on my daughter while winking at me behind her back and that made my whole life ridiculous.

At least I gave Barry a good send off. That was the only thing I'd done since having my daughter that I was really proud of, which was sort of pathetic when I thought about it because that meant in seventeen years I hadn't done much worth bragging about.

Tom tried to speak with me several times and I told him to go away, even though he was crying and blabbering on and on about how sorry he was. He even passed a note underneath our bedroom door. I didn't read it. I shredded it into about five hundred little pieces. I told him I needed time alone before I could speak to him and told him to check in at the Hilton Garden Inn.

Calabasas used to have the Calabasas Inn as our main hotel, but it had closed down which made me depressed. We had our recommitment ceremony there a few years before in their garden. Our first wedding was atrocious. It was a quickie wedding in Tom's backyard. Instead of a sit down meal, we had a serve yourself banquet, so I decided to redo it. I got tired of refusing to show people my wedding pictures. I needed a new set I was proud of that matched my life now.

The Calabasas Inn had a fabulous fountain at the end of a large grassy area. It was so beautiful there that they booked back to back weddings every weekend. We had the recommitment ceremony right in front of the waterfall. I had a chuppah even though I'm not Jewish, because I like the way they look. The florist decorated it with pink and white lilies and I stood under it wearing a Vera Wang Collection strapless mermaid taffeta gown. I swear on my life that I looked better than Pamela Anderson when she got married to Kid Rock in her bathing suit. There's something to be said for class and when you put on a Vera Wang gown, you turn into the classiest bride in town, even if you were a former stripper.

My first wedding I wore an absolute disaster of a dress that ripped in the seat of my pants when I bent down to kiss the flower girl. The poor girl had to stand behind me the entire ceremony to hide the rip so I promised I'd give her my wedding dress. I have no idea where that girl is today. She was the daughter of one of the Mexican men who was working on Tom's house. Tom picked up her father on the side of the road.

The San Fernando Valley has all these streets lined with men who don't have green cards, don't speak English and work hard at a cut rate. Your drive up and hire them. It's an easy system for them to find a job. Instead of getting trained and putting together a resume, all these guys have to do is make sure they're standing on the right corner. It's like being a prostitute, but instead of giving you sex for money, they'll give you a paint job, a toilet repair, a sprinkler fix. I've always felt it's so cool that illegal immigrants can come to America and find work just by standing on the street. Even if you just got out of jail, you can get hired to go into someone's home to fix their toilet because there's no way to check your background or references. It just proves that this is the land of opportunity.

Tom wore a classic black tuxedo from the Armani Collezioni, which I think is just a fancy way of saying collection in English. Mindy told me it might be how you say collection in Italian, but I told her she was wrong. The suit had satin trim and a one button front. We tied it together with a white shirt, and skipped the tie, because Tom looked so cool without it.

Tom, even though it breaks my heart to think of it, was the most handsome groom in the world. When I walked towards him on the green and white carpet made of freshly plucked lily pads, that the florist had made fresh in Brazil and flown in earlier that morning for my wedding, I felt like the luckiest girl in town. I couldn't believe I picked so well. But that dream is over. It turned out that Tom's a schmuck. The man I based my entire life on is a no good worthless piece of dirt on the bottom of my shoe.

And Mindy, my best friend, is a lying sack of scum.

I kept trying to think of where I was when they were having the affair. Shopping? No. Mindy always shopped with me. Getting my nails done? No, Mindy always got her nails done at the same time. Playing tennis? No, Mindy always played tennis with me. I searched my brain to find out when they got together to cheat on me, and just couldn't see when it had happened. Either I was a total idiot, or Tom and Mindy are just so damn sly they were able to pull it off underneath my nose for years.

Years!

How long had their affair been going on? If it had been years, I'd be even more mortified than if it had just been a few weeks or a few times. Or maybe it happened just that once, in Mindy's bathroom, on the day of Barry's funeral. That could be, I decided. I hoped it was just that once, because one time felt better than if it had been many times. Don't get me wrong, one time still felt horrible, but if they had been sleeping together for a long time, that would be like, unforgivable.

I needed to get some answers, so I called Katie. After all, she's the one who started it. I begged her to come over right away. This was a bit odd since Katie wasn't really in my inner circle. She was one of my outer circle friends. We never spent time alone and I never invited her to my house unless it was for a party. You know, when there's someone you might like, but you've never given them the time of day so you don't know if you like them. Well, that's my relationship with Katie. I never gave her the time of day because I had Mindy, and Mindy completed me.

Katie arrived eight minutes later. I kid you not. I wasn't sure where she lived, because she didn't live in the Calabasas Oaks. I assumed she lived somewhere in Calabasas because she always hung out with us Calabasas moms, and figured she might live by the lake. Calabasas has a man-made lake with attached homes surrounding it. You have to be a Calabasas resident to get a key that gives you access to it. I like to run around the lake. They have this great path that goes near the shore. There's no swimming, though. The water has bird poop and fish and old line and hooks because some idiotic people actually fish the water. But still, the lake is pretty to look at. If I became friends with Katie and she lived at the lake, we could hang out on her deck and watch birds fly by as we drink cocktails.

Once Tom and I went to a boat party on Calabasas Lake. We cruised around while having cocktails and thought maybe we should get a vacation home on the lake. We'd never have our first home there, because they're small, like only twenty-five hundred square feet and not behind a guard gate, but we'd be perfectly comfortable saying it was our second house.

"Mama!" Maria called out and knocked on my door. "Amigo aqui." She said.

"Katie? Is that you?" I called out.

"Yes. It's me." She said.

"You can come in." I yelled.

Katie entered my room and immediately started coughing. "Oh, god, what's that smell?"

I sniffed my arms. I think the smell was me since I hadn't showered in four days, but I wasn't going to admit this to her.

Katie looked around the room. She walked over to the swing. "Wow, some decorating job. She looked at me, resting high up on my four poster bed. "Are you still wearing the same dress you wore to the funeral?" She asked.

"Katie, I need you to promise me what you're seeing here today, you won't tell anyone."

"Of course." Katie said. "It's our secret."

"Tom is sleeping with Mindy." I said and started crying.

"I know." She said. "I told you."

"I found them together in Mindy's bathroom at the reception."

Katie gasped. "No." She said. "How tacky."

"I know. It's like the tackiest thing you could ever do."

"Wow, you must feel awful."

"I'm a mess. You have to tell me who saw them. Who told you they were cheating on me?" I said they because it felt not only that my husband was cheating on me, but that my best friend was too.

"Look, I'm sworn to secrecy." Katie said.

"But the secret's out. It doesn't matter anymore."

"I don't know if I can trust you."

"You can trust me. Actually, out of all the people we know, you can probably trust me the most." I said because between me, Mindy and Stacy, I definitely was the nicest out of the three.

"Candy, we're not really friends, you know." Katie said, and she was right. We weren't really friends, but who cares.

"Katie, I need to know the details. You have to spill it. I'm dying here." I begged. "Look at me. Do you ever think I would let you see me like this if I wasn't totally sincere?"

"You have to promise that you'll die with this secret." She said and I was really worried that it was something horribly awful, like terribly awful about Mindy and Tom.

"I promise, promise, promise."

"Okay. If this gets out, I'll know it was you. It wasn't a friend of a friend of a friend who saw them. It was me."

"You? When? Where? How?" I asked.

Back in middle school, I took a journalism class and learned all good reporters ask who, what, when, where and how. I was a Jessica Savitch fan for about a month because I liked her hair style, and everyone kept telling me I looked like her. I already knew who and what, I just didn't know when, where or how.

The how was going to be the hardest to figure out and accept. I kept asking myself, how could this have happened? Every answer I gave myself didn't flush out. Tom was unhappy in our marriage? Nope. I knew he loved me and I loved him, and he never went more than twenty-four hours not getting sexually satisfied. Now I watch Oprah, so I know that's pretty good, especially coming close to twenty years of marriage. I was losing my looks? Nope. With Botox, spray tans, my breast augmentation and realigning my body with Pilates, I looked better than when he married me.

The only how that made sense was that Tom was tired of sleeping with the same woman year after year. If that was the answer there was nothing more I could do. I invented positions keep him happy, and believe me, it's not easy doing the splits upside down at my age. I even installed a swing in my bedroom when all the other Calabasas moms were installing a stripper pole. I like trends, but I opted for the swing because it was unique. I didn't know anyone else who swung naked in their bedroom as a form of foreplay. I tried to keep our sex life from getting boring, because there's nothing worse than being boring, except being poor.

"Look Candy, Jack's business is way down so I had to take a job." Katie said. I gasped and put my hand to my mouth. This was worse than I thought.

"I know. I know. It's totally embarrassing. I'm a bartender in a restaurant called Chapter 8 in Agoura."

Agoura? No one goes to Agoura.

"I got a job there because I thought I wouldn't see anyone I know. After all, no one from Calabasas goes to Agoura." Katie said and I wondered if she could read my mind.

"Before I married Jack, I was a bartender at the Rainbow Bar & Grill on Sunset so getting another bartender job was the fastest way to make money. Please don't tell anyone."

"I won't." I promised.

I considered telling her that being a bartender has a lot more dignity than being a pole stripper like I was before I married Tom, but I held it in.

"Not that I was a bartender before I got married, I don't care if you tell anyone that, just don't tell them that I had to go back to work." Katie made clear.

OMG! She is reading my mind. I hope she isn't a gypsy.

"I was just about to get off work when they came into the bar. The place is sort of dark, so they didn't see me. They took a booth in the corner. Mindy ordered a Cosmopolitan." Katie said.

"How predictable." I said. The Cosmopolitan drinks were all the rage since the Sex and the City movie came out.

"I know. I didn't think it was a big deal at first, you know, 'cause I thought you'd be coming in to join them, but then they started kissing."

I gasped.

Katie stopped talking while I took in the horrible news.

"Oh, my God." I said, because in times like this, I couldn't think of anything else to say.

"I know. OMG is exactly what I said. I couldn't believe it because Mindy is your BFF. Then I didn't know if I should tell you or not. I walked around for days tortured over it, but decided if I were you, which thank God I'm not, that I would want to know."

But I didn't want to know. I wanted the world back the way it was where I believed my life was perfect and that Mindy, while a bit needy and self-centered and annoying at times, had my best interests at heart.

Katie and I swore each other to secrecy. I would not tell anyone that she was working nights as a bartender in Agoura and she would never tell anyone that I didn't shower for four days. She told me I smelled really bad and then left. She's blunt, but still, I like her. Compared to dealing with Mindy, having a heart to heart with Katie was a piece of cake. She actually let me finish my sentences, and then responded to them.

After Katie left, I thought about getting out of my black dress and getting a shower, but I was in mourning. Not over Barry, over the death of the life I used to have. The black dress was the perfect outfit for the occasion.

It was only when I was able to smell my own body odor that I considered calling Nancy for an emergency session to cut it off of me, but thinking of Nancy and Zen Spa reminded me of Mindy. I tried to shut out thoughts of her as much as possible, because every time her name came into my head, I felt a sort of shock, like my brain was having an electrical shortage.

Mindy hadn't called to see how I was or to apologize or to beg for my forgiveness. I hadn't heard a peep from her. The nerve, I thought, after all I did for her before and after Barry's death. I was her 100% BFF and she stomped all over my heart like it was no BFD.

I heard a splash out in the pool. I got out of bed and walked over to the window. My legs felt weird, like after you've been riding on a horse, because I had only walked to the toilet and back to bed for the last four days. Down below I saw Kelly and Brad swimming in the pool and on a lounge chair I saw another lifeguard from the club. Brad looked up, but I don't think he saw me because I ducked down.

"MARIA!" I yelled.

Maria opened the door and stood at the threshold. For two days she refused to come into the room because I refused to take a bath. She brought me food on a tray she set inside the room and said ay yi yi, over and over.

"You can come in now. I'm going to take a bath."

Maria was so happy. She ran over to the bathtub

86

and set up my bubble bath, lining the edge with lit candles, turning on my spa music that had sounds of the forest so I could hear birds chirping and wind rustling through pine leaves. She put two fluffy white towels monogrammed with my initials on the towel warmer and dropped in three teaspoons of my Chanel No. 5 Bath Gel. I was told by the sales lady at Neiman Marcus that it has Pro-Vitamin 5 and Vitamin C and E derivatives that are anti-oxidants that fight free radicals. I wasn't sure what made it a pro-vitamin as opposed to just a regular vitamin, and I thought derivatives had something to do with the stock market, but I guess I was wrong.

I did understand anti-oxidants and free radicals, because Helga, the lady at Zen Spa who gives me my bi-weekly facials, explained to me that anti-oxidants are little soldiers that attack the free-radicals on my skin. She described the free radicals as microscopic terrorists that damage my pours with their toxins.

Maria held her nose the entire time she set up my bath so it took her a while since she only had one free hand. When she was done, she went out of the room and closed the doors behind her, and finally, after four long days, I peeled that black dress off and threw it in the trash instead of the dry cleaning bag. There's no way, even with multiple cleanings, that that dress could ever be worn again.

I put my toe in the water. It was scalding hot. I think Maria felt I needed a good cleansing. I added cold water, put my head back on my bath pillow and turned on the jets. It was a Jacuzzi tub of course, because Tom and I always had to have the very best.

I tried to relax, but my mind kept thinking over and over, Tom, Tom, Tom, and Mindy, Mindy, Mindy, and how could you do this to me. Mindy wasn't prettier than me. I was sure of that. I tried to be a whore in bed, like all good wives are supposed to be, and happily embraced that side of marriage. After all, it's the only time in a woman's life where being a whore is a good thing. I know this because I watch TV, and every TV sex therapist I've seen on Dr. Phil, the View and even Ellen, insisted it would keep my husband from straying.

I was there for Tom. I supported him when he worked long hours. I never demanded he be home at a certain hour or that he spend more than two hours with me on a weekend day. I let him come and go as he pleased, and kept myself busy with tennis, shopping and hanging out with Mindy. I mean really, I asked nothing of him and in return he slept with my best friend.

It was turning into a horrible bath. Even the birds on the soundtrack annoyed me. I didn't want to think. I didn't want to feel any of these horrible feelings. I closed my eyes to relax, but kept reliving the scene inside Mindy's bathroom where my husband was standing with his pants down. It played on my closed eyelids like a movie, over and over.

Then, I had this odd feeling that someone was looking at me. I opened my eyes, and I kid you not, Brad was standing by my bathroom door.

I screamed.

"Sorry." Brad said. "I thought this was the guest bathroom."

Sly dog, there's no way in hell he thought this was the guest bathroom.

I glanced down at my body. Luckily, with the jets and the bubble bath, he couldn't see any part of my nude body.

"Brad." I said.

"Yeah." He answered, while standing there with a sly smile that told me this kid wanted to jump into the tub with me. He was only wearing board shorts and a pucca shell necklace. I don't think this kid ever got dressed properly. He probably went to school dressed like that.

"Get out!" I said sternly.

"You sure you don't want me to wash your back?" Brad said.

"I will call the cops on you." I warned him and he just laughed, and I'm telling you, this kid was more attractive than Clooney, Pitt and Cruise all meshed together.

"Wouldn't do that, Mrs. Katz. You'll get in trouble for messing with jailbait, remember." He said with a smile and ran his fingers through his hair and unhooked his pucca shell necklace that was stuck on his right nipple.

"Brad?" I said, quietly.

"Yeah, Mrs. Katz." He said.

"Get out or I'll call your parents." I insisted.

He didn't have a reply. He just walked away slowly, stopping for a moment to glance at the swing hanging from the ceiling before leaving the room.

Holy crap! Of all the nerve!

I got out of the bath once I knew the coast was clear and wrapped myself in a towel. I had to do something about the mess I was in. I had to decide if I wanted Tom in my life. I had to decide how I was going to kill Mindy so it looked like an accident. I had to decide how I was going get Brad away from my daughter without her hating me more. Feeding starving children in Africa was way off my list. Yes, I may be shallow and I may not have done any charity work in my life so far, but my life was crumbling in Calabasas, California, and I no longer had such a strong desire to head on over to Africa to help fix their food shortage.

I got dressed in a comfortable, yet sexy and stylish Juicy Couture jumpsuit and went downstairs.

"Maria, get me an Evian.' I ordered. I was going to be the kind of person who orders people around from here on out, I decided. No more Mrs. Nice.

"Si, Mama." Maria said and rushed to the refrigerator and got me an Evian.

"And don't call me Mama. I'm young enough to be your daughter.' I told her.

"Si Mama." She said as she poured my Evian into a glass that had ice made from tap water. I almost said something too her about how when the ice melts, it's going to contaminate the water, but when she added an orange slice, a small umbrella and straw to the glass, I kept my mouth shut.

I went out to the backyard where Kelly was having her after school playdate with the two hunky high school boys.

"Mom, you're out. This is Chris." Kelly said.

"Hello." I said with attitude, because I was in a bit of a mood. I always prided myself on making Kelly's friends feel welcome in our house, but this day I was having a few issues and didn't feel like being a good hostess. "Kelly, I need to talk to you, now. Inside." I said.

Kelly rolled her eyes at me and informed Brad and Chris that I was always too needy for her attention.

I headed back inside, expecting Kelly to follow me, but when I turned back, she was on a lounge chair again and Brad and Chris were checking out my ass.

"Kelly!" I said, and the guys laughed.

"Mom! What? Can't we talk later?" She asked.

"No. Now." I told her.

We went into the family room where Maria was going through my wedding photos, the good set from the second time I got married. She was crying, as if she was the one who had been cheated on. She probably was afraid I'd be sending her back to Tijuana if Tom and I got divorced.

"I want you to stop seeing Brad." I announced. "He's not good for you."

"Mom, my love life's none of your business." She informed me.

"Yes it is. You're my daughter."

"Look, just because everyone in the neighborhood is talking about Dad and Mindy, that doesn't mean you can take it out on me."

"You know?"

"Of course I know. I knew before you. Angela's mom told Sarah's mom and Sarah's mom told Lilly's mom, who told Lilly, who told Cindy, who told me."

I sat back on the couch. "I'm such an idiot."

"Mom, you're not an idiot, you're just, I don't know, you're like one of those people everyone just walks all over."

Wow, to hear it put that way by my daughter was truly awful.

"I don't like to be mean to people." I said.

"I know. That's why everyone treats you like crap. I mean look at the way I talk to you. I do it because I can get away with it. I'm only telling you this straight because I think you need to hear it. I think it's time we had this talk, don't you?"

I started crying.

"Don't cry, Mom. It's not a bad thing that you're nice. It's just not that smart. Oh, and don't worry about Brad. I think I'm sort of over him. He's too into himself and I need someone who is more into me, like Chris."

"You like Brad's friend. Kelly, that's sort of tacky, don't you think?" I asked, while wiping away my tears.

"No. It's only tacky when you're older and married, like Mindy and Dad. I'm only seventeen. It's expected, but it's a good thing, Mom. I've learned from watching you, that if I'm too nice to my husband, he'll walk all over me. That's why I'm going to marry someone nice, like Chris, so I can walk all over him. That way I'm not the one who gets hurt when the marriage ends."

"Your father and I haven't talked about divorce yet." I told Kelly.

"Mom, come on, the divorce rate is like, so high. The fact that you and dad are still married sort of makes me a freak. Anyway, I have to get back to the guys. You okay? Did this talk help?" Kelly asked.

"Uh, huh." I said.

"Oh, and I'm glad you got a bath. The house was really starting to smell." She added, before heading back out to the pool.

Divorce!

I hadn't thought of divorce yet. I'd only thought of Mindy Klein kissing my husband.

Mindy!

What a horrible person she was. She hadn't even called or sent a note or come to my door begging for forgiveness. No wonder Barry had a smile on his face when he died. He knew he'd be through with her. If I was Barry, I would have hung out with Nina on my lunch hour too. She seemed like a pretty sweet girl even though she was a porn star, unlike Mindy who couldn't be trusted.

I went back to my bedroom and got on my swing. The only good part of the week was that I'd hardly eaten so I lost about ten pounds. Maria tried to get me to eat, but I refused. She kept bringing me Evian and saltines, and even though the crackers were carbs, since I didn't eat anything else, I didn't get fat.

It was then that I decided it was time to make a list. I mean, isn't that what everyone does when their life is a mess. You make a list. You get an action plan of steps to take and then you just follow those steps and suddenly everything falls into order. I was so excited and wondered why I hadn't thought of it days before. It would have saved me hours of having to smell my own body odor.

I took a note pad out of my side table drawer, grabbed a pencil, and hopped back on my swing.

Candy's Action Plan

I.   Tom
     1. Will I divorce Tom?
         a. Do if I want to see him again?
         b. Do I want to sleep with him again?
         c. Can I look at him without vomiting?
         d. Do I still love him?

II.   Mindy
     1. How will I kill Mindy?
         a. Shoot her?
         b. Stab her?
         c. Run over her with my car?
         d. Poison her?
         e. Beat her?
         f. Cut off her head?

Roman number one was a bit harder to deal with than number two. After all, how do you decide if you still love someone? I'd known Tom since I was eighteen. He came into the strip joint I worked at with a group of business men and slipped a fifty, along with his telephone number, inside my G-string. Yes, he was twenty years older than me, but he was handsome and he had money so I went on a date with him, not thinking I'd fall in love so fast, but I did. After just two dates, I decided Tom was the only one for me for forever and luckily he felt the same. We were married soon and three months later I had Kelly. We were the all American family. I mean, who would have thought that swinging on a pole would get me this great life with this great guy. It was a dream come true, until Mindy Klein came in and shattered it all apart.

    Yes, I still loved Tom, but should I divorce him was a little bit harder to decide. What would life be like alone? I couldn't even imaging dating again or getting married again. I was stumped. I loved Tom, but he was a lying cheat, so to save what little dignity I had left, I decided I had to divorce him.

Number two I was absolutely sure about. I knew I was going to kill Mindy, I just needed to find the most efficient, fastest way possible that would be easy to disguise as an accident since I didn't want to go to jail. Nowadays there's all this ballistics testing and DNA stuff that it's pretty hard to do away with someone unless you find a way to get rid of their body so evidence can't be found. The idea of chopping up Mindy's body or burning it all sounded so gross, so once I thought about it, I decided I couldn't kill Mindy. Not because I wanted to leave her alive, but because I didn't want to have to dispose of her corpse.

I crumbled up my action plan and tossed it across the room.

"Candy." I heard a voice say on the other side of my door and it wasn't just any voice. It was Mindy. She tried opening the door, but it was locked. "We need to talk." Mindy said with a tone in her voice that made it clear to me that she did not feel bad about what she'd done.

I got off my swing and walked closer to the door. "Go away, you backstabber." I yelled.

I heard a scraping sound and saw the doorknob giggle, then the doors opened. Not only was I horrified by her betrayal, now I was also horrified by the sight of her wearing a tank top with her double D's.

"That door was locked. How did you get in here?" I asked.

Mindy held up a small metal tool. Not only was she a husband stealer and a gypsy, apparently she was also a burglar.

"Jesus, Mindy, you can't just come in here." I said.

"Oh, knock it off." Mindy told me. "We need to talk." She sat down on my swing.

"I don't want to talk to you. In fact, I never want

94

to see you again." I told her. "You backstabber." I added to make her more upset, but she started swinging back and forth and wasn't bothered at all.

"Look, the way I see it. Barry's dead, I'm broke, Tom's into me, he's got money, and I'm stealing your husband." She said, as if rattling off a recipe.

I actually couldn't speak. I was so stumped, that my mouth came open and instead of words, I made a horribly embarrassing squeaking sound. The first thing I could get out of my mouth was, "Get off my swing." I grabbed the chain to stop her from swinging.

"My life is ruined. I'm taking yours." Mindy said.

"How can you be so cruel?" I asked her. "What is wrong with you?"

"Candy, look, I'm not nice like you. I've never been nice. I wasn't born nice. I don't aspire to be nice. I actually like being mean. It feels good. You should try it sometime."

"Are you like possessed with the devil or something?" I asked, and thought back to all those séances I had with my Malibu Barbie and wondered if I conjured up a wicked spirit that's come to haunt me in the person known as Mindy Klein."

"Oh, God, no." Mindy said and laughed. "I'm not possessed, Candy, I'm just trying to survive. It's a jungle out here in the suburbs. Nice girls finish last and it's your turn to get pushed out.

I really wanted to hit her on the head with my imitation of Michelangelo's Statue of David. It was made out of marble and stood three feet high. It probably would have cracked her skull pretty good, and wondered why I didn't add it on my list of weapons when I was trying to decide how to kill her. Tom took me to Florence to see the original for our second honeymoon after our recommitment ceremony. I instantly fell in love with David. I purchased miniatures and placed them all over our house. There's one in our garden, one in our guest bathroom and one in my foyer.

I have about fifteen placed all around our house so when guests come over, they know I have an appreciation for art.

"You're not getting Tom." I told her.

"Yes, I am. And I'll also get this house and all the furniture in it." She told me. "Including this swing."

My mouth fell to the floor and my eyes went wide. Something snapped in me. I hated Mindy Klein, and realized maybe I always hated Mindy Klein. She was superficial, materialist, self-centered, and yes, Mindy Klein was really, really shallow!

"We'll see about that." I said to Mindy and poked my finger into her chest with every word I said. "Now get off my swing, get out of my house and crawl back from where you came from, you… you… gypsy!"

Mindy gasped. "How do you know I come from a family of gypsies?"

"I know all about you, Mindy. You're going up against the wrong girl. I'll fight you teeth and acrylic nails and I'll win."

"I don't think so. You know how deceptive we gypsies are." Mindy said and started laughing as she walked out. "See you around, Candy." She hollered back at me and even though I was really, really scared, I didn't pee in my pants even a tiny bit.

Gypsies, I thought, what do they all know about gypsies that I don't. I grabbed my notepad and started a new list.

Candy's New Action Plan

1. Find out about gypsies.
2. Win Tom back so Mindy can't have him.

CANDY SCREWS TOM TO SCREW MINDY

CHAPTER FIVE

It didn't look good for me that I was going up against a gypsy. Apparently, they're a bit self-centered and don't have much of a conscience. That described Mindy exactly. Too bad I never thought of her being a gypsy earlier. All the signs were there, I just missed them. She found backstabbing to be the funniest sport she'd ever played and never felt guilt. I just thought she was a little selfish like the rest of us Calabasas women, but then I found out I'd been hanging with a gypsy.

I read over my action plan. Number one, find out about gypsies, was completed. Now I was moving on to step number two. Win back Tom so Mindy can't have him.

I called Tom's office. His secretary went into a coughing fit when she heard it was me. "Wait." She said. "He's in a meeting for real this time, but I'm under strict orders to pull him out so he can take your call. Don't hang up or you could get me fired." She begged of me.

"I won't." I told her, feeling proud that I was so important to Tom that he threatened to fire his secretary if she didn't put my call through.

"Mindy." Tom said when he got on the line.

"Mindy?" Oh, my God repeated in my head, over and over and over and over.

"It's Candy."

"Candy, I knew it was you."

"So why'd you say Mindy? If it was as a joke, Tom, it's not funny. It's not funny at all."

What on earth was going on? What was wrong with the world? My husband of eighteen years had gone totally bonkers.

Then I remembered why I was calling. I was trying to win him back.

"Tom, I'm ready to talk." I said while thinking I'm ready to beat you to a pulp. "Can we have dinner tonight?"

"Tonight sounds great." Tom said.

"How about 6:30 at Riviera?" I asked.

Riviera was our favorite Italian restaurant at the Calabasas Commons, the main shopping, eating and entertainment center in town where I spent much of my time. They had a Barnes & Noble, an Edwards Theatre, Starbucks, a Ralph's grocery store, and a bunch of boutique clothing stores. My favorite is Belle Gray by Lisa Rinna. You know, she's the one who is married to Harry Hamlin and was on Day's of Our Lives and Melrose Place and then Dancing with the Stars. I have absolutely no idea who Belle Gray is or why she didn't name the store Lisa Rina, but the store has awesome clothes that you'll find the stars wearing. I like to zip in there to get the latest t-shirt worn by Jennifer Anniston or the latest dress worn by Britney Spears.

"Sounds good." Tom said. "Oh, Candy, this is great. It's been a hard week for me, you know. I've got a lot to get off my chest and I haven't been able to talk to my Candy Cane."

I wanted to vomit. Never before when Tom called me his Candy Cane had I wanted to hurl. Usually I melt like a high school girl with a crush.

"Whatever." I heard myself saying.

Whatever!

How would I win him back saying something like that? This was going to be harder on me than I realized. Seems the feelings you get when your husband has bonked your BFF are so strong, it's hard to be nice.

"What did you say?" He asked.

"It's not forever." I said.

"Good, because I just don't know what I would do without you." Tom said.

I gave the phone the middle finger.

Tom was being sweet considering I'd called him a scumbag, a dirt bag, a douche bag, a trash bag…. I called him all the horrible bags I could think of as he whined outside my bedroom door four days earlier, but he deserved it.

After hanging up, I took out Nancy's emergency session business card out of my wallet that looked blank, because the numbers on the card were so small. Normally appointments at Zen Spa had to be made two months in advance. Using up one of my three emergency sessions was the only way I was going to get in that day, and I did consider this an emergency. I held it up to the light, but remembered most of the numbers from when I called Nancy for Mindy the day of Barry's funeral. Even though I dropped out of high school, I kind of had a photographic memory. I don't consider myself smart or educated, but if you rattled off ten sentences, I could repeat them one to ten and then ten to one.

"What's your emergency?" The voice asked.

I was annoyed by the voice on the other line this time. I never knew who it was, but it wasn't Nancy. It probably was the receptionist she trained to talk like that when she answered that line. I mean, yes, while taking care of us Calabasas ladies is a high priority, it's not like she was answering the President's red phone when there's a super emergency. Well, I think he has a red phone. I saw it in a movie last year and Mindy assured me that he did have a red phone for emergencies, but who knows if that's true. Obviously, Mindy is a liar.

"This is Candy Katz. I need to look fabulous for a dinner with my husband who is having an affair with my BFF."

"Ooohhh. That's a good one. Is he the one sleeping with Mindy Klein?" The voice said, out of character. "Sorry, I'm not supposed to say anything like that. One minute."

As I expected, they got me right in. I was sure Nancy wanted to hear my side of the story since Mindy had probably told her hers. She knew more secrets about everyone in town than the nannies and would probably write a tell-all book one day.

Nancy didn't use common beauty techniques. She had a way of blending the mind, body and soul together through the use of heated rock massage, which she says brings us closer to the earth and infuses our body with natural energy. She also had her clients look at themselves in the mirror and say positive affirmations. It was kind of like that skit that used to be on Saturday Night Live where Stuart Smalley told himself he's good enough, smart enough and dog gone it, people like me.

Once I did a spoof of it and Nancy was not happy. She told me that she took her work very serious and if I did not come to Zen Spa to unify my parts, mind, body and soul, through massage, steam-room, Jacuzzi, and beautifying treatments such as hair, nails and make-up, that I should go somewhere else for my treatments. After that, I made sure to never joke when I looked in the mirror and told myself that even though I had them reduced, my breasts were big enough.

Before opening the spa, Nancy worked as a therapist. She actually had a PHD and was a family and marriage therapist for fifteen years before making the change. She told me she didn't feel she could do as much with her clients by just talking to them. She wanted to transform their inner selves, but also beautify them. She felt most of the married couples she was working with wouldn't have any problems if the wife dropped twenty pounds, changed her hair style and evened out her skin tone with a high-quality make-up. But, when she suggested this to her clients, they always got mad at her and stopped coming.

Nancy was on fire, and I mean on fire. Forty-eight, five foot ten, she looked like my Malibu Barbie. I kid you not. She was the whole package, and if she didn't switch to women when she ended her marriage five years ago, every husband in Calabasas would be trying to date her. Now all they do is talk about how exciting it is that she likes girls. Nancy's had a few flings with clients who have just gotten out of a long term marriage and always wondered if they were lesbians. Ninety-eight percent, Nancy confided in me, return to men after a few dates because as she says, women mostly love other women because we want to look like them, not make-out with them. I just love her. She's so insightful and smart. She's one of the few women I aspire to be like.

When women were in a real bad way, like I was, she offered what she called a psycho-spa-therapy. It's totally confidential and what she does is follows you from room to room as you get different treatments and she talks to you like a friend. Her philosophy is that we have the answers to our problems, but as women, we need to talk it out to get to them. She backs her research up with the book "Women are from Mars and Men are from Venus." It's expensive therapy because on top of the rate for the treatment, Nancy charges $350 an hour. She says it's worth it because with her, you're not only getting someone who has credentials in spa treatments, you're also getting someone with a PHD in treating head cases. I know a lot of women who've paid the price, because desperate times call for desperate measures. I don't know where I heard that, but I feel so smart when

I say it.

The first order of business is to get a cleansing shower. They won't touch you if you haven't used their anti-bacterial soap that is infused with a scent of lavender. I scrubbed and scrubbed, because even though I had a bath at home, I could have sworn I could still smell my body odor, and the lavender scent helped me relax.

When I came out of the shower, Nancy was waiting for me. She said nothing at all, not hello, not how are you, she just put her arms out for a hug and that was all it took for me to start sobbing. She held me as I cried, while wearing their Egyptian cotton robe they heat before you put it on, and I swear, I felt like a little baby being held by her mama. When I stopped crying, she looked me in the eyes.

"There, there. Feel better?" Nancy said.

I shook my head yes, because I did feel better.

I had the urge to ask her questions about Mindy's emergency session. What did she say about Tom and did she know all about their affair? And if so, would she give me all the details.

"You understand, Candy, that although I know all about Mindy's affair with Tom, as a psychologist, I am unable to give you any information. We here at Zen Spa take pride in our confidential services." Nancy said.

Damn!

"I know." I said, while thinking she shouldn't have told me that Mindy was sleeping with Tom because that's confidential.

"I'm only telling you that I know about Mindy and Tom because I know you know finally and that everyone in town knows." She said.

"Everyone?" I asked.

She shook her head up and down. "Yes. I'm glad you're facing it. Let's talk. It's time to begin your body spirit rejuvenation. You've come to me just in time. I can feel that your parts are all out of sync."

Nancy took my hand and we walked together into the massage room where I was prepped for my rock massage. I squeezed in between heated sheets that had to be at least a seven hundred thread count. It was like going back into my mama's womb, it was so cozy. I went on my stomach and a round foam piece was placed under my ankles. My arms were positioned by my side and the sheet was lowered to just above the crack in my behind. My head was turned towards Nancy who sat in a chair beside the table. She was still holding my hand. She hadn't let go of me since I cried in her arms.

"So let's talk." Nancy said.

I didn't think I had so much to say, but once she told me to talk, I didn't shut up. I went on and on about Mindy betraying me and Tom breaking our wedding vows that we recommitted a few years earlier. And then I told her about how even my daughter, Kelly, thinks I'm a rug everyone walks on.

"Stop right there." Nancy said to me as the masseuse rubbed the edge of a soft heated stone around my shoulder blade. "Do you know why I start all my extreme cases with a sacred stone therapy massage?" I was about to answer when she said, "Don't answer. Just listen. Native Americans believe the stones have heaving powers. These warm stones are not only releasing stress out of your muscles, they are also opening energy pathways through your spirit."

I was impressed and made a mental note to buy some Native American stones for home right after I left. I was feeling different since the therapist started rubbing the stones all over my body, I just didn't realize it was because my energy pathways were opening up.

"Your daughter is here to guide you." Nancy continued.

"Guide me? But I'm her mother."

Nancy started laughing as if that was a funny thing for me to say. "You sure?"

"Yes, I'm sure." I snapped.

103

"Kelly can bring into your life the one thing we lose as we get older that Botox can't." Nancy said.

"What?" I asked.

"Honesty. It's through the children that we get our honesty. They haven't developed the lying skills yet that are necessary to be a successful adult. Kelly's telling you that you're not taking care of yourself." Nancy said.

"I do. I exercise. I rarely eat carbs. I get my hair, make-up and nails done every week. I take great care of myself." I said.

"What Kelly and I are talking about doesn't have to do with beauty regimes."

Oh, great, now I get therapy based on my daughter. Nancy was off her rocker. My seventeen year old daughter was honest only because she had such an attitude and Nancy didn't understand this because she didn't have kids. I was not going to let my daughter's opinion of me be the basis for my emergency session with Nancy.

"You're wrong." I told her. "There's nothing wrong with being nice to people all the time."

"Yes there is. " Nancy said. "Because there's no way you can be nice to people all the time and still be nice to yourself."

Now this damn session was turning into a mind twister. I repeated her sentence in my mind over and over. I just didn't get it.

"Nancy, I don't get it. What's your point?"

"You're hitting resistance." She told me.

"Resistance of what?" I asked.

"The truth. You don't want to face the truth so there's nothing more I can do for you. Until you're ready to understand that you have to stand up for yourself, no one can help you. You have an addiction." Nancy said.

"No, I don't." I told her because I was not addicted to drugs or alcohol.

"Yes. You do. An addiction to pleasing others and it's going to ruin your life if you don't stop. Just think about that." She said, and left the room.

Wow, I was an addict. Did I have to start going to twelve step meetings? At least I didn't have to do that step where I apologize to people I've upset. I didn't have anyone in my past mad at me except for my mom who stopped talking to me when I became a stripper instead of a doctor. With my memorization abilities, she thought I was so smart that I'd find a cure for AIDS, but I needed to make money fast. If I waited to get through medical school before making a wage, I swear I'd have died from starvation.

We didn't have money when I was growing up. My mom divorced my dad when I was one because he was a gambler. She said she had enough after he went into my hope chest, which wasn't a chest really, it was just an old cardboard shoe box, stole my silver baby cup and sold it. It was from Tiffanies, but she found it at Goodwill and spotted its value right away. The three initials were SAW which didn't match my maiden name, Candace Marsha Bundy, but my mom told people she had SAW engraved on the cup because the first time she saw me was so magical.

After their marriage ended, she started slinging hash over at Burt's Grill. I kid you not. When someone ordered hash browns, she tossed a slab of crunchy fried shredded potatoes with her spatula onto their plate. She got pretty popular. People came from all over Riverside, the town I grew up in an hour from Los Angeles, to see her fling hash while they ate breakfast. She made pretty good tips, but then got addicted to this white powder she used to tell me was Sweet n' Low. She said it really helped her concentrate on the heaving the chunks of hash across the restaurant so quickly. By the time I was sixteen, she was way addicted to Sweet n'Low. She sniffed it all the time and spent all her money on it.

Later, of course, since I'm not dumb, just nice, I

found out that the white powder was actually speed her friend in the apartment next door made. It was a pretty dangerous job, because he had to mix chemicals and one day there was an explosion that burned his hands and blew a hole in the wall between our living rooms.

I had been hungry for most of my childhood, so medical school was not an option. I became a stripper and stayed clear of all white powders, even the real Sweet n'Low you can get for free at restaurants that is FDA approved, because I didn't want to grow up to be like my mom. I watched her, year after year, pace in our living room, sweating and grinding her teeth, and maybe I'm too judgmental, but it didn't look like much fun. Then I met Tom and my whole world changed. I had money, so why would I go back and get an education.

I, Candy Klein, am an addict.

I practiced this in my head as I was moved from my spiritual rock massage to a rather aggressive facial. I always thought my skin was clear until I met Helga. This woman could find a blemish on a baby's bottom. A pore is the trashcan for the air's debris, she liked to say, and since Los Angeles had its fair share of smog, according to her every person was riddled with acne.

I told her I was getting treated for an evening out with my husband and that I didn't want my skin swollen and red, and I thought she was going to beat me up.

"I never swell or redden the skin." She told me with her Hungarian accent. "That is for amateurs. I've cleaned the faces of over one hundred thousand clients." She insisted.

I thought it sounded like a lot of facials for one woman to have done, but without a calculator, I couldn't do the math to see if she was lying.

At least with Helga torturing my face, I was too preoccupied to think about Mindy and Tom. That was a nice break since it had been an entire week of my mind spinning out of control about those two. The break was short, though. When Helga was done cleaning out my acne, and mentioning that I had hairline wrinkles developing around my mouth and needed to stay out of the sun, she sent me down the hall to rejuvenate in the Niagara waterfall rain shower. I was looking forward to relaxing, but as soon as I stepped in, my mind went bonkers again.

Mindy and Tom are having sex!

What the F!

Ever since Suzy, my mentor at Hot & Sexy, the first strip joint I worked at, told me never to say the F word even if I was getting F'd, I didn't. Her philosophy was if you speak like a lady, you'll be treated like a lady. Even though we gave lap dances to vulgar men and did splits in our G-strings onstage, she insisted that if we spoke properly we would get respect. Words have power, she told me, and a lady chooses her words carefully. I just adored her and attribute her advice to how I was able to hook Tom. When we made love on the fourth hour of our first date and I didn't talk trashy like the other girls from the club he'd slept with, he says he knew I was the marrying type.

Mindy Klein and my Tom were having an affair!

I still could not believe it.

Nancy came back to talk to me before my make-up was applied by Tamara, an ex-make-up artist to the stars who left the feature film world to work with Nancy. She claims she gave her career up in films because she believed in Nancy's mind, body, spirit philosophy. Well, at least that's what she told me. I knew from Helga that Nancy and Tamara used to date, but Nancy dumped Tamara. She was crushed, so she came to work at the spa just to be near her one true love. Anyway, before getting my make-up done, Nancy brought me into a quiet room and held my hand so we could talk about all the emotions I'd been experience since I came through the door. I started crying.

"I'm angry." I said.

"Good. It's the first stage of mourning." Nancy

said.

"I'm dehydrated." I said.

"Good. That's the second stage of crying." She said.

"I'm hungry." I said.

"Good. That means you're going to live." Nancy said. "Because without food, we wither and die."

She held both my hands and looked at me, waiting for more.

"That's it for now." I said.

"I think you're holding back. I think you don't want to admit what you're up against."

"What am I up against?"

"Mindy Klein."

I broke down into tears again. "You know, I was her best friend."

"Yes, you were her best friend, Candy, but she wasn't your best friend back."

I got a little confused and had to think about what she was saying.

"You're right. I was too nice to her and she walked all over me."

"Exactly. There's hope for you. You're getting the point."

"But she's not going to win. She's not taking my husband, she's not taking my house and she's not taking my swing."

Nancy looked at me weirdly. I almost explained about the swing in my bedroom that I installed instead of a pole, but I was getting tired.

"Whatever." She said. "The point is, you've got the point."

Nancy had a way of talking sort of backwards. I always had to stop talking a minute to give my brain time to decode her message. Therapy was exhausting. Analyzing me took a lot of work. No wonder I was so happy being shallow for so many years. It's so much easier.

Nancy vowed to keep our talk confidential, then she sprinkle sage all over me to get rid of any evil spirits that might be attached to my aura. I don't see how it could have worked. The stuff looked just like cigarette ash and didn't smell much better. Then she gave me a great big hug and told me to live strong. I wanted to tell her that was Lance Armstrong's saying before his fall and that she should think one up for herself, but I didn't want to be rude. And she's such a terrific gal that I didn't even get upset when at the end of getting my hair and make-up done, I learned she'd raised her rates $200 an hour. She apologized over and over that she forgot to tell me. I told her not to worry, because she really was worth $550.00 an hour. She really knew her stuff.

Refreshed, enlightened and looking like a knock-out if I do say so myself, I returned home and carefully searched through my closet for the turquoise chiffon halter dress Tom bought me when we were in Hawaii on our second honeymoon. He liked it because if he looked real hard, he could see the outline of my nipples. He said it was a turn-on to be out to dinner with me and to be able to see them. You see, that's the kind of extra stuff I did for Tom. How many other wives wore see through dresses so their husbands got to eat with a woody? I gave and gave and gave, and still, he cheated on me with my best friend.

I found the dress in the back of the closet still in the dry cleaning plastic bag from when I had it cleaned years before. Well, maybe I only wore it for him once, but still I wore it even though I knew you didn't need x-ray vision to see my tatas. But tonight I was winning my husband back from Mindy. I was in a war and had to use whatever means necessary. I put on the dress, and with my long blonde hair straightened and my make-up done to perfection, I was feeling confident that I could pull this off. After all, not only was my marriage on the line, so was my reputation, my furniture collection and my swing.

I put on my Valentino Bow Detailed Slingback pumps in fuchsia. I bought them to wear when I swung nude in my fuchsia Moulin Rouge bedroom for Tom. Yes, fuchsia shoes didn't really go with my turquoise dress, but I was dressing to impress my husband and hoped seeing the shoes would remind him of our nights alone in our bedroom before Mindy came between us.

I took out my Ilana Wolf Silk Wrap and cleverly disguised my tatas with it, planning to dramatically reveal them at the table when I was eating with Tom. There was one weakness Tom had and that was women's breasts. Sometimes when he saw a pair, he couldn't speak, which is probably why he cheated on me with Mindy. After all, she went up to a double D and I went down to a C. I'd hate to think that might play a part in ending my long marriage, but you know, there have been worse excuses. Woody Allen fell in love with his adopted daughter. Who would have thought that would ever have happened from such a smart guy.

It was 6:45 p.m. when I arrived at the restaurant. I was intentionally late because I didn't want to look desperate, but Tom wasn't there yet.

Of all the nerve!

The hostess sat me at a table in the back where I waited, I kid you not, for another ten minutes before he showed up. I thought he couldn't live without me. I thought he was tortured over me kicking him out of the house. Apparently I thought wrong.

I sat with my back to the door and pretended to read the wine list, but the names were all fancy and I had no idea how to pronounce them.

"Sorry, my meeting ran late." Tom said and sat down. "You look amazing, my Candy Cane."

I wanted to be sweet and nice, because after all I was up against Mindy who was ruining my life, but when I saw Tom I wanted to slap him.

"Don't call me that." I said and tears started

110

pouring out of my eyes. "How could you?" I asked him.

"Mindy's just, I don't know. I'm sorry, Candy Cane. It'll never happen again. Don't cry. I'm an idiot. I don't want to lose you." He said. "I don't want to lose what we had."

He reached out for my hand. I pulled it back.

"How can I trust you?" I asked him.

"Look, after you ran out of Mindy's house, I told her never again. I realized just how much you mean to me." Tom said. "I ended it and haven't seen her since."

"Really?" I said.

"Yes. You and Kelly mean the world to me and I'm begging for your forgiveness."

Take that Mindy Klein. You are so out and I am so in!

"It's going to take some time for me to get over this."

"I understand, but I'm willing to do whatever it takes. I'll even go to marriage counseling if that's what you need."

Wow, Tom always said therapy is for the dopes that can't figure out life on their own and need someone to confirm this for them.

Tom took out three carat diamond solitaire necklace he had wrapped with fuchsia wrapping paper since he knew it was my favorite color. He said there was only one diamond because I was the only one for him, and that he bought a three carat to signify the triangle of our family, Kelly, me and him. I was hooked.

Dinner was a blur after that. I took off my silk wrap and Tom was grinning from ear to ear as he stared at my chest and kept begging me to come with him to his hotel room because it would be more exciting for us to do it there instead of our house. I told him he'd have to wait until he ate all this dinner because he'd been naughty and I wouldn't let him have his dessert first. It felt like when we just started dating, except for when I thought about him with Mindy, which happened every other minute or so, but there was a crazy sort of excitement between us again. Tom seemed sexier and more handsome now that he cheated on me, which is absolutely crazy when I think about it.

We drove to the Hilton Garden Inn that was right down the street. We took Tom's BMW and left my Mercedes in the parking lot at the Commons shopping center. We could hardly keep our hands off each other enough so that he could drive and practically ran to his room when we got out of the car. Tom wanted me to keep my turquoise dress on since he bought it for me on our second honeymoon. He said it made him feel like he was recommitting to me again and that it was easier to lift my dress up than take it off. We made passionate love and I started crying like I did after my first time when I was thirteen, because I was so full of emotion. After, he held me in his arms and rubbed the contour of my shoulder. It was right then that I knew I would love Tom forever.

"Tom, let's never fight again."

"Never. I'm checking out of here and coming home." Tom said. "We belong together, Mindy."

I gasped and sat up. "What did you just say?" I asked.

"I said we belong together, Candy." He said.

"No, you didn't. You said Mindy, not Candy." I demanded.

"Candy, what's wrong with you. I did not." He insisted. "Your mind's playing tricks on you."

I wasn't sure now. My mind had played tricks on me before and this had been such a trying week that I wasn't sure if he was lying or not.

"I'm sorry." I said. "It's just, it's been a long week. I'm sort of tired." I told him.

"I know. Come here." He said and I cuddled in

his arms and turned to the side.

We spooned like, well, spoons, and I closed my eyes to try to relax, but I could have sworn he said Mindy. I opened my eyes and in the dim light, I saw a piece of long brown hair on the sheet.

I jumped up, turned on the light, and pulled the sheet back.

"What are you doing?" Tom asked, and he held his hands over his private area.

"You haven't seen Mindy since the day of Barry's funeral, huh? What about this?" I said and held up the long piece of brown hair. "Mindy's been here, Tom. I may not have finished high school and I may not have gotten my GED like I tell everyone, but I know a piece of hair from India when I see it." I said.

"India? What are you talking about?" Tom asked.

"Mindy's hair is fake. She has hair extensions. This is from her." I told him, while gathering up my things. "You are a liar and a cheat. I don't ever want to see you again."

I stormed out of the room, holding my shoes in my hand, and slammed the door behind me. I stomped down the hall.

"Candy, you don't have your car." Tom yelled out of the room.

"I don't care. I'll walk." I told him.

That's what I did, I walked the street, a little wobbly I might add because I did have quite a bit to drink, back to the parking lot at the Commons shopping center. I wasn't worried about running into a dangerous homeless person strung out on drugs who might attack me and steal my three carat necklace or my seven hundred dollar shoes because in all the years I lived in Calabasas, I'd never seen a homeless person walking the streets. Our neighborhoods are too upscale for them, which is why I thought it was a bit odd seeing that homeless woman in Beverly Hills. Really, she didn't have the economic status to walk those streets. She didn't even have shoes to walk those streets.

I made it back to the Commons, crying the whole way and was sure that whatever mascara and eyeliner Tamara expertly applied to my eyes was now at the base of my cheeks. I was worried about running into someone I knew when I reached the parking lot, because the shopping center is where we all go on the weekends to eat and walk around.

I looked in the side mirror of a Lexus parked on the street and it was worse than I thought. I had so much black underneath my eyes that I looked like I was playing football. I tried wiping it off with my silk scarf, but the car alarm went off and a voice started yelling at me. "Step away from the car! Step away from the car!" It said over and over and sounded just like Darth Vader. I ran away before I got caught. If I got arrested for trying to break into a car, I don't know how I would explain that to the neighbors.

I spit, and I know this is gross, on my silk scarf to get it wet so I could wipe the mascara off my face. I ruined the scarf, but I planned on burning that outfit anyway, except for the shoes, of course. I would never wear that ridiculously see-through recommitment dress ever again. In fact, I planned to burn it in the gas fireplace in our backyard just as soon as I got home.

Tom! What a putz. I married a putz. After all those years of doing séances with my Malibu Barbie, I got a putz. I planned to dig that doll out from my hope chest and burn it with the dress.

There was no more hope for my marriage. It was over, I decided. If Mindy wanted Tom, she could have him. In fact, they deserved each other and I deserved to be happy with someone as nice as me. There had to be a man out there somewhere who wouldn't take advantage of the fact that I would let him walk all over me and I vowed to find him.

When I reached the parking lot, I walked on the outer edge, as far away from the restaurants and shops as possible. I put on my three inch heels and hid my tatas with my white silk scarf that was now dotted with spots of black, and made a beeline for my car. I got inside, turned the engine on, but when I went to put the car in reverse, I got a warning light that said my tire pressure was dangerously low. I opened the door and ducked my head down by the asphalt and looked at my tires. All four of them were flat.

Mindy Klein!

She had sabotaged my car. The odds of having one flat tire were pretty good. The odds of having four flat tires meant only one thing. I was the victim of a gypsy attack.

I turned off my car and called AAA Roadside Service. A tow truck arrived thirty minutes later and the driver got out.

"I'm here to bless you, little lady. I'm Bob, the tow-truck driver with a heart." Bob said while looking at my car. "You got yourself four slashed tires. Looks like a one inch blade."

"How do you know?" I asked.

"Been driving a tow truck for a lot of years. You must have yourself an enemy. Going through a nasty divorce? Sleeping with someone else's man?"

"Something like that." I told him.

"Uh, huh. I knew it. Where should I tow it? You're gonna need a whole new set of tires and all the tire shops are closed this late."

"Just tow it to my home in the Oaks." I told him. A crowd was forming over on the sidewalk. I was hoping not to be seen. "Listen, Bob, can I just hide in my car while you do your job. It's sort of cold out here."

"Sure. You sit in your car, little lady and I'll get you home in no time."

I hid inside my car, hoping no one I knew would see me in such a ridiculous state. And then, before I knew it, my car rolled and Bob pulled it up onto the flat bed of his truck with a cable. I was sitting in my car up on the tow truck for the whole world to see, like a trophy girl at a car show.

I rolled down the window. "Bob." I yelled, but he couldn't hear me. The sound of the crane and the tow truck engine was too loud.

A huge crowd had gathered and some of them were pointing to me and laughing. And there, standing in the midst of them was my enemy...

MINDY KLEIN!

She smiled and waved at me as the tow truck pulled away and I was paraded in the Commons parking lot for everyone to see. I wanted to die. This was not how the night was supposed to turn out. Yes, I did get a very expensive necklace out of the deal, but somehow, while being driven home in my car on top of a tow truck, I didn't feel so lucky. In the old days, getting a diamond necklace could make me happy for like five days, but this time I wasn't feeling so good. Tom was still a cheat. Mindy was sabotaging my life, and I was stuck driving humpback on a tow truck like the space shuttle when they fly it back to California from the Kennedy Center.

We reached the Oaks guard gate. Carl came out of the security booth. I waved at him from high up inside my car.

"Hi, Carl, it's just me, Candy." I said to him.

He came out to talk. "Having some car trouble?"

"Yeah, just a few flat tires. Well, got to go. The tow truck is on an hourly rate." I hated to lie, I really did, but my life was in a bit of a mess and I just didn't have time to talk to him.

Carl opened the gate and we wound through the streets of the Oaks. I scooted low so no one could see me. I could explain the four flat tires. I could explain how I got stuck inside my car on top of the tow truck. But, I did not want to explain why my hair and make-up looked so bad.

Bob backed into my driveway, raised the front of

the tow truck bed and lowered the back. It felt like I was on a roller coaster at Magic Mountain as he unclamped the tethers and rolled my car onto the driveway.

"Sign right here." Bob said as he handed me a form to sign through my car window.

I signed the form and handed it back to him. I was mortified by the experience, and didn't have the strength to get out of my car yet. Plus, Bob was blocking my car door.

"Have a nice night." He said.

"I will." I told him and smiled, but I think he could tell I was upset.

"You know, little lady." He said while leaning down into my car window. "I'd watch out for whoever did this to your car. I've been in this business for a lot of years. I've seen a lot of slashed tires, but usually it's only one or two. It's hardly ever three. Only in extreme cases are all four tires slashed at once. Whoever it is that's got it in for you is real mad. Be careful."

With that, Bob got in his truck and drove away, leaving me alone in my driveway, sitting in my Mercedes with four flat tires.

CANDY SCREWS WITH TOM BECAUSE HE SCREWED MINDY

CHAPTER SIX

I woke up the next morning and reached over for Tom out of habit and he was there! I sat up, confused.

"Tom, what are you doing here?"

My head pounded as if I had a drum inside it. It was then I was pretty sure I drank too much the night before.

Tom moaned and his eyes blinked open. I glanced over at the clock. It was almost eleven in the morning. What on earth was going on?

I hit his arm again. "Tom? Wake up. It's almost lunch time. Don't you have to go to work?"

"I called Sasha earlier and told her I wouldn't be coming in." He said groggily.

"How did this happen again?"

"You don't remember?"

I didn't remember when I first woke up, but I was starting to remember. Bits and pieces were flashing in my mind.

"You called me to come over. You told me I was the only man for you for the rest of your life, that you forgave me and were sorry for acting so weird at the

118

hotel."

Yep, that was matching what was popping into my brain. It was painful to think about, but whether I liked it or not, it was all coming back to me.

After Bob, the tow truck driver, literally dropped me off in my car on my driveway, I came into the house and made perhaps one of the worst decisions of my life. I went straight to the bar and took down Tom's prize bottle of Chinaco Blanco tequila. Nothing good ever happens after drinking tequila. I knew that from experience, but I was distraught so I didn't hesitate.

Tom was in New York on a business trip when one of his employees insisted on buying him a shot of Chinaco since Tom had never tried it. Well, Tom fell in love with it and ordered nine more shots, then stripped down to his boxers and danced with two drag queens on the bar. He had to pay the employee a large Christmas bonus to keep it quiet, but he said it was worth it. He had the time of his life and ever since he's always had a bottle of Chinaco in our bar.

I, thank God, didn't do ten shots. I only did six, but I remember feeling emotional after the third one. I was in my backyard sitting alone at the fire pit burning my black Robert Rodriquez Bow Strap Double Knit Dress, my turquoise recommitment dress and my Oprah Chenille robe that was contaminated with reclaimed water, and finally, my Malibu Barbie. The tape I used to reattach her head when I was twelve after my dog bit it off, had lost its sticking ability and her head came off again. I tossed Malibu Barbie's body in the fire first and then her head. Her blonde hair went up in flames, and there was a poof of smoky air that swirled up like a spell or something was concocted. The whole thing was a horror to watch. All my dreams and hopes and two sexy dresses, up in flames.

I called Tom crying and begged him to come home and oh, my God, I told him I forgave him, loved him and could not live without him. I gave him the easy ticket. I told him it was over and that he didn't have to make amends because I knew he really loved me and I knew deep down he was truly sorry. Man, Nancy was right. I was a pushover.

Tom walked to the bathroom nude and for the first time I was so grossed out by seeing his body. It was contaminated with Mindy Klein and I didn't see how on earth I was ever going to get over it. I found myself making the face I make when I eat something that tastes nasty, scrunching up my nose and eyes.

Tom got into the shower. "Candy Cane, come in with me." He called.

My head felt like it was going to split open. "I need coffee." I told him.

And just like that he was back in our house and we were back on our schedule and I was expected to be back to being his sweet Candy Cane.

As if.

I tried hard, so, so hard to be the way I was before. Easy going, always smiling, never demanding, but I could not keep myself under control. I was possessed, I tell you, with the fact that he cheated on me.

I asked him why he always came home late from work and accused him of having been with other women our entire marriage. I demanded he write a list of all the women he cheated on me with. When he refused, I insisted it was because he had slept with so many women, he couldn't remember their names. I demanded he tell me which women in the neighborhood he had been with besides Mindy. I followed him around the house every minute he was home, asking him about each and every woman I knew who lived in the Calabasas Oaks.

"What about Charlotte?" I asked.

Charlotte was a Southern Belle. She always wore bright colors to stand out, something her mama taught her. And even though having flat hair was in style, she always had big hair like Jane Fonda in Barbarella. Worse part is it looked good, even though it was out of style, because like Jane Fonda in her younger days, Charlotte had a knock-out figure, large breasts and the face of an angel. Mindy was always jealous of her.

Charlotte married for money just like Mindy. Hugh was a tall cowboy who wore a black cowboy hat, black cowboy boots and lots of silver and turquoise jewelry. He had pockmarked cheeks from a bad bout of adult acne Charlotte said appeared after they were married or else she might not have married him. That wasn't the worst of it. He had a round stomach that poked out like a nine-month pregnant woman. It was the oddest look. He was one of those men who only gained weight in his tummy.

"What about Samantha?" I asked.

Samantha was a corporate lawyer who paid her way through college by being a dominatrix. Her husband was impotent and had one of those devices that pumped air into him so he could make love. I overheard Samantha saying at the pool at the Calabasas Tennis and Swim Center that she was dying to know, since turning forty this year, if she was still attractive enough to make a man get excited without using a pump. The pump was crushing her ego and even though it allowed her husband to do it anytime and for as long as she wanted, she wanted to have a natural experience with a man again that proved he was sexually aroused by her.

"What about Hunter?" I asked.

Hunter was one of those naturally beautiful women, like Jane Seymore. Yes, she had her breast augmented, but she was thin and active and even her hair didn't look colored. I, of course, knew that she did color her hair that perfect shade of light brown that young girls have that doesn't have a hint of ash or gray. I also knew that she had such clear skin because she did colonics like every other day. She was way in to taking out the toxins in her diet and by the looks of her, she had a clean system, but I wasn't willing to get my body cleaned out like that. There was a lot I would do to be beautiful, but colonics wasn't one of them.

Hunter was happily married. I knew that, but there was a rumor going around the neighborhood that she and Francois, her French National husband, were swingers. Tom once asked me if I had any interest in swinging and that's when I installed the swing in our room. When he explained to me what he actually meant, I told him the only swinging I would do was on the swing in our bedroom.

I went over every female Oaks resident we knew and even their nannies and maids. When I started going through their gardeners, Tom told me he had had enough, and insisted he hadn't slept with anyone in the neighborhood except Mindy, of course, which set me off into my next round of interrogations. I had a list of questions I needed answered, I told him, in order to get over it. That was the only way I could go back to being the way I was before. Reluctantly, Tom agreed to answer them, because I was driving him crazy and I promised to stop interrogating him after he answered my questions.

"Was Mindy better in bed than me?" I asked.

"I can't answer that."

"Yes, you can. Was she?"

"Candy, I changed my mind. I don't want to do this." Tom said.

I didn't care. I went on for days. Question after question popped into my head, and even if I asked the question like twenty times before, I asked it again because Tom wasn't answering me. And, I needed the answers. I couldn't help it. I was poisoned with jealousy over his affair with Mindy Klein.

What positions did you do?"

Missionary?

Does she smell better than me?

Does she make you feel happy?

Is she smarter than me?

How many times in one day did you do it?

Does she make you laugh?

Do you love her?

Do you love me?

How did it first happen?

How long did it last when it first happened?

Are you sorry?

Is she sorry?

Are you sorry that I'm sorry it happened?

Do you miss her?

Are you thinking about her right now?

Did you notice that her boobs are lopsided?

It took God seven days to create the earth, but it took only five days before Tom had enough of me.

"I've had enough." He told me.

"Of what?" I asked.

"The interrogations. The jealousy. The questions! Candy, you've become so pathetic."

"Excuse me!" I yelled. "I am not pathetic, buddy, I'm a woman scorned and this is how women scorned act." I wasn't exactly sure what scorned meant, but I saw a woman say that exact sentence in a Lifetime Television Movie to her husband who had cheated on her so I said it to Tom.

"I can't do this anymore." He said.

"You're lucky you're alive." I said.

"Are you threatening to kill me?" Tom said.

"Well? The thought has crossed my mind a few times."

"Mindy never acts like this." Tom said.

That did it. He compared me to Mindy Klein right when I was standing next to my imitation Statue of David in the foyer. I hurled it at him. He ducked and the statue went through the window behind him. It shattered, and it wasn't just any window, it was a ten foot window in our living room.

"I can't stay here anymore. It isn't safe." Tom said. "I'm leaving you."

"You're leaving me?" I said.

"Yeah, and I want a divorce." He added.

"You want to divorce me?" I asked, because I just couldn't understand his reasoning.

"Stop asking so many God damn questions." Tom yelled.

"You had the affair." I said.

"Your behavior is out of control. I can't live this way." Tom said before moving back in at the Hilton.

My daughter told me the neighbors were talking about me in a bad way. There was concern that I was a candidate to go on a 72 hour hold in the psych ward because first I hit Stacy and Mindy on the court and then I tried to kill Tom with the Statue of David. My daughter was mortified, especially when I had to hire a window company that had to use an enormous crane to replace our front living room window. It was obvious to everyone that the window was broken in a fight, especially since I threw the imitation Statue of David so hard it landed on the sidewalk.

I cannot tell you the relief I felt right after I threw the statue and saw the glass shatter. I mean, of course I was scared and mortified and it made Maria have to vacuum the living room for hours every day for the next week because we kept finding little pieces of glass everywhere, but just to get all my frustration out felt great. I felt alive. I took David by the head and threw that beautiful work of art as hard as I could. And even though I have fake boobs, a fake nose and fake eyelashes, I felt totally real in that moment.

That only lasted for about ten minutes though, because after Tom left me, I went back to my bedroom and cried for the rest of the day. I tried so hard to be the loving wife again, I did, but it's really difficult to love a rat, you know, even if the rat gives you a three carat solitaire diamond necklace and even if the rat has been your husband for almost twenty years.

This time, however, I wasn't about to stay in my room for five days and not get a bath. I needed to be an example to my daughter on how to act when your husband's betrayed you, so only three days later, I got up and acted as if nothing unusual was going on. Then I found out from Maria that Kelly decided to stay at her girlfriend's house the day before until the situation at home cleared up. I got dressed anyway because it was time to get my life in order. I was a grown-up and couldn't sulk around the house crying like a two-year-old.

Ready to tackle the day, I went down to the kitchen and poured myself a cup of coffee, trying to ignore Maria crying over spilt milk. Literally, she spilled a little milk on the counter and she started crying, so I started crying. Ridiculous, I known, since such a little thing as spilt milk shouldn't make us cry, but it did. It was the stress of the times that got to us. Plus, Maria had a way of crying that was way over the top, like when you see women in a village crying in some far off place where a bomb's just gone off, yowling and mumbling in another language.

Maria kept talking to me in Spanish, so distraught, while I held her in my arms. I don't know what she said to me. I only understood "ay yi yi" and "Mr. Tom" and "hiho de puta" which meant motherfucker. I did learn a little Spanish when I worked one pole over from Chica Bonita at the Nasty & Nice Strip Club. Her act was all about insulting the customers and the meaner she was to the men, the bigger tips she got.

As I ate poached egg whites on lettuce that Maria made for me, I thought about what I would do that day. I had three options, workout, shop or go to the spa. I decided, since I had to burn some of my clothes, that I needed a few new dresses so I opted for shopping.

With my day set and my mind feeling together, I read my horoscope on my iPad. Maria always had it ready for me on the table because I read it every morning. In fact, it's the only thing I read from the Los Angeles Times. Once in a while I'll check out the Calendar Section, but really, who has that much time in the morning to read an in-depth article. I'm a Gemini, which as Mindy used to say, meant that I had two sides to my personality. She never told me what those two sides are, though.

"Maria, here's my horoscope." I always read my horoscope to her. She looked forward to it every day. "You look for the good in every situation. You are a genuine person who has everyone's best intentions at heart, but beware. There are others close to you who don't share this belief." Like duh? I could have written my horoscope this day.

Heading out to shop for a new dress, I stopped at the gate to chat with Carl, but he said he was too busy to talk. I think this was a lie, because he was just sitting there twiddling his thumbs. Maybe he was thinking about something and needed quiet, but in all the years I'd seen him at the gate, Carl was never too busy to talk to me.

I drove over to Belle Gray at the Commons shopping center, ready to drop a few thousand on a few dresses. I strolled around the store, trying not to look for Lisa Rinna, but every time I was there I couldn't help searching for her. I was in need of a new BFF anyway and Lisa would do just fine. We were both the same size and not only could we share clothes, I could get clothes from her store at cost if we became tight. And, if Lisa Rinna was my new close friend, Mindy would be so jealous. I'd get into all the fantastic Hollywood parties and maybe Lisa could find me a star for my next husband. I'd even settle for a television actor, so long as he had at least a Golden Globe nomination.

I took five dresses off the rack, and not that I was trying to look like an angel, but all five were white. I was tired of wearing black. My new life was coming around and it was time for me to lighten up. I was done grieving. Yes, I had been dumped by my cheating husband of twenty years who slept with my BFF, but I could not let that be the end of me. I needed to move forward with a new attitude and new dresses.

Sarah, the sweet salesgirl, helped me with my purchases. "That looks fantastic!" She said about each dress I put on.

"Really, 'cause I think this one makes my legs look stocky." I said about the third dress I tried on.

"Fantastic." She said again, so of course, I believed her. This girl was the poster child for the well put together woman and I did not believe even for a second that she would lie to me. Never before had a shopping trip gone so well.

I came out of the dressing room beaming with happiness. Shopping has a way of doing that to me. When the whole world feels like it's crumbling around me, well on this day it actually was crumbling around me, I find that if I go shopping and get some stunning outfits that all is right with the world for the next hour. That's how long the shopping high lasts for me. It used to last weeks when I first met Tom and he would take me shopping. Since before my off the rack clothes were from the Salvation Army, it felt unbelievable to be purchasing clothes that were actually bought off the rack for the first time. I didn't have to take them home and use Spray 'n Wash to get out the stains and I didn't have to wash them three times to get the thrift store smell out.

I handed Sarah my credit card. Outside the store, a crowd was gathering. People were looking in at me and pointing.

"What's going on?" I asked. "Are you guys having a sale or something?"

"No." Sarah said as she took my five dresses and rang them up. The total was $2,549. "I think they're looking at you Mrs. Katz."

"Me? Why?" I asked.

"You know?" Sarah said.

"No. I don't." I said.

"The affair you're husband's having. How you've gone suicidal and threatened to kill everyone. In fact, when you came in here, I was a little nervous."

"Oh, my God. I'm not suicidal." I said, and noticed Sarah pulling a sharp letter opener away from my end of the counter.

"I believe you. Look, it's none of my business, but whenever I'm having a hard time, I go see Randolf and it really helps." She handed me a card for Randolf Psychic Palm Reader for the Wealthy.

"Thanks." I said and gathered up my bags and headed for the door. The crowd backed away as I neared. Mindy had to be behind all this. She had to be ruining my reputation and was managing to do it fast. Maybe seeking counsel with a psychic palm reader wasn't such a bad idea. Who else would give me insight into how to go up against a gypsy?

I called Randolf immediately when I got to my car. He said he was booked that day, but if I drove right over he could see me right away. Turns out a client had just cancelled when I called. Feeling lucky, I looked at his address and nearly had a heart attack when I saw that it was in Van Nuys. I hated Van Nuys. It was deep in the San Fernando Valley and riddled with poor people. I grew up with poor people and my goal when I turned eighteen was to stay as far away from poor people as possible. I had only been to Van Nuys once, when I was called to jury duty because they have a city courthouse there, but I was dismissed right away because I broke out in a rash all over my arms. I'm not sure what it was, but as soon as I left Van Nuys the rash went away.

I called Randolf on the phone. "Randolf, is there any way you can come to me?" I said.

"Impossible. The energy won't be right." Randolf said.

Reluctantly, I drove to his house that was in the

middle of a rundown neighborhood a mile away from the courthouse. Everywhere I turned I saw women walking with babies and strollers and VPL's. I kid you not. I watched a countdown show on VH1 about the top 100 fashion mistakes and VPL was number one.

I parked my car in the closest parking spot I could find, but it was about half a mile away from Randolf's apartment. I was worried that what I was doing wasn't the brightest idea, so I called Belle Gray on my pink iPhone to confirm with Sarah that this guy was not a total weirdo.

"Belle Gray. This is Lisa Rinna. How can I help you?" I heard.

Holy crap! I was talking to Lisa Rinna, the Dancing with the Stars diva, that TV Guide channel hostess of all red carpet galas. The fashionista of Calabasas, California.

"Hello." She said.

"Lisa, uh, Mrs. Rinna. This is Candy Katz. I was in today and purchased five white dresses, and one was one of your "Lisa's Picks." I said, because I wanted her to know that I was a real client, not just some Hollywood wannabe who strolls through her store with only $100 in her checking account just to meet her.

And then I saw them, a swarm of gang looking guys approaching my car.

"Yes, yes. Is everything all right?" Lisa said.

There were about thirty or so hard looking guys, who all wore the same clothes, a white t-shirt and dark blue jeans riding so low that the crotch seam almost touched their knees. God, if ever there was a place that could use my fashion help, Van Nuys was it.

"Yes, but I was wondering if I could speak to Sarah." I asked.

One of the men opened my door. How nice, I thought.

I stepped out of the car. "Thank you." I said to him.

"Eh, no problem, mi amore." He said.

In this area, not only was I the only size two walking the street, I was the only size two with fair skin, blonde hair and a decent pair of jeans on. I had on my True Religions I purchased last season, but they were still in style. All the women around me had on stretch tapered jeans. Anyone who knows anything about fashion will tell you that it is the few, the very skinny and not many, who can wear a tapered jean.

"Sarah stepped away. Is there something I can help you with?" Lisa Rinna asked on the phone.

I was walking down the street, searching for Randolf's apartment and feeling a little bit vulnerable, since four of the guys were following me and the rest were checking out my car.

"No, thanks. I'll call back."

I wasn't sure what to say to Lisa Rinna. We didn't seem to have that chemistry Mindy and I had. It was boring talking to her, like being on a horrible date when you know that it's going to take about a million years for the guy across the table to finish a boring story. Not that Lisa Rinna's boring, it's just, we didn't have that snap me and Mindy had. I think that's why I always let Mindy slide. Even when she was being a bitch to me, at least I was laughing.

"Excuse me, you wouldn't happen to know a Randolf." I asked one of the men following me.

"You looking for Randolf?" He said.

"Yeah, that's what I said. I'm looking for Randolf."

"Down there. The beige building."

I looked down the street. All the apartment buildings were beige. The men laughed. Apparently, this guy was playing a joke on me. I stopped, turned around, and faced the men.

"Excuse me, gentlemen. But if any of you are thinking of trying to rob me or take parts off my car, you should know that I have a photographic memory. I never forget a face, and I know your names."

The men laughed again. They didn't think I was serious.

"You, over there looking at my new set of Pirelli tires, your name is Herman, and you…" I pointed to the man who told me Randolf's apartment was beige, "Your name is Carlo."

The guys looked freaked out.

"How do you know my name?" He said really close to my face.

I looked away and swatted the air in front of my face away from my nose.

"Those cigarettes you smoke really make your breath stink."

I didn't want to tell him that I'd been listening to their conversation and had counted that the guy next to him had said Carlo about fifty times in the last minute.

"When I come back out, I expect my car will be perfect or I'm calling the cops."

The men stopped following me. I think they were freaked out.

Randolf lived on the top floor of a beat up four story building. Built in a square, it had a dingy pool and courtyard in the middle. Kids were everywhere and they were all crying, as if they were hungry. There was one young mother standing at her apartment door, holding a baby. The girl must have been only eighteen and she looked so tired already.

I thought about Angelina Jolie walking in Namibia surrounded by so many hungry children and I didn't know how she did it. Just going to a rundown apartment in Van Nuys made me upset. Suddenly, helping poor people didn't sound so good. It was horrible there. Everyone looked so desperate and although the women had their hair, makeup and nails done, the colors were all wrong and they wore too much black eyeliner.

I found myself wishing for Calabasas. I liked living

131

in the Oaks. I liked shopping and dropping thousands of dollars in five minutes. I liked over paying Nancy for her therapy session. I liked my expensive life. Being at that apartment in Van Nuys reminded me of my childhood. There was no way I was going back to being so poor that I had to live in an apartment like that again. Good for Angelina Jolie. She was able to meander in the world of poverty and not get stressed out, but I was, I decided, too shallow to follow her. I decided I needed to divorce Tom, take him for every penny he had and find another sugar daddy to replace him. After all, I am a nice person. I deserve to be self-centered and have a rich husband to pay for my expensive lifestyle.

I found apartment number seven on the top floor, which was odd since I'd already passed a bunch of apartments that were numbered in the twenties. The door was freshly painted a bright red that I took as a good sign, because it matched exactly the fire red polish I had on my acrylic nails. Just as I was about to knock, the door opened.

"Come in." Said a voice. Damn, I thought, another mysterious voice. I didn't want to walk in because I was scared.

'Don't be scared." The voice said. "I won't hurt you like Tom and Mindy."

Bingo! I stepped in. This voice understood me. This voice was on my side.

The door slammed behind me and the place went completely dark.

"Oh, shit." I said.

Then bam, the lights turned on. Randolf was laughing and standing behind me. He was a little person, literally, he was really short. He gave me a big hug which was like getting half a body hug.

"You passed the test." Randolf said.

"I did? You were testing me?" I asked.

"This whole set-up is a test of your character. You wouldn't believe how many people chicken out and don't walk through that door."

"Well, okay. But I am a little scared." I admitted, because I was shivering.

"I know. I know. It's a difficult road you're traveling down."

Damn, I love this midget, I mean small person. He so gets me. I'm never leaving.

"Candy, I'll be honest with you. Sarah called me and filled me in on your situation. I don't just know this stuff from the cosmos. I'm good, but I'm not that good."

"Oh, I thought maybe you could read minds or something."

"Well, I can, just not in such detail. My gifts come out in a very fuzzy way. I don't get hard facts or clear pictures. I get energies, and I can tell you, you're radiating a sad, sad energy."

"I know." My voice cracked and I started to cry. He gestured to a big red circular chair that I saw for sale at Cost Plus. "I'm a wreck."

"Well who wouldn't be. Your husband's been sleeping with your best friend." Randolf said as he sat across from me in a blue circular chair, and went into a meditation pose.

I love this man. If he didn't live on the fourth floor of a Van Nuys apartment building, he could be my next husband.

Randolf closed his eyes and went very quiet. He stayed that way for a good five minutes and I was beginning to worry.

"Randolf?" I asked.

He shushed me, so I shushed, but only for a few more minutes.

"Randolf?" I asked again. "You okay?"

He opened his eyes and wiped his forehead. "Wow. That was intense." He said.

For you maybe, I thought.

"Candy Katz, it's an honor to be in your energy. I'm not worried about you anymore. You're going to be just fine. That'll be five hundred dollars. I take cash, check or credit card."

"You're kidding me, right? I may be blonde and only have my GED…"

"Ah, ah, ah." Randolph said, and shook his finger side to side.

OMG. He knows I'm lying.

I looked at him, so surprised. "How do you know I was lying about my GED?"

"Your energy darkened."

I looked around myself and didn't see any energy field.

"Look Candy, you're a nice lady. You're going to do great things with your life. You just have to remember to keep it real." Randolph said and then stood up. "I have another client on the way. That'll be five hundred dollars." He held out his hand for payment.

"Do you take American Express?"

"Of course."

While he ran my card through the machine, I walked around his living room looking at a bunch of pictures of him. In one of them, he was standing with Richard Geer and some other funny looking guy who was wearing a white sheet for his clothes.

"Wow, you know Richard Geer?" I asked. "Whose the other guy wearing a sheet?"

Randolph just laughed and laughed, "Candy Katz, you keep real, one day you'll be loved and respected just like that man. He's the Dalai Lama." He said as he handed me my credit card and slip for me to sign.

"Huh, never heard of him."

"Get out now. I've got another client."

It was good that he was a psychic instead of a doctor because he had horrible bedside manners.

"You're a funny guy, Randolph."

"Eh, part of my profession."

We hugged goodbye and it was a little odd because his face went right between my breasts, but that's what happens when you hug a short guy. I promised to come again and left.

When I came out of the apartment, Carlo and his gang were waiting for me by my car. They whistled as I strolled down the street towards them. It made me feel good. Not only was I going to be loved like that sheet wearing guy, apparently I was still sexy. That's good to know when you're being dumped by your husband.

"Eh, lady, we watched your car for you." Carlo said.

"Thanks, guys." I told them and unlocked my car with the remote. Carlo opened my door. "Thank you." I said.

"No problemo." Carlo said.

And just because he was so nice to me, I gave him a hundred dollar bill and told him to take his buddies out for a sandwich. Then Carlo explained that buying lunch for everyone in his gang would cost more like three hundred dollars. I counted the guys and had to agree, so I gave him two hundred more.

I drove away in a good mood. I didn't like going to Van Nuys and I didn't like how upset I felt being in that apartment with all those poor people, but I was buying lunch for disadvantaged gang members. That made me feel good, just like when I gave the homeless lady Mindy's shoes. It gave me a bigger high than the first time I had a g-spot orgasm, which took me five years to find, and the feeling lasted a lot longer.

TOM SCREWS MINDY TO SCREW WITH CANDY

CHAPTER SEVEN

The minute I got home, I looked up the Dalai Lama on the internet. He's this really well known spiritual leader of a country called Tibet and they call him His Holiness. How I could ever be respected like the Dalai Lama was beyond me. I'm a former stripper, the daughter of a hash slinger and a dead beat gambler. I didn't do all that studying the Dalai Lama did. In fact, I can't remember studying even once during the entire time I was in elementary and middle school. He has a Nobel Peace Prize for trying to get the Chinese to stop picking on Tibet without using violence. Just in the past month I hit Stacy and Mindy, and tried to kill Tom with a priceless piece of art. Well, that Statue of David was an imitation of a priceless piece of art, but it did cost a lot. I'd become so violent that people in the neighborhood were scared of me. Randolf had to be a total nut. I wasted five hundred dollars that could have been used to buy clothes.

My life was so messed up. I kept going over the end of my marriage in my mind. I broke it down into three simple parts so I could understand.

1. Tom cheated.
2. Tom left.
3. Tom wants a divorce.

I couldn't get over it, even though divorce happens all the time. Three couples on our street divorced in the last year. When I heard about their breakups, I didn't think it was a big deal because all three husbands were really unattractive, so I figured the women were happy they were free to find a good-looking guy. But now that it was happening to me, it felt worse than the stomach flu I got between Christmas and New Year's when I dropped six pounds and didn't have to make the same New Year's resolution I made every year to lose weight again.

My divorce was more tragic though because Tom's the total package, rich and good-looking, not like some of the other husbands who, quite frankly, wouldn't have found attractive wives with their looks if they were poor. It sounds shallow, I know, but it's really not. It's just the truth.

Look at Barry. The guy was Fred Flintstone's twin and if he was penniless or made only forty thousand a year which is considered poor in Calabasas, Mindy would not have given him the time of day. I once saw her spit at an ugly guy who tried to pick her up at the bar in the Regent Beverly Hilton Hotel because he worked at Jiffy Lube. We were at a luncheon for my thirty-fifth birthday. I picked this hotel because it's where they filmed my favorite movie, "Pretty Woman." I identified with Vivian, a prostitute who turns her life around when Edward, played by Richard Gere who is a friend of the Dalai Lama in real life, decides he loves her enough to make her his kept woman. It's as if the movie was based on my life, except I was never paid for sex, I gave it away for free.

Even though it was my birthday, Mindy insisted I sneak out with her to the bar in the lobby because she said my party was boring. I don't know how she could think it was boring. All the women were dressed like hookers in mini-dresses and old scuffed up knee-high black boots. As a party favor, all the tables had black Sharpies for the women to use to cover-up the scuffs on their boots, like Vivian did in the beginning of the movie before Edward bought her all those fabulous clothes in Beverly Hills. I had the I Love Lucy episode Vivian watches when she gives Edward a happy ending repeating on four TV's. I had a Richard Gere look-a-like playing piano in the center of the room and a Barney look-a-like, who was the hotel manager in the movie, teaching the women table manners. That was popular, because most of us still didn't know which was the salad fork and the entree fork.

It was a lot of fun, but Mindy hated that she had to dress up so she was mad at me. And because she wouldn't stop bugging me, I snuck out to the bar with her for a quick drink and that's where we met the drunk ugly guy without money. Mindy was flirting with him because she was mad at Barry for cutting her off from shopping. Then the drunk ugly guy told her he worked at a Jiffy Lube.

"How can you even talk to me on your salary?" Mindy hissed.

The drunk ugly guy looked like he was about to cry. He just finished telling us his fiancé had dumped him. "You money grubbing bitch." He said, then turned to walk away and Mindy spit on his back, I kid you not. Thank God he was too sloshed to notice.

Now that money grubbing bitch had stolen my man. Dumped by my friend and husband, I didn't know what to do for the rest of the day. Shopping for clothes was over. My trip to the psychic was over. The house was clean, because Maria cleans it all day even if it's not dirty. The grocery shopping was done, because Maria does all the shopping. I didn't have my daughter to talk to because she was laying low at her friend's house. She was upset that I broke the living room window and there was one tinny fight on the front lawn that really embarrassed her. I chased Tom out of the house as he was leaving me. We played tug-a-war with his suitcase and I begged him to stay. I got a horrible scrape on my butt too from him pulling me across the sidewalk, because I was only wearing only my bra and underwear.

It was all too depressing. I went back to my bedroom and got on my swing to relax. Since I was a little girl, swinging always made me feel better. When I was seven, we lived in an apartment by my elementary school. When there were a bunch of people hanging out in our living room, sometimes my mom took in homeless people for a few days if they brought her Sweet n' Low, I'd sneak out and swing for hours alone at the school and I'd forget about all my problems. This time, however, it wasn't working. I had real problems. I was to become a divorcee and Tom, the man I thought I would grow old with, was having sex with my BFF.

When my butt started hurting, I got off the swing, pulled out the first season of Sex and the City on DVD and ordered Maria to bring me a bottle of wine. I got in my white Victoria Secret sweat pants that say pink across my butt. When designers started putting their names across the butt of sweats I thought it was sort of weird, but after I kept seeing all of Kelly's friends wearing them, I bought a few pairs. I topped the sweats with a white spaghetti strap tank since I was sticking with my white phase in hopes of getting out of my depression, curled up in bed and turned on the show. Just as I was about to watch my tenth episode, I heard the front door open and slam shut.

"Mom!" Kelly screamed.

I was so relieved Kelly was home. I'd been calling her over and over, worried that she was freaking out that her father was divorcing me, but she wouldn't answer my calls. Her phone went straight to voicemail and I'd left so many messages her mailbox was full. I rushed out of my room. Kelly was sitting at the bottom of the stairs crying.

"Kelly, I was going to tell you. It's why I've been calling you so much." I said.

"What are you talking about?" She asked.

"About Dad and me getting divorced." I said.

"God Mom, you are so self-centered. Everything is about you." She said and stormed up the stairs, walking right passed me and screaming. "God, I hate my life!" before going in her room and slamming her door shut.

This was worse than I thought. She was really upset about the divorce. I walked up to her door and I could hear her crying. I knocked gently. "Kelly Bean, can I come in?" I said as I walked in.

Kelly was on her bed with her face hidden under a pillow and she was kicking her feet up and down. It reminded me of when she was two-years-old and would throw the cutest temper-tantrums. I sat at the top of her bed and stayed clear of her feet so I wouldn't get kicked.

"Kelly Bean. Don't cry. What is it?" I asked

"I can't tell you. It's just awful." She said.

"You can tell me, Kelly Bean." I said. "I'm your mommy."

She came out from under the pillow. "I'm in love." She said.

"Oh, that's it. With who?" I asked.

"Chris. How did this happen. I'm too young to fall like this. It's all over for me." She cried.

"All over. Wait, you're not pregnant, are you?"

"Oh, God, that is so like you to think that. I'm not pregnant, mom. In fact, I'm not having kids ever. It'll ruin my body, so just get over it."

I wanted to tell her that my body wasn't ruined from having her and that since I exercise and eat right, I look pretty good naked even though I'm over forty, but I'm sure she'd just yell at me for being all about myself, so I kept quiet. After all, if there's one thing I've learned as a parent, it's that teenagers are unpredictable.

"My life is over. No more making out with some random guy at a beer bong party…"

"Wait. You do that?" I said.

"No. I don't do that. I would never drink from one of those disgusting beer bongs. They've got everyone's germs on them, mom. Like duh." Kelly said.

"Oh, good." I told her and stopped there. I didn't want to go into this, but once a stripper I worked with at The Booby Trap got a rash around her lips after drinking from a beer bong. It was so bad that the customers threw their empty beer bottles at her when she was on stage. Woody, the bar manager, had to pull her until it cleared up and she lost hundreds of tip dollars. I loaned her a hundred because she needed to pay her phone bill and she never paid me back. I wanted to ask her for my money, because that week I was broke and living off Jiffy Pop popcorn which of course was before I knew about carbohydrates, but I didn't want to be rude.

"I'm too young to be tied down. Being in love destroys people. It makes you all insecure and co-dependent. You can't do anything fun anymore. It ruins people. I'm a mess. I can't even think about myself, because all I think about is Chris. This is a disaster. I might as well die."

"It's your first crush, Kelly Bean. It's so sweet." I said.

"Mom, uh, God, this is love. My first crush was on Mr. Parsley. I know the difference between love and a crush. I'm a senior."

"Your fifth grade teacher?" I asked.

"Like duh. Don't you remember when I had you tell Maria to buy me parsley all the time? It's not because I liked to eat it. I felt closer to Mr. Parsley after school if I had parsley to eat."

I remembered her parsley phase, but I didn't know it was because she had a crush on her teacher. I thought it was because she was suffering from a poor body image and was on the verge of becoming an anorexic because all she wanted to eat was parsley. I sent her to a weekend seminar for girls who think they're fat, but none of them weighed more than 80 lbs. My therapist thought it was important for Kelly to go because she was on the dangerous path of eating only greens. I thought the food disorder clinic was a success because Kelly never became anorexic, but I guess it was because she had a crush, not a disease. There was one good thing about it though, our house smelled really fresh, like a spring salad, that entire year.

"Chris doesn't think it's right to be with me because I've made-out with Brad. Apparently guys think that's a big deal."

'So, are you and Brad over?" I asked, because I was hoping the answer was yes.

"Oh, God, Mom!" She yelled again. "You are so nosey."

"I'm just thinking, If Brad doesn't care if you date Chris then have Brad tell Chris that. You know Kelly, we women have to manipulate men to get them to do what's right"

"It's not just that, okay."

"What is it then?"

"Chris likes big boobs and I'm only an A cup. But I love him. I really, really, super love him and if I can't have Chris, then I'm just going to die."

I put my daughter in drama when she was five because, well, she was so dramatic. I was trying to push the one thing I knew she was good at. She didn't like math, science or English. Shopping, cheerleading and drama are the only extracurricular activities she liked. I wanted her to go to one of those really good state universities I couldn't get into because you need a high school diploma, and I wanted there to be more on her resume than just school. Kelly wasn't a good student. She got by with passing grades, which, you know, still made me happy because a C- gets you through the same as an A+.

"Do you want a breast augmentation?" I asked. Normally I call it a boob job when I'm talking with my friends, but with Kelly I wanted to set an example. If she wanted a boob job, I would get her one. There was no way my daughter was going to be ostracized for being an A cup. That's total discrimination based on her looks, not the kind of person she is inside, and unlike skin color, this was something doctors could fix.

"Oh, God, Mom, it would be like, so embarrassing to show up at high school with bigger boobs. Everyone would know." Kelly said, and I was so proud of her. What a terrific daughter Maria and I raised. "I want them done right after graduation and I don't want them too big because I don't want to look like a stripper." She added.

Kelly knew I was a stripper before I married her dad, and sometimes she'd throw comments into our conversation like this just to let me know she didn't approve, but I just ignored them. I'm proud of my days as a stripper. If it wasn't for the stage and the pole, I would have been homeless and starving to death. Kelly had no idea what it felt like to be poor, which was okay because I didn't want my daughter to ever go through what I experienced because even though Kelly was spoiled and selfish, she still was my little Kelly Bean.

"Deal." I said, and I went to high five her, but she didn't put up her hand.

"No, mom. Let's not go there." Kelly said. "It's just not cool."

Kelly and I watched TV in bed together the next day. I called her school and told them she was sick, which I explained to Kelly wasn't a lie because being in love can actually make you sick. We got through three seasons of Sex and the City, ate popcorn and laughed.

Kelly was fine with the divorce. It didn't even seem to register. Maybe it was because Tom was rarely home when she was growing up or maybe she was more mature than I realized. I still looked at her as my baby Maria took to the park and took to get a picture with Santa. She said she'd been waiting for the divorce to happen for years. It's like a rite of passage as a teenager when you go through your parent's split. She heard about it on My Space. For her generation it's considered a good thing, because it makes them closer to being adults when they've gone through such trauma. When I was a teenager, which was before the Internet, we talked about our feelings standing on a street corner smoking a cigarette.

My time with Kelly was wonderful. She even told me she loved me, which she hasn't done since she was twelve. I had pry it out of her, and even though she said, "God, Mom, there I said it." I didn't get upset. But then it was over.

"I've had enough. I'm going out." Kelly said. "Teenagers can only be around their parents for so long before we get a rash."

Even though it was almost eleven o'clock on a school night, she met her girlfriend at Starbucks. I almost told her she should go to bed and gets some sleep, but Kelly had been through so much already, I didn't want to upset her more.

The next day was the third Thursday of the month, which is when I have my book club meeting with the gals. I started the club four years earlier because I felt so smart whenever I said I was in a book club. We didn't read the entire book. We skimmed, used Cliff Notes, and I would go on the Internet and print up blurbs. When we got together and everyone added their thoughts on the sections they read, we all got a sense of what the book was about. Usually we read the Oprah Book Club selections, but sometimes the books she picks are depressing, like the book "Night" about a guy who was in a Nazi prison camp. I learned by reading that book that even though I had a chuppah at my recommitment ceremony, I didn't want to know the history of the Jews, especially the Holocaust. It was just too depressing.

After that book club meeting, we decided to read only chic lit or self-improvement books. The chic lit novels, even though they could be over three hundred pages, were so much fun to skim. Most are about women in their twenties, just starting a career and trying to find a man, but still we related to them because they all love to shop. And, even though we were in our late thirties, we felt and acted like we were in out late twenties. But the best part about switching to chic lit was that many of the books get made into a movie so we got to plan a girl's night out where we'd go see the movie and go out to dinner after to discuss the movie compared to the book. Sometimes the movie was so different from the book, I wondered if the producers read it.

This month we were reading "A New Earth" by Eckhart Tolle, which is such a funny name for a guy. I was absolutely convinced it was the book for us when I saw Jenny McCarthy on Oprah talking about how great the book is. Her hair was bleached blonde and she had it cut into a sharp bob that made her look so smart, I almost forgot she was a Playboy Playmate. Jenny talked about how the book taught her to be present in the moment. I haven't actually read it yet, but I'm sure she's not a liar.

Mindy was in the book club too, but I was sure she wouldn't show since I'm the one who started it and she always hated going. If she showed up after what she did to me, I would be shocked if the other women even spoke to her.

I made a plan to get the book in the morning at Barnes & Nobel and then lounge at the pool and read it before our three o'clock meeting. I got ready for bed feeling better about my situation. I wasn't standing by my man after he had an affair like a politician's wife. I'm not really into politics, but I can tell you that I did pay attention to John Edwards and his affair with that TV producer. His wife had cancer and he chose to bonk a scruffy looking woman who didn't know how to run a comb through her hair. I know politics is a brutal business, but this was just disgusting. I could understand if he cheated with a pretty girl like that New York Attorney General Elliot Spitzer who had an affair with that gorgeous call girl, but John Edwards didn't even trade up. Especially when you're running for President, you have to trade up because it's going to come out eventually and everyone's going to see who you're bonking. I'm only a middle school graduate and even I understand this.

I brushed away the rose petals Maria places on my pillows every night to show how much she appreciates me and hopped in bed positive that even though Tom cheated on me and dumped me, that my life was heading in the right direction. I fell asleep fast, because I'd been drinking merlot for two days and had the best dream. I was an angel flying in the sky with a bob haircut just like Jenny McCarthy and was dressed in a little white mini-dress. Mindy was the devil. She wore a red dress and had big horns on her head. I shook my angel wand. Angel dust sprinkled on her breast and they shrunk to a double AA. Devil Mindy hissed fire out of her mouth, so I shook my angel stick again. Water poured on her head, putting her fire out. Smoke steamed out of her mouth when she hissed at me again. It was the best dream I've ever had.

The next morning I felt a little embarrassed to go outside, because like Nancy and Kelly said, apparently everyone knew my husband was sleeping with my BFF. But I couldn't be a hermit, right. I had to start living my new life, which I planned to be the same, except Tom and Mindy would no longer be in it.

I put on the smallest bikini I had, because I was really skinny from hardly eating and looked smoking hot. I tossed on my Hot House Orchid Chiffon Tunic by Tommy Bahamas over my swimsuit and my Leopard Kitten Heel Tommy Bahamas flats, and headed out the door. I put the top down on my Mercedes and it was such a gorgeous day, that I didn't care that a bug flew into my teeth when I was driving. I was just happy that I was smiling. It'd been weeks since I'd been able to.

I stopped at a light. In the car next to me was a hot and I mean really hot guy driving a BMW. He lowered his sunglasses so I could see his eyes and checked me out like I was a steak and he was a hungry bear. I kid you not. It was just like something you'd see in a movie. And it was then that I realized I could have sex with him if I wanted to, because I was getting divorced! I had been so upset, that I hadn't considered the possibility that I could bonk anyone I wanted, whenever I wanted, wherever I wanted. I was a free woman. This positive side to divorce I'd never considered. Thank God I wasn't a hag yet. I worked out four times a week and was in the best shape of my life. I only had three pockets of cellulite I couldn't smooth out, one on my left leg and two on my right, but for my age that was pretty good. If Hugh Hefner saw me in the nude, he'd stick me in Playboy. I even had a high school'er trying to pin me down, so at least, even though my husband dumped me, I still look good enough to pull a demi.

The light turned green. I turned up Beyonce's "Put A Ring On It" and moved my head to the beat. I was feeling totally hot and totally bitchin as I pulled into the Commons parking lot and found a parking spot close to the book store. Unfortunately, it was right in front of Belle Gray. I wasn't in the mood to run into Lisa Rinna. I was still bothered by our lack of chemistry on the phone. You'd think, since we have the same taste in clothes, that we would've hit it off better. I was worried when we met face to face we'd have nothing to say and it would be really awkward so I rushed by her store.

Inside Barnes & Noble, I asked a clerk where I could find the book. He directed me to the best sellers table by the front door. I found the book and was shocked that it was 336 pages. How would I be able to skim all that in one afternoon was beyond me, so I asked the clerk if there were Cliff Notes I could buy, and I may be wrong about this, but he seemed annoyed when he told me not yet and suggested that I should just read the book. He had such an attitude, that I almost complained to the manager, but I didn't want to get him in trouble.

With the book in my Prada bag, I drove next door to the club hoping Brad wasn't on lifeguard duty. I wasn't in the mood to be bothered. I got out of my car and walked through the club and out to the pool. After my eyes adjusted from the sunlight bouncing off the water, I scanned the lounge chairs for the perfect spot and...

Oh, my God!

Mindy was there!

And, she was there with Stacy and Katie!

And, all three of them were reading A New Earth!

Mindy actually thought she was allowed to stay in my book club!

As if!

I set up my towel on a lounge chair so no one else would take it, put my new copy of A New Earth on the towel and walked over to them. Stacy and Katie's eyes went so wide, I thought their eyes were going to pop out of their sockets.

"Mindy, I need to talk to you." I said.

"So talk?"

"Alone."

Mindy and I walked over to the other side of the pool.

"The book club is mine. I started it. You can't go anymore." I told her.

"Oh, really? Is that what you think?" She said.

"That's what I know."

"I've made some calls. Me and the girls think,

given your violent history, that we're voting you out."

"I started the book club and you didn't even want to be in it."

"So, I've changed my mind."

"I'm the president. You can't vote me out."

"God, Candy, you're so stupid."

"I am not stupid."

"Yes, you are. Don't you know presidents can be impeached and thrown out of office?"

"So this is how it's gonna be, huh? War?" I said.

"If you want to call it that. You're not much of an enemy, though." She said and laughed. "You're just too nice, Candy. You'll never beat me."

And I couldn't believe it, but I started getting tears in my eyes.

"How can you be so cruel?"

"I don't know. It comes naturally. Probably just the way I was born. Honestly, I can't help myself. It's all so easy."

"We were best friends."

"Look, Candy, don't take it personally. I'm just doing what I have to do. Some people go to work to make money, I find a man to give me his money. Think of it like my career."

Tears fell from my eyes and even though I was embarrassed, I couldn't stop them.

"See how sweet you are. I'm not like that. I'm a bully. I prey on people like you." She took a deep breath. "I can't talk anymore. I have to go read my book for my book club today." Mindy said.

As I watched her gorgeous long brown hair sway side to side as she walked away, I started shaking like a crazy person.

"Not so fast, Mindy."

She stopped and turned back to me with a smile on her face. "Oh, Candy, please, just face up to your life now. It's all over. Tom hates you and I've managed to turn…" She started counting on her fingers… "one, two, three, four, five, six, seven… seven of your friends against you. It's time to see the writing on the wall."

I walked up to Mindy and was about to cuss her out, but thought that wouldn't be the best behavior in front of the Calabasas residents lounging by the pool and the group of kids in day camp in the shallow end. I was boiling over with hatred and anger and I wanted to scream and hit her. I even wanted to light her hair on fire.

"Say it, already, Candy. You're turning red."

I looked her in the eyes and for the first time in my life I actually hated someone and I felt bad about this.

"There's a lot I could say to you… you… you husband stealer, but I'm not going to waste my breath."

I grabbed a huge chuck of her hair and pulled on it hard, thinking her extensions would come off.

"Take that, you insensitive witch."

"Candy, stop it!." She screamed.

I tugged and tugged, but none of the hair came off. Ricardo really is a good hairstylist.

She dug her nails into my arm. I let go of her hair and she pushed me in the pool. I screamed and landed in the freezing water. My Tommy Bahamas tunic went up over my head on impact and twisted around my face and arms so I couldn't get free to swim to the top. I thought I was going die, for real this time, not for fake like when I saw Mindy and Tom together in the bathroom. Unless someone rescued me, it was entirely likely that I would drown. Then finally, someone grabbed me from behind and swam me to the surface. I unwrapped the tunic from my head, and saw that it was my knight in surfer wear. I started coughing and gasping for air.

"Hold on to the rescue tube." Brad said.

The kids in the day camp parted in the water so he could pull me to the steps. I sat down and continued coughing.

"Geez, Mrs. Katz, it's a good thing I was here." Brad said.

"Where did you come from?" I said.

"The locker room."

"See, she's crazy." I heard Mindy say to Katie and Stacy. "This is what Tom and I have been dealing with. She's totally violent and out of control. Come on girls, let's go hit some balls on the court.

I looked over at the three of them as they packed up to leave the pool area. Stacy, who I was pretty sure hated me since I pegged her in the face with a tennis ball, gave me a dirty look as she packed up. Katie went along with the group, as if she wasn't in charge of anything. It was sort of pathetic. I wondered if people looked at me that way when Mindy used to boss me around.

"Kelly broke up with me." Brad said as he wrapped a towel around me and helped me to my chair.

"I heard."

"She told me she's in love with Chris. She thinks I'm too into myself." He ran his fingers through his hair and checked out his appearance in the reflection on the metal umbrella pole.

I was too depressed to talk. I was wet and tired, which I found hard to believe since I slept for twelve hours the night before, but my body wasn't used to all this chaos. For years I had a stress free life where I didn't even have to clean a toilet, was dishes, do laundry, make dinner or get a job, and now I was up to my eyeballs with anxiety.

"So, like, you know, I'm a free man again." Brad said. "Thought you and I could go out sometime?"

"You're not a man yet, Brad. You're seventeen."

"Having the big birthday soon and turning legal."

"Look Brad, you're a sweet kid and I really appreciate that you just saved me from drowning, but... but... my life...." I started crying. I couldn't even get a word out that didn't sound like Mini-mouse because my mouth was sort of frozen in this really funky, and I'm sure really unattractive, position. "My life is falling apart and I…."

Brad looked so upset. "Geez, Mrs. Katz. I know Mrs. Klein's been sleeping with your husband, but I thought you were all right with it. It's been going on a while and thought, you know, maybe you were swingers or something cool like that since you two stayed friends for such a long time after they made out at the New Year's party here at the club."

"They did?"

"They got caught kissing in the men's locker room by Chris's dad."

"They did?"

"It wasn't full-on. Their clothes were on, but they were, you know, mackin hard."

"I had no idea." I buried my head in the towel and cried like a blubbering idiot.

"Wow, that's harsh."

The female lifeguard on duty waved at Brad to come do his time up on the chair.

"Got to get back to the station or I'll get fired. So, what'a you say about that date?"

"Brad, you're a sweet kid, but there's no way in hell that I'll go out with you." I said and Brad just laughed, as if even though I said it, he didn't believe it and that pretty soon I'd be his.

"How about just friends?" He said.

"That I can do."

He stood up, but before he walked away, he leaned down close to my ear and whispered, "You know Mrs. Katz, lot of people sleep with their friends."

"Brad, I will call your parents."

He smiled and walked away holding his rescue tube over his privates and I was pretty sure I knew why.

I laid down on the chair, wanting to die. Mindy

kicked me out of my marriage and now she wanted my book club. This gypsy would stop at nothing. She may have damaged my relationship with my husband, but she was not going to stop me from going to my book club. I was going to show up so informed they would keep me in the group.

I studied for the next three hours. Even when I had to go to the bathroom, I held it in so I wouldn't waste time. The book was sort of good. It wasn't blockbuster good or fun like Sophia Kinsella's books, but that little Eckhart Tolle dude had some interesting things to say. I didn't understand a lot of it, but I got that my ego was a problem and that I was supposed to live in the now because now is all we have. That was a problem for me, though, because the now was crappy. I was losing my friends. Tom didn't love me anymore. Everyone in Calabasas thought I was going postal. In the now I was totally fucked, and no one, even a prostitute, wants to admit they're totally fucked.

I went into the locker room, took a shower and changed into my Elizabeth and James School shirt that I got at Belle Gray. It has lovely detailing on the back, tapered and with a line of cute little buttons and since it was white, it made me look professional. I paired it with my Phillip Lim Tiered Ruffled Pencil skirt that is ultra-short and my Jimmy Choo Premiere Slingback Snakeskin pumps and I looked ready to hit a board room. Armed with the power of now and a really awesome outfit, I drove to Starbucks at the Commons and got a table on the walkway. I was 45 minutes early, but I wanted to be there before Mindy so I could win some of the women back to my side.

I glanced over at a woman at the table next to me. She was reading The Secret which was so passé. Didn't she hear, the secret about "The Secret" was out? I was just glad we were all out of our "Eat, Pray, Love" phase. Seemed like an eternity that we women were idolizing Elizabeth Gilbert like she was the second coming of

Christ. I mean please, that woman was crazy. She went to Italy to explore pleasure and instead of having sex with a bunch of Italian men, all she did was eat.

First to arrive was Tatonka, a gorgeous Native American whose parents named her the Indian name for buffalo. She was mortified when the movie Dances with Wolves came out, because she had to explain why she was named after buffalo, over and over, to everyone she met. Before the movie, everyone thought her name was sophisticated. Now they laugh.

"You're here." Tatonka said. "Rumor has it, you're out."

We kissed cheeks, both sides like the Europeans, but we didn't actually touch lip to skin because that would mess up our lipglass application. Lipstick was out of style. We all wore sheer and shiny glass with plumpers to make our lips bigger, since we were all still afraid to have a lip augmentation. Some of them don't turn out so well.

"I'm not giving Mindy my book club. She has my husband, don't you think that's enough?"

Tatonka was about to answer, but Katie, Stacy and Mindy walked up.

"I'll call you later. I don't want Mindy mad at me." Tatonka whispered. She was shaking a little at the sight of Mindy.

"You've dried off. Did that cute lifeguard feel you up when he rescued you?" Mindy said to me.

"Shut up." I said.

"Girls, let's not fight." Stacy said, as Hunter, Charlotte and Samantha from the Oaks sat down. These were three of the women I accused Tom of sleeping with in our neighborhood, but they were in my social network so I had to be nice to them.

'Why are you here, Mindy? Can't you leave me alone and let me go on with my life? You don't even like to read." I said, and all the women turned their heads to Mindy to hear her answer.

"No. Why should I change my social calendar for you?" She said, and brought out her copy of "A New Earth" and it had sticky notes inside it marking important pages. This was the first time she'd ever read a book for the book club. I gasped at the sight of it.

"Ladies, let's get this out in the open. I'm having an affair with Tom. We're in love."

I started gagging.

"In love?" I said.

"Yes. He's moved in with me…

"Moved in with you?" I started wheezing.

"Yes. I know it's hard to face, Candy, but this is what's happening now, and you should know after reading this book that we have to live in the now because now is all we have." Mindy said.

She was so charismatic, that if it wasn't my husband she was taking, I would worship her too.

"You all should know that after Tom divorces Candy, we're getting married." Mindy said to the women. "You have to pick who you want to stay in the group. It's me or Candy. I'm not threatening any of you, but it's in your best interest if you pick me. I'll still be around, and Candy will be living in an apartment in some horrible place like Woodland Hills or Tarzana."

The women took the debate pretty seriously. They chose Mindy, explaining that it would be awkward seeing her around if they didn't and asked me to leave. Unbelievable!

Exiled from my book club and my group of friends, I cried all the way home, but when I pulled into my driveway there was a flower delivery man on the front porch holding an enormous bouquet of white roses. It was so big it could have housed a bird's nest. I was sure they were from Tom and that meant Mindy was so out and I was so in again.

"Hello." I said to the delivery man.

"Candy Katz?" He asked.

"That's me." I said, happily.

"These are for you." He handed me the heavy bouquet. "You've been served."

I looked inside the bouquet of flowers and instead of birds nest inside it, there was a large manila envelope.

I read the return address. "Huckabee, Finstock, Merrigold & Meringue. That's a stupid name for a business." I told the man.

"Yeah, yeah, sign right here." I signed a paper he put in front of me. "You have to vacate the premises in thirty days." He said, before getting back in his car and driving off.

"What do you mean by premises?" I hollered back, while opening the manila envelope. I pulled out divorce papers. It was official. Just like Mindy said, Tom was going through with it and giving me the boot.

There was a letter from Tom.

> *Dear Candy,*

> *I am in love with Mindy now.*

No f'ing way! You do love her!

> *I know this is all a shock to you, but Mindy is the most amazing woman I've ever known. I can't live without her and I'm not going to deny my feelings anymore.*

Yeah, why should a little thing like a marriage vow get in the way of you denying your feelings, you rat!

> *I'm giving you one month to move out of the house,*

What! Why?

> *so Mindy and I can move in. Her house is being foreclosed on since Barry left her penniless.*

I'm not moving out of this house!

> *You have to move out of the house as stated in the pre-nup you signed.*

Oh, shit, I forgot about the pre-nup.   I'll fight it.

> *Don't try to fight this in court. I've already consulted with five lawyers who've told me there's no way you'll win, especially since you tried to kill me with an imitation Statue of David.*

> *Tom*

I searched behind a row of bushes along the brick wall on the side of our drive way, and glanced up in the large birch tree in our front yard for a film crew. I had to be getting punked, but there was no one around, not even cars driving on the street. The place was deserted. Even a flock of birds flew out of a tree when I looked their way. It was as if everyone in the neighborhood knew Tom was serving me divorce papers and disappeared, worried I might go postal.

Mindy Klein, the gypsy, was behind it all and winning. She was ruining me, just like she said she would. She took all my friends, my husband, my book club, and now she was getting my house, my furniture and my swing. The only friend I had left was an underage horny teenager who was only interested in scoring with me.

CANDY'S SUPER-DUPER SCREWED

CHAPTER EIGHT

I found a one bedroom apartment miles north of Ventura Boulevard which we considered deep inside the San Fernando Valley in an area called Canoga Park. It wasn't too far from away from Kelly so I moved in. She decided to stay in our house with her dad and Mindy. She said she would be ostracized if her friends found out she shared a one bedroom apartment with her mom north of Ventura Blvd. and I couldn't afford a two bedroom. When she reminded me how she was never home anyway since it was her senior year and that right after graduation and her augmentation she was moving out, I agreed she should stay in the house. Kelly had been through so much. I wanted her to be happy, so I left my home, my husband, my maid and even my daughter with Mindy and moved out.

My pre-nup with Tom gave me $1500 a month to live on. When I agreed to that amount years ago, it was a lot of money. Now it was hardly anything. My rent was $795, which was the cheapest place I could find that I would actually live in and then I had to pay my utilities. I asked Tom for more money, but he said Mindy said no. He was being such a jerk. He even transferred my club membership at the Calabasas Swim and Tennis Center into Mindy's name. Hers expired not

158

long after Barry died because he hadn't paid the dues for a year. There was a two year waiting list to join again so Tom added Mindy to our family membership and deleted me.

"Mindy doesn't want to see you at the club." He told me.

"You're whipped." I told him.

"Look, Candy. We're in love. You don't understand."

"Denial ain't just a river in Egypt." I told him.

My mom taught me about the Denial River one night when she couldn't sleep, even though it was a school night and I was only in first grade. She said it was okay that I was going to bed at 3:00 a.m. since she was giving me a history lesson.

At least Tom let me keep my Mercedes. Since it was paid off, he gave it to me as a bribe. "I'm giving you the car." He said, "As a gesture of good will. I hope we can still be friends."

"Fuck off." I told him and then he said the rudest thing ever.

"Before I met you, you were just a stripper. I was the best thing that ever happened to you."

Oh, please! As if! And vice versa!

"Go fuck yourself." I yelled into the phone. "And I hope you catch a gypsy disease from Mindy that makes your dick shrivel up and break off."

After that conversation, he refused to take my call, even when I called his office a hundred times a day, five days in a row. Maybe I was a little harsh, but considering he bumped me out of his life and replaced me with my best friend, I didn't think so. But Tom was a fool because there was such a thing as a gypsy disease. Rose Roop, the tarot card reader two doors down in my apartment building put a curse on Tom to make sure he'd get it from Mindy, and she only charged me forty dollars. "May God give you luck and health, sugar." She said to me after we made the deal, which seemed sort of

159

weird, you know, because I didn't think God would be so nice to me after putting a curse on Tom.

My tiny apartment was just awful. It had horrible brown carpet that had been there since the 70's. I'm not kidding. Henry, the manager, told me so. He was one of those guys who looked like a circus clown without dressing up. He had rosy cheeks and nose full of red varicose veins that stood out against his white skin. Henry was as soft and round as a marshmallow, but I liked him. Even though I didn't have a credit rating, because I never had a real job and all our credit cards and mortgage were in Tom's name, he rented me the apartment because he said I was the kind of tenant he wanted to see around. He wasn't lying either, because every time I walked by his apartment, he stood at his doorway and said, "Welcome home, pretty lady." And then he'd watch me walk up the stairs. Once I asked him if he was checking out my ass, but he said he was just making sure I got inside my apartment safely.

Henry was a good apartment manager. He spliced off his cable so I could get it for free. The cable company wanted $95 a month to get all the TV channels. You would think, even if you're poor, you could have HBO and Showtime, but apparently they consider those channels a luxury. After hearing me complain, Henry spliced off his cable line if I agreed to go to the liquor store for him every now and then. He told me he had a condition that made it hard for him to walk. I almost told him that if he exercised and drank less his condition would get better, but I didn't want to be rude. And anyway, it wasn't a big deal going to the liquor store. It was in walking distance, so I didn't have to use money on gas.

Money was tight. I didn't even have enough to get my acrylic nails filled. After two months four of them came off, so I borrowed pliers from Henry and snapped off the others. It only hurt a little. He gave me sand paper to file off the glue, and then I bought a bottle of nail polish for $1.99 at the pharmacy and did my own nails.

I kept my poor life hidden from Kelly. Instead of having her come to my apartment, I met her at Starbucks or Coffee Bean, pulling up in my Mercedes and wearing one of my fabulous dresses Tom bought me over the years. Besides my jewelry and car, the only thing I got out of the marriage was my wardrobe. The only problem, as Kelly pointed out to me while I sucked in a venti mocha with whole milk, whipped cream and caramel sauce dripped on top, was that I was getting too fat to fit into them.

"Mom, God, I can't believe you didn't get a nonfat latte. Have you seen yourself in the mirror lately?"

"Why?"

"Seriously, and I'm not saying this to be mean, I'm saying it because I care, but I think your ass is totally a size eight now."

I knew I was pushing it by not exercising and eating everything, but I figured I had a six month window before it was obvious. When Kelly said that, I thought I was going to have a heart attack, but I just laughed it off.

"Oh, you know, I haven't been working out as much lately. That's all."

"Well you better start, 'cause I've seen pregnant women smaller than you."

Oh, my daughter, she was so honest. I thought about telling her she was being rude, but I didn't want to upset her. Life was getting hard at home. Cindy had moved in along with Mindy and not only was Cindy screaming all the time and making out with her 100% Bitch lover in the Jacuzzi, Mindy was redecorating.

She tried to have all my Statue of David's donated to Goodwill, but the Hispanic man who came to the house with the Goodwill truck rejected them. He was Catholic and thought the statues were pornographic. Kelly said she laughed for five minutes, though, when

Mindy yelled at him and he made the sign of the cross, mumbled a prayer as if he'd seen the devil, and drove away. Chuck and Chip, a terrific gay couple three doors down, took the statues and lined their driveway with them until the homeowners association threatened to sue them. Now, apparently, my statues are hidden in bushes all over their front lawn.

But the worst part, Kelly said, was that Mindy hired a guy in the Home Depo parking lot with horrible body odor to glue crystal balls on the statue pedestals and the smell stayed in the house for two weeks. Mindy told Kelly that the crystal balls would absorb all my energy out of the house, and Kelly told her she wished they absorbed all the smell out.

After seeing Kelly that day, I fell into a deep depression. Two more months passed and I gained twelve more pounds. My life was a complete disaster. When I watched every episode of a Jerry Springer marathon for three straight days, I hit rock bottom. It wasn't all the alcohol or food I'd been eating or the fact that my hair had been so neglected that I had four inches of roots, it was that I'd become so white trash again that I actually thought the Jerry Springer Show was good.

Then I had an ah-ha moment, you know, the kind where a light goes on in your head and you understand something. I was on the path of becoming my mother. Soon I'd be slinging hash browns and sniffing illegal Sweet n' Low. It was all just too depressing. I felt suicidal. I went downstairs crying to Henry. "Without money, I'm nothing. " I said.

He gave me a real tight hug and rubbed me on the back. "That's not true, pretty lady. You're a hot mama."

"I am?"

"Sure you are, even though you've gained a hunk a weight since moving in. Don't mean to be a downer, but if you get to a size 10, I'm gonna have to go back on my agreement to wave the $500 deposit."

I went back to my apartment and tried to look at

my butt in the medicine cabinet to see how big it was. I had to jump up five times to see it and what I saw in the mirror made me even more depressed. I'd pushed myself to the limit. If I didn't fix myself up now, I might never return to being a hot mama.

My hair needed to be colored and cut, so I went to a salon on Reseda Blvd. where I didn't need an appointment. I couldn't believe it. They had a big sign that said walk-ins welcome. No pulling out a card and calling "the voice." And the price for a cut and color was only $24.95, a total bargain. It wasn't the nicest place, but at least there wasn't hair all over the floor. The place was clean, but the lighting was florescent, the counters weren't granite, and the chairs had holes worn through the upholstery. I was used to five star facilities designed by… well… designers. This place looked slapped together twenty years ago by someone who hadn't studied design and only had a thousand dollar budget.

Barbara, a short-haired, tall and skinny woman with a bad spray tan, well, maybe she was tan from being in the sun too long, had me sign in at the cashiers desk, which seemed odd because I was the only one there for a haircut. She sat me at her station and under the florescent lights, I looked horrible. My face was fat, my skin tone was uneven, my skin was dry and in desperate need of exfoliation. I needed an emergency session with Nancy, but couldn't afford Zen Spa. It was then that I realized just how much my life had turned to shit.

"How much do you want for it?" Barbara asked me.

"For what?" I said.

She held onto my long hair and flipped it in front of my face. "Your hair. I can cut you a bob that'll make you look smart." She said, and hacked like she had a hair in her throat. I think the non-smoking campaigns went right over her head, because she sounded like an old lady and she had a lump inside her shirt by her bra that was the shape of a cigarette pack. "I'll pay you $80 for it." She said. "It goes to make wigs for women with cancer."

"Oh, my, gosh. That's such a good cause."

I thought of all those women in India who got pennies for their hair that was in much better shape than mine because it wasn't processed. Then I thought about all the stars chopping off their long hair into bob haircuts and decided it was time for a change.

"Cut it off, then."

Barbara whipped out scissors and cut off my hair in seconds.

"Wait!" I shrieked, but it was too late.

"Whooo hooo. I just love doing that. All you gals squeal the same. It's like cutting off the tail of a pig." She said, and doubled over with laughter while holding my long blonde hair in her right hand. Then she stood up, put her hands and my hair in the air and waved to the ceiling. "Thank you, Jesus. Whooo hoo!" She added. I might be wrong, but I don't think she was really religious, because right after she said, "Fuck'n A, it's a good day."

My eyes filled with tears as I looked at my short hair in the mirror.

"Don't cry, darling. Give me twenty minutes and you'll be looking sharp as a tack." Barbara put a pony tail band around my hair and placed it in a drawer lined with felt, like a jewelry case.

"Don't cut off more. Keep it as long as you can." I told her.

"Honey, it's gone. You're short and sassy now. Ain't no turning back."

She was right. My life as I knew it, and now my hair had been cut off. There was no turning back, so I stopped crying and faced that what's done is done.

Barbara cut my hair into a straight line, bleached my roots and surprisingly it looked good, and I only owed her $5.99. She deducted my cut, color, tax, tip, and a storage fee to hold my donated hair and a shipping fee to mail it in to the wig making place from the eighty dollars she owed me. I walked out of the salon smart looking and fired up to go back to my disgusting apartment and find a way to turn my life around, but there was a homeless woman blocking me from getting into my car. She was looking at her teeth in the side mirror.

"Excuse me." I said. "I need to get in my car."

The woman looked at me and started shaking her head. "She got you. I leave my post for one minute and she's got a new one. How much did Barbara give you for your hair?"

"Oh, you know Barbara?" I asked.

"We used to be best friends, before she stole my husband."

I gasped.

"My best friend slept with my husband too. Now she's living in my house and I'm so poor I have to get my hair cut here."

"No, no, no, Barbara didn't sleep with my husband, she stole him. He was an illegal and wanted for a crime he did years ago in Tijuana. She turned him in at the police station for the $1000 reward."

"What was he wanted for?"

"Just a small armed robbery. No big deal, right. We all make mistakes."

"Yeah, nobody's perfect." I said, but that was a white lie, because while nobody is perfect, most of us don't have armed robbery in our past.

"What'd the lung hacking bitch give you for your hair?"

"Eighty."

"Girl, you just got taken by a pack a day smoking cigarette hag. Now she's gonna put your hair on The Hair Trader.com and get $1500."

"She told me it was going to make wigs for women

with cancer."

"She's full of crap. You go in there and tell her she's full of crap." She pushed my back just a little towards the salon doors, but I was too scared to stand up to Barbara.

"I… I…"

"Go on, woman, get in there. Ain't you got any backbone?"

My lips started quivering. "No. I don't. I don't have a backbone. I never stand up for myself and everyone always hurts my feelings because of it."

"You can't be like that sister. Got'a be tough. Look at me. I'm a nobody. Got no one and nothing but this grocery cart I stole from the Ralphs parking lot, and all because I let that woman steal my husband. I used to have a good life, a one bedroom apartment and a man who worked day after day cleaning gutters so our cupboards were stocked with Spam and Cup o' Noodle soup. I trusted that woman. I told her about his past and she ruined me. People don't care about other people any more. Users. That's what everyone is. Users! Now get in there and tell her you want more money!" She yelled at me.

"All right! I will." I wiped the tears from my eyes and went inside the hair salon. Barbara was spraying Aqua Net on her hair and using a hair pick to make the top real high.

"Barbara, I know you're going to sell my hair on the internet for over a thousand dollars. I want a bigger take."

"Christ, did that nut job in the parking lot tell you that? Woman's playing you. When you go back out there and tell her how much you got, she's gonna insist on a 50/50 split. You're being scammed, and I'm not giving you any more money because a deals a deal. Not my fault you were too stupid to fall for it." She said and lit a cigarette. There was still some Aqua Net floating in the air. It caught on fire and then blew out quickly.

"Whoa." She put the cigarette out. "Better wait 'til my hair spray dries or my head's going up in flames."

I started crying again. I couldn't help it. I was so tired of everyone being so mean.

"Damn it. Crocodile tears. I'm a sucker for crocodile tears. Here, take this twenty." She handed me a twenty that had a ripped corner and a bunch of writing on it. It didn't seem like anyone would accept it. "Now go on. Get out." She said.

I left and went back to my car. "How much did you get?" The homeless lady asked.

"Twenty."

"Shit, you gotta stand up for yourself better."

"What do you care? You don't know me. You trying to scam me?"

"Look, you're on to me, but don't you think I deserve ten out of that twenty? I am the reason you got it, and I did give you a free counseling session."

I handed the twenty dollar bill to her. "Take it. You need it more than me."

I got in my car and cried all the way home. Everyone took advantage of me and I was so tired of it. Didn't these people feel bad about themselves? I once took an extra piece of gum from Kelly's pack and I felt so guilty I apologized for days. She was only two years old and after she thought my name was Mommy's Sorry. She called me that for the next year.

All I wanted to do was stay in my dingy disgusting apartment and hide out, but when I got home, Katie was waiting for me at the top of the stairs. When she saw me, her mouth went really wide and I thought it was because my hair looked so great, but then she said, "Oh, my God. Look at you. You're a mess."

"What are you doing here?" I asked her while I opened the door to my apartment.

"I heard you lived in a crappy apartment in Canoga Park, but I had to see for myself."

"See" I gestured to the apartment building. "It's true. Now go away." I went inside my apartment and shut the door right in front of her face. I didn't usually act like this, but I hated everyone right then, except my daughter of course.

Katie knocked again. I opened the door.

"What do you want?"

"Stacy dumped me and replaced me with Mindy. I'm out."

"Now you know how it feels. What do you want from me?"

"Just to talk I guess. I feel like I ruined your marriage. I never should have told you Mindy was sleeping with Tom. Should have let you stay ignorant."

"Did you just call me stupid?"

"No. Ignorant."

"Oh. Okay. Look Katie, I would have found out eventually, so don't feel guilty." I was relieved that there was one person in the world who actually felt guilt.

"Look, my husband's still out of work. Pretty soon our house will go into foreclosure. If it wasn't for my bartending job, we wouldn't have money for food. I just want you to know you're not the only one having a hard time."

"Jeez, Katie, I'm sorry."

"God, you're so nice. I feel so bad about dumping you after the split, but I knew I'd get picked on by Mindy and Stacy if I talked to you. They cut me out anyway, so…" Katie's voice cracked. I thought she was going to burst into tears, but she made this ridiculous looking face, like the face you'd make if someone is pulling out your fingernail, and then she burst into tears and fell down to her knees on my doorstep.

"Do you want to come in and have a drink?"

Katie glanced inside my messy, dark and dingy apartment. "I'm not sure. Is it safe?"

"I guess. I'm still alive."

"Barely." She added as she walked in.

Even though Katie spoke every rude comment that came into her mind, I liked her. At least I knew where I stood which was refreshing after being friends with Mindy.

"I can't stay long. I have to work at eight o'clock."

I cleaned up as I walked fifteen feet through the living room to the small kitchen and grabbed my bottle of Two Buck Chuck from Trader Joe's. I poured us each a glass, keeping the label turned away so she couldn't see the brand.

"Wow, you got fat really fast." Katie said. "But I like your hair. It makes you look smarter, even though you're not."

"Thanks." I said and handed her the glass of wine.

We sat down on the couch after I got Katie a towel to sit on. She said she was allergic to certain kinds of upholstery, but I think she thought the couch was dirty. I didn't make a big deal out of it, because it was. The apartment came furnished and the furniture had been there as long as the carpet.

"It's really depressing here." Katie said. "You need to redecorate."

"I'm broke. Tom only gives me $1,500 a month and rent here is more than half that."

"Man, Mindy did a number on you."

"Yeah. She's a gypsy, you know."

"Oh, I didn't know that." She said and there was this lull in the conversation which I just hate. It's how I felt on the phone with Lisa Rinna. I never had lulls with Mindy in conversations. Even if she was telling me to shut up or get out of her way, I'd rather have that than uncomfortable silence.

"So, what do you do all day?"

"I do my nails, drink, eat, cry, walk to the liquor store and watch Jerry Springer."

Katie started crying, again.

"Don't cry. I'm fine, really."

"No, you're not. You're disgusting now. You used to be this woman I idolized."

"You did?"

"Yes, but I've helped ruin you. Now you're fat and broke, your nails are short and your manicure looks cheap. I can't believe this could happen to you."

"Katie, I'm getting by. I'm happy."

"No, you're not. You're just too stupid to see how miserable you are." That sounded like a cut-down, but I wasn't sure, so I let it go.

"I can't believe you're getting this upset about me? We're like, not really friends."

"Oh, God, Candy, you are so self-centered. I'm not upset about you, I'm upset about me?"

I felt like I was talking to Nancy. You know how Peter Piper Picked a Peck of Picked Peppers is a tongue twister, Katie was speaking sentences like Nancy that were mind twisters.

"This is my future. Any day now we're getting booted out of our house and I'm going to have to live in some over-priced apartment in the Valley that comes with a family of cockroaches."

"I don't have cockroaches."

"I just saw two crawl across the wall."

"Holy shit!" I screamed. I grew up in apartments with cockroaches and I hate, hate, hate, those bugs more than I hate Tom, but not more than I hate Mindy Klein. I vowed, when I was old enough to become a stripper and make enough money to move out, that I would never live in a bug infested apartment again.

Katie suggested I turn all the lights on to keep the bugs from coming out, and I did, but told her I couldn't do it all the time because I had to keep my DWP bill low.

I started crying and Katie started crying and then we started chugging our wine, which Katie said was the best wine she'd had in weeks and I lied and said it was a Kendall-Jackson merlots I stole from Tom.

"Come to Chapter 8 tonight. The place'll be crowded with cougars and even though you're a lot fatter, compared to the divorced moms in Agoura you still look good. You have to get out there and find young guys to have sex with before you hook up with you next husband, and you better do it fast, before you get too fat."

"I am not a cougar."

"Yes, you are. It's the next stage after divorce. You have to go through it whether you like it or not. Odds are, the next rich guy you find's not going to be as attractive as Tom. You got lucky there, so you better find some hot guys to have sex with before you find an old ugly rich guy to marry."

If she was right, my life was is worse shape than I thought. Not only was I destined to have sex with a lot of young men, I was destined to get married to someone who looked like Barry and smelled like salami, bless his dead soul.

I promised Katie she would see me there that night and told her not to worry. Her husband would find a job and they'd be able to save their house and she could go back to being friends with Mindy and Stacy and not talking to me. I said it as a joke and Katie swore that would never happen, but we both knew it would. I didn't want to hold that against her though, because at least she came and checked on me, which was more than anyone else had done.

As soon as she left, I stormed downstairs to Henry's apartment and pounded on the door. He opened it.

"I want an exterminator immediately."

"No, can do, pretty lady. Don't got the dough."

"There are bugs in my apartment."

"There are bugs in every apartment, darling. I can't get you an exterminator and no one else."

Depressed, I walked to the liquor store and bought myself a National Enquire because Jessica Simpson was on the cover for being fat, and she was a lot fatter than me so it made me feel better about myself. I bought a frozen Lean Cuisine from the freezer section, and a sixteen ounce can of Budweiser. It was the cheapest, and laughed like a crazy woman for a moment because just six months before, I wanted to help feed starving children and now I could hardly feed myself.

I went home and while eating dinner with all the lights on, I saw how dirty my apartment was so I spent an hour cleaning. Cleaning was a lot of work. Poor Maria had been cleaning our huge house for $75 a week. Now I felt bad for underpaying her. I had no idea it was so hard to get the scum between the refrigerator and the cabinets.

After cleaning, I searched inside boxes looking for my Christian Audigier studded medallion Cross Flower halter dress in leopard. It flared out around the tush, so I was sure I could still fit in it. My wardrobe overflowed the closet, so I had boxes of expensive dresses, designer jeans and shoes stacked in my tiny bedroom. I found the dress on the bottom of the fifth box and hung it in the bathroom while I showered to steam the wrinkles out.

I shaved for the first time in months. I could see why European women didn't shave. Once you get used to it, the hair doesn't look that bad, and it's so much faster getting through a shower. I blew my hair dry and applied all the appropriate ingredients necessary to my face for a flawless look. I used the last of my Epicuren moisturizer, and when that was absorbed, I applied my Mac foundation and eye make-up. Mac isn't the most expensive cosmetics, but no one else has the color selections they have.

It took me one hour and thirty minutes to complete my look. It was only 7:30 so I sat on my towel covered couch and watched a rerun of Sex and the City. Sarah

Jessica Parker was prancing around in her apartment in a pair of boy shorts and her body was so toned that I threw my National Enquirer at the TV. I used to look that good. I used to be fun like her, but everything had been taken away from me. I was over forty, I was broke and I was almost real fat. I started crying, and grabbed toilet paper off a roll I kept on the end table because I couldn't afford to buy a box of tissues. I fanned my eyes real fast with my short nails and my cheap manicure, hoping to stop the tears so I didn't ruin my make-up. I dabbed the corner of my eyes, scrunched up the tissue and threw it at the TV.

I had to get out of my apartment before I had a breakdown. Katie told me not to get there before nine o'clock or I'd be sitting in an empty bar looking desperate. Not wanting to be pathetic, I left early with a plan to drive slowly, but Agoura isn't that far. It was only a fifteen minute drive. We always talked about it like is was some suburban far away land where moms are more dedicated to their children than getting spray tans and shrinking their waists, and how we so did not want to become that kind of woman.

Since I was early and nervous, I stayed in my car in the parking lot and made a list of what I would do when I got inside.

Candy's Chapter 8 Action Plan

> 1. Sit at bar.
> 2. Buy a drink.
> 3. Drink the drink.
> 4. Go to bathroom.

I figured I could repeat steps one through four the entire night. There was one thing I knew for sure, though, I was not going to do any dancing. I was just out for a little socializing. This was what divorced women did, right. Go to bars, have a martini, go to the bathroom, over and over.

I got my courage to go inside and waited in line with ten other women who were all wearing mini-dresses like me. We tried not to look each other in the eyes, but Katie was right, this place was swarming with cougars and even though my butt was two sizes bigger than it was before, it was two sizes smaller than any of theirs.

The bouncer checked our I.D.'s and it was sort of embarrassing because the guy probably just turned 21, and here we were asking this kid for permission to get inside. None of us looked under the age of thirty, so it was ridiculous that he carded us. I think he abused his position of power because he asked each of us the year we were born, and then he asked the lady ahead of me, what year was she divorced. Really, how rude.

I handed him my driver's license. He looked at my left hand.

"No ring, huh."

"I'm cleaning it." I lied. "Just meeting a couple girlfriends." I added to my lie because sometimes in life, a lie is a horrible thing not to say.

He leaned in close to my ear. "Got a tan line on your finger. Just separated, huh?" The weasel asked.

"Can I have my driver's license back?"

He leaned in close to me again. "Yo, cougar, if you're looking for a young guy to take home for a night of sexual pleasure, I'm your man." He said and winked, then gave me my license. "Yo, Gerome, got a hot one!" He hollered inside the door.

Gerome was the D.J., dancing to "Don't Have To Be Rich" by Prince. He did a double finger point at me as I walked in, and then spun around twice in the same spot.

Chapter 8, unlike Barbara's hair salon, had been designed by a designer. The entire place was covered with three colors, red, black and white. The booths had red and white leather, the bar counter had sleek black granite and a large dance floor had a strippers pole center of it. I had no idea Agoura was this hip. No wonder Mindy and Tom came here to cheat on me. The place reeked of sex.

The Prince song ended, and Justin Timberlake's "I'm Bringing Sexy Back" boomed out of the sound system. I looked around, wondering which booth Tom and Mindy were kissing in, and suddenly I felt nauseous just thinking about it.

"It's that one over there." Katie said from behind me. "You know, the booth I saw Tom kissing Mindy."

Katie was standing behind the bar, wearing a low cut tight black button up shirt that was hardly buttoned and skin tight black jeans. She was a hot bartender.

"What can I get you?" She yelled.

"Apple martini." I yelled back.

I did a little dance move to the music, in an attempt to look cool, sat at the bar and crossed my legs. The place was filling up, but there were five women for each guy. Katie served me my martini and told me it was on the house. I drank it fast and ordered another that I insisted on paying for, but she insisted on sneaking me another one since I was poor and I never told Mindy and Stacy that she was working nights as a bartender.

After the second martini, I had two shots of tequila. I couldn't afford them, but I didn't care. My mom told me during the great depressions when a lot of people were depressed, they spent what little money they had on alcohol. Anti-depressants hadn't been invented yet and the alcohol made them feel better, like medicine, so being in a great depression, I planned to get real drunk.

It didn't take long for the alcohol to work. Soon I was smiling and chatting with another depressed woman sitting at the bar whose husband left her because she didn't lose weight. My right foot tapped as I watched women dancing together on the dance floor. They were having fun. They didn't care how they looked, and I admired them. I was so sick of being depressed.

Gerome put a remix of Aretha's R.E.S.P.E.C.T. on and the women started singing and cheering. I chugged the rest of the martini the lady sitting next to me was drinking when she looked the other way, kicked off my shoes and hit the middle of the dance floor. Me and twelve depressed, overweight and lonely women, busted out R.E.S.P.E.C.T. as if we'd never wanted anything more.

Panting, I went back to the bar and asked Katie for a glass of water. Then I heard his voice.

"Hey, Mrs. Katz."

I turned and there was Brad, my knight in surfer wear, but he wasn't wearing his surfer clothes. Brad was in a casual blazer over a button up shirt and he looked old enough to be my date. After all, I was a cougar now and if my calculations were correct, which I wasn't sure because I'd had a lot to drink, he was eighteen now.

"Brad! How'd you get in here?"

"Fake I.D. My eighteenth birthday gift from my buddy. Been hanging out here lately. Agoura's got a lot of cougars to choose from, if you know what I mean."

"Yeah, I know what you mean, Brad, and don't give me and you a second thought. Unlike all these women here, I'm not desperate." I turned to the bar to order another drink from Katie, but she was gone.

"Yeah, I know. We're just friends." He said.

"That's right. We're just friends." I confirmed with an adult tone in my voice. I was trying to act dignified, but I was drunk and hanging out in a bar like a pathetic divorcee.

Brad smiled at me, ran his finders through his hair and gestured for me to go with him. "Well, how 'bout you and me go sit in that booth over there and talk. As friends, of course." He said while looking me up and down, even glancing back behind me to check out my ass.

"Keep your hands to yourself.'

We walked to a booth in the corner which was

176

dark and off to the side, the exact type of corner you'd find a couple making out in. I got nervous that it wasn't a good idea.

"Brad, I don't think we should do this." I told him.

"Don't worry Mrs. Katz. I'm not into you."

"You're not? Why?

We sat down in the booth.

"Forget it." He said.

"Tell me. Why don't you like me anymore? I know I've put on some weight and I cut my hair…."

"That's not it. I like your short hair, and you know, your butt's bigger, but still, it's not bad."

"Then what is it?"

"You have a reputation."

"Please. I haven't had a reputation for being a slut in twenty years?"

"It's not for sleeping around. People think you're psycho."

"What!"

"Sorry, Mrs. Katz, but I don't want you coming after me with a hatchet after we make it, you know. I'm going off to college and plan on getting married some day and having kids. You could be a liability. My dad's a lawyer. He showed me Fatal Attraction and warned me to stay away from crazy women."

I started crying.

"Oh, come on, Mrs. Katz, I'm sorry. I didn't mean to make you cry." Brad said. "Just, you know, I didn't want you to think I was gonna try to feel you up while we were sitting here."

"Why wouldn't you try? I'm still pretty, aren't I?"

"Yeah, yeah, it's just, you know, there's something different with you now. It's sort of unattractive."

"What is it?"

"You're insecure."

"I am not insecure and I am not psycho. I'm really, really nice, and I am totally hot still." I said. "Just watch this."

I stood up, chugged down his bottle of beer, went to take off my shoes, but they were already off, and strutted over to Gerome.

"Put on Aerosmith's "Love in an Elevator." I yelled. He double pointed at me, spun around, and got to work switching the track. When I headlined at Boobs & Babe's, the crowd came to see me perform to this song every night. I thought back to my routine and concentrated. The song began. I strutted to the stripper's pole and the minute I grabbed hold of it, it all came back to me. I slipped and spun around. The crowd back away. The women stopped dancing and cheered me on. I cat crawled on all fours and went into split position. It hurt, but I was so drunk, I could take the pain. I raised my legs up, wrapped them around the pole and slid hands free to the ground, ending right when the music stopped. The crowd loved it. They whistled, screamed, clapped and gave me a standing ovation as I took a bow.

I walked back to the booth. Brad's mouth was open, frozen in shock, and I could tell he was completely in love with me again. I was happy to have one thing in my life back on track. I didn't want to sleep with Brad, but needed Brad to want me. I used to be his milf and I wasn't give that up.

I sat down and the room started spinning.

"Mrs. Katz, you toast? Mrs. Katz, you about to bite it?" I heard Brad say, but his voice sounded muffled and faint, like he was real far away.

I remember slipping down under the table, but after that I can't remember a single thing, which is why I freaked out when I woke up in my bed the next morning, wearing just my G-string and saw Brad in bed next to me. Not only did I want to scream "Oh, my God" but I actually did… about a twenty times!

"Oh, my God. Oh, my God. Oh, my God." I yelled over and over, sitting up and covering my chest with a sheet. I smacked Brad on the head.

"Get up. Get out. Oh, my God, I'm going to hell."

Brad was still in his clothes, though. This was a good sign. Maybe I wasn't going to hell for taking away his innocence. I hit him in the head again.

"Ouch!" Brad said.

"What are you doing here?" I yelled again, and popped him in the head again. "You can't be in my room! You can't be in my apartment! And you can't be in my bed! This just can't be happening to me."

Brad crawled out of the bed, stood back against the wall, cowering with his arms shielding his body. "Stop! Don't go all psycho on me."

"What happened? Tell me, tell me. What did we do? Oh, my God!"

Nothing." He said, then yawned and started laughing.

I grabbed a shirt and threw it on without him being able to see my tatas. Strippers know how to get dressed that way fast. It comes from years of sharing a dressing room with other strippers.

"Tell me everything. What did we do?" I asked him, real hysterical.

"Man, Mrs. Katz, you're making me kind 'a worried that I helped you out. You're going all fatal on me."

Yes, I was going all fatal on him because if I made it with my daughter's ex-boyfriend, there would be no turning back for me. I might as well retire in a mobile home park in the middle of a desert until I wither and die.

"Please, Brad. I can't remember anything after dancing on the stripper pole." Yikes, that' was not something I wanted to remember the next day. Yeah, I was good on the pole, but at my age, I shouldn't be putting on shows for ten men and sixty lonely women.

"Nothing happened. You got sick so I drove you

home."

"Did we kiss? Oh, my God, did we do more than kiss?"

"No. We stopped a couple times so you could throw up. You smelled really awful, too. We came home and you took off your dress... and..."

"Wait. In front of you? Did you see my breasts?"

"Yeah, but it's no big deal. I've been with a lot of women. I've seen 'em before. I do like that tiny tattoo you have."

"You saw that?" I have a tiny heart tattoo on my right cheek. I got it for Tom after he told me I stole his heart. What an idiot I was.

"Yeah, when you crawled from the living room into bed like a cat, it was sort of hard to miss."

It was official. I deserved to die, and just as soon as Brad left, I was going to kill myself with a butter knife, because Mindy got my good set of steak knives.

"I didn't want to leave you here alone, being so drunk and all, especially since you kept making this really weird breathing sound. I was afraid you'd choke on your vomit and I'd be brought up on murder charges, so I rolled you on your stomach and watched you 'til five, but couldn't stay up any longer. And honestly, I was kind of afraid to leave you here a lone. Doesn't seem like the safest neighborhood. I'm kind of worried that my car got stolen."

Okay, I love this kid. Someday he's going to grow up to be a really great husband. I still think he'll cheat on his wife, but at least he'll watch out for her.

Brad left after I made him coffee, apologized for my behavior and begged him never to tell my daughter. He said he had a good time and that it'd be one of those nights he'd never forget. He wanted to drive me back to Agoura to get my car, but I insisted on taking a taxi. He was already fifteen minutes late for school and had an Algebra test in second period he couldn't miss.

I showered and waited on the curb for the taxi to

180

arrive feeling pathetic. The taxi pulled up and I got inside. I explained where I needed to go and why, which was so dumb because the taxi driver was from Saudi Arabia and the entire drive he lectured me about how a woman should behave.

"In my country, women do not drink or sleep with a man not her husband. We cut off your hands and feet for such things. In my country, a woman's place is in the home. In my country, women wear burkas to cover their boobies." He looked back at me and gestured to my C-cups. "Look at you. Look at those you wear. Look what you do to me. You tempt me like a devils child. You make me think vile thoughts about those."

Thank God I had them reduced from a D Cup, or else this guy would probably really lose it. He kept looking back at me and pointing to my breasts. I was worried we were going to crash. It was a long drive. I was hung-over and his voice was loud. He yelled at me the entire drive. The night before I thought Agoura was close, but this morning it seemed so far away.

Finally, we reached the parking lot.

"Get out, you devil temptress." He said, after telling me I owed him thirty dollars.

"I'm sorry for tempting you. Really, I'm a nice person." I said as I handed him $40 dollars, the last of my money that was in my wallet. "Here's a ten dollar tip for upsetting you."

He grabbed the money out of my hand. I shut the door and heard the lock click. He peeled out, leaving tire marks on the asphalt and a cloud of exhaust smoke in my face.

Across the parking lot, I saw another hung-over cougar getting out of a taxi. Embarrassed, we both tried not to look at each other as we walked the walk of shame. My shoulders slumped forward and I walked to my car. Someone had written "wash me" on my back window. I started crying because the reason I hadn't washed my car was that I couldn't afford to. It was the worst moment of my life. I just wanted to get to my car, forget that the night before I'd stripped and barfed in front of a high school senior, and think of some way to turn my life around.

CANDY'S LIKE SERIOUSLY SUPER-DUPER SCREWED

CHAPTER NINE

I knocked on Rose's apartment door at 9:30 in the morning, even though I knew she was sleeping. She took her last client at midnight, and rarely got up before noon, but this was an emergency.

"Rose. Open up."

She opened the door wearing a zebra print muumuu and a purple bandana covering her dreadlocks. She was a large Jamaican woman with full lips and warm brown eyes. She told me all about her childhood one day when we went to the mailbox at the same time. Her father brought her family to America because when she was a little girl, he made his living by having her dance on the street for tourists and the Americans gave the most money.

"Girl, my father always said to me, America is the land of the giving people. He said it all the time, sugar, especially when he got his welfare check in the mail."

"Does he live around here?" I asked her.

"Sugar girl," she said and got real upset, "He died after eating moldy government cheese." She pounded on her chest. "But girl, he spoke to me from the grave."

"He did?" I said with a little bit of an attitude. I didn't believe her, because when my granny died of alcoholism when I was four, I talked to her all the time and she never answered.

"I was mixing a gallon of powdered milk, and girl I heard him same as if he was standing right next to me."

"Dead people talk to us?"

"Sugar, they do, but you can't hear 'less you have the psychic way."

"What did he say?"

"Get off the dole. It'll kill you."

"No."

"Yes. I was so shocked, I spilt the milk and ate my corn flakes dry. Then the next day there was a recall for government powdered milk. Some factory worker tainted it with rat poison."

"Oh, my God!"

"I know. My father saved my life. It was then, girl, that I knew I had the gift for real and went after my dream of being a medium.

"Oh. Good for you." I said, while thinking, you're nowhere near being a size medium, but I didn't want to say anything to her because that would be rude.

Rose squinted. Her face was in bright sun and her eyes were barely open. I watched her nose scrunch up to half its size, amazed that it could do that. "Girl, get away from my door. You're breaking my dawn."

"Rose, I need some backbone." My voice cracked. I started crying. "My life's a mess. I'm broke. I need a job. I need some respect. I need your help."

"Hell, sugar, backbone ain't a hard bitch to get. You come back at lunch time with a sandwich for Rose and you and me'll make a deal." She said, and slammed the door in my face.

I went to my apartment and scanned the cabinets. Peanut butter and jelly was my only option, but when I looked at my loaf of bread, I saw mold growing on it. I couldn't give Rose moldy bread after what happened to her father with moldy cheese, so I decided to make her the lunch I ate every day growing up. Peanut butter and jelly on saltine crackers.

When the big and little hands on my battery operated clock hit twelve, I had a plate full of them ready to give to Rose. I knocked on her door three times.

"Rose, it's me, Candy. I'm back."

Rose opened the door in a yellow and red muumuu that made her dark skin glow. "Come in sister. Let's get to it."

"You have another client coming?"

"Not till 2:00, I'm just hungry. What'd you bring me?"

I handed her the plate of saltine peanut butter and jelly crackers.

"Jeez girl, Rose was hoping for some lunchmeat?"

"I'm sorry. It's all I had." I hunched over, defeated.

She pushed me on my back over to a large pillow. "Sit down, sugar. Rose don't discriminate against food." She said, and popped a cracker sandwich in her mouth as she sat down on the pillow across from mine. Between us was a low table with candles, incense and a stack of Tarot Cards.

"I like your apartment." I said.

It wasn't my decorating style, but it was colorful. She had mismatched pillows and carpets all over her floor and on the walls. It sort of looked like when you go into a rug store and everywhere you turn you see a rug and another and another.

Rose ignored me. She popped the cracker sandwiches into her mouth so fast that she couldn't speak. Then she turned red and didn't move. I was worried she was choking, but finally she swallowed, licked peanut butter off her fingers and took a deep breath.

"Uh, sugar, good PB&J's. I'm good now. Let's see what you've got going on." Rose lit a candle. "Stare into the flame. Show me your soul."

"How do I show you my soul?"

She rolled her eyes. "Girl, like I said. Stare into the flame."

"Oh."

I stared at the fire without blinking and the flame got taller and taller and Rose started humming like an idling car, louder and louder. I got kind of scared, so I closed my eyes. A wind rushed by me and when I opened my eyes the flame was out and a line of smoke twirled up to the ceiling from the wick.

"Is that supposed to happen?"

"Whew, sugar, your soul is big. Ain't never, ever, seen that flame fire up so high. You tell Rose all about yourself now 'cause I got to know who I'm dealing with."

I started with my first memory which was when I was still in diapers. There was a black cat my mom had that always hissed at me. One day I poured baby powder on it which turned it white and it never bothered me again.

"Black spirits been chasing you since you a pup. Go on, sugar."

I gave her every single detail I could remember about my childhood, my mother, my father, the eight apartments we lived in, and all about my marriage to Tom, my fabulous daughter and my fabulous life that was taken away by my horrible ex-best friend Mindy.

"Mindy's your teacher." Rose said.

"Oh, please. What course? Husband stealing? Life ruining?"

Rose shushed me. "You talk too much. Don't listen. That girl's teaching you not to be stupid. She's a blessing, sugar girl, without Mindy shittin' up your life, you'd die getting nowhere."

"I am nowhere. Look at me. Look where I live. I'm a nobody. I've got nothing."

"Girl, you got a rock in that head of yours. Soul's off the chart, but that rock's like a cork stuffing all the good in you and not letting it get out, but I'm gonna help you 'cause I like what you got going on inside."

"I don't have any money to pay you."

"Bring me a sandwich a day and I'll help you grow a backbone."

"Thank you. Thank you." I said, and gave her a big hug. "This is so exciting!" She pushed me away so she could smack a bug on the wall with her napkin.

"Girl, I've had it with these bugs. You're first assignment from Rose is to get that cheap bastard down those stairs to pay for an exterminator."

"I already tried. He won't."

She smacked her napkin at another bug.

"You want my help and I don't want any more bugs. You find a way. Don't come back here tomorrow, girl, don't you show your face at my door 'til you found a way to convince that slum lord to hire a bug man. "

It took me three hours to get the courage to go up against Henry again. Finally, after I saw a bug in the kitchen, I went downstairs to Henry's apartment. I figured I'd start out nice and then get mad only if I had too.

"Hi, Henry, I was just wondering if you changed your mind about getting an exterminator?"

"Nope." He said, looking straight at my cleavage. I wore a tight tank top and jeans, because I wanted his full attention.

"Henry, I'm a nice lady, but when it comes to bugs, I get mean. What's going on here, I think it might be illegal. You don't get rid of the bugs, I'm gonna call the cops on you?"

"You mean the health department, idiot." The guy

from apartment six yelled out his window.

"Ah, yes, the health department. You get an exterminator in here or I'm calling the health department." I told Henry. "And don't call me an idiot." I yelled up to the guy in apartment six.

"Sorry." The guy yelled back.

"It's okay." I yelled back at the guy.

Henry scowled and held his breath. All the broken blood vessels in his skin filled up with blood so his face turned red. He looked like he was going to hit me or yell at me or. Then I got worried that he was gonna spit on me because he started swishing his jaw around.

"You know, pretty lady, I let you move in here 'cause I thought you wouldn't be any trouble, but now you're coming home with minors and demanding exterminators."

"He wasn't a minor. He turned eighteen two weeks ago." I said, then realized just how bad that sounded. "Why are you always watching me anyway? What I do is none of your business. I'm starting to think you let me move in here so you could check out my tits and ass every time I walk in and out of my apartment."

"Yeah, I did, but now you're getting fat and you cut your hair. I hate short hair on women. Everything was fine with me and my ex-wife until she cut her hair and got an ass bigger than a diesel truck!" He yelled.

"Threaten a sexual harassment lawsuit." The guy from apartment six yelled out his window.

"You get an exterminator in here twice a month or I'm filing a sexual harassment lawsuit against you."

Henry got red again and I saw his fists bunch up into a ball. "Why I ought' a…"

"You hit me, you'll go to jail. I have witnesses." I pointed to the faces looking out their apartment windows.

"Fork out the money, cheap bastard." The little old lady in apartment three yelled. Her voice was so cute, like the same way you'd expect a little old lady to say, come on over here and give grandma a kiss.

"You go, sugar." I heard Rose yell.

"We're tired of sleeping with bugs." The man from apartment eight screamed.

"Homey don't play with crickets." The little old lady yelled.

"I'll pay for once a month, that's it. You want any extra bug spraying, get a can of Raid!" Henry yelled at me and at all the faces in the windows.

"Oh, my God. This is so great!" I jumped up and down and clapped, then stuck out my hand. "Deal." I said all business like. He shook my hand and tenants cheered through their open windows. I leaned in to Henry's ear and whispered. "Thanks, buddy, I owe you."

"Ah, shucks." Henry said and blushed so that his cheeks were fire red. I worried some of the varicose veins were going to burst. "I'm a sucker for pretty ladies." He said and pulled me into a tight hug.

"Henry?"

"What?"

"Let go of me."

"Sorry." He said like a sly dog. I'll be damned, as he took his hands away from my back, he rubbed them over my ass. I smacked his arm.

"Henry! Watch your hands." I told him real angry, but he just laughed and laughed as he walked back into his apartment.

The next day, I went to my appointment with Rose with a turkey sandwich and sat down on the pillow.

"You did good with the slum lord, sugar girl." She said, and then looked at me sort of weird.

"What? Is there something on my face?" I asked.

"No, girl, just after one lesson you're sittin' up straight now."

I looked at my posture and she was right, my back

was straight. "Wow."

"See how being certain of yourself and mixin' in attitude can get you some self-esteem?"

"Yeah, I guess, but Rose, I got a problem. I'm broke. I can't stand living this way. I need your psychic powers to help me find a job."

"What skills do you have?"

"None."

"Sugar, think harder. You got to have something going on in you."

"Really, I don't. I don't have any skills. I don't have a high school diploma. I don't even have my GED."

"Ain't you ever had a job, sugar?"

"I was a stripper."

"Oh, Lord, you too old to get back on the pole." She said.

I almost told her about my great performance at Chapter 8 and how I was still able to do the splits, lift my legs up to wrap them around the pole so I could slide upside down onto my hands, but I didn't want to brag.

"Let's see what the flame can tell me." Rose lit the candle between us and set out her tarot cards. "Get your eye on it, sugar."

We zeroed in on the flame and then her eyes got real big, as if she was getting a message, then she closed them and poof, the flame blew out again. She opened her eyes and only had one word to say.

"Run."

"Why?" I asked.

"Candy, message ain't mine. Just comes here through me and you. I ain't in a position to question it, girl."

"Who sent the message?"

"Sugar, ain't you getting the work we're doing here. We're tappin' into your soul. It's a message from your soul so there ain't nothing you can do to change it, girl.

You better run."

"Oh, okay." I didn't want to argue with her, in case she wasn't a quack like Randolf.

Running had never been my sport. Tennis was my game, but what the hell. I had time on my hands and a big butt, so I put on my tennis shoes, an adorable Hard Tail sweat suit and went for a run. It was a beautiful fall day, not too hot and not too cold. There was a breeze that made all the leaves on the trees shake a little. Except for the trash in the gutters, the boarded up crack houses and the road kill smashed into the asphalt, it was beautiful being out on the streets. After five minutes, I ran back to my apartment, panting and sweating. Turns out, running isn't the easiest sport.

I checked in with Rose every day and the only message she got from my soul about my job was to run, so every day I went running. Neighbors got used to seeing me. They waved hello and kids would follow me like I was Rocky Balboa. My body started craving vitamins, so I ate better and swore off alcohol. On my budget, I couldn't afford to drink anyway, so even though I didn't have a job, I felt richer because I had more money to buy food with. I met Juan who lived three streets over and grew produce in his backyard that he sold in his front yard. I started buying vegetables from him. His prices were half the cost of the grocery store, so I started eating salads instead of ice cream and frozen dinners.

Some days if I was feeling stressed or bored, I would run twice, in the morning and the evening. The pounds were melting off me. My thighs were getting muscle definition and my arms looked as if I was lifting weights from pumping them back and forth. Henry was so happy I was losing weight, he brought in the exterminator for an extra bonus spray as a surprise. Even Kelly told me she might take up running because she'd never seen someone change their body so quickly.

My body was getting back in shape, but I still didn't

have a career. I wanted to be rich again so I could move back to the Oaks and rub it in Tom and Mindy's face.

"Rose, isn't my soul giving you another message yet?"

"No, Candy Cane. Just run."

"I keep running and running, but I'm not finding a career. I know every pot hole in this neighborhood by heart."

"Maybe run on different streets?"

I took her suggestion and drove to different neighborhoods, parked my car and ran. I ran around Woodland Hills, Tarzana, Agoura, Encino, Sherman Oaks, Studio City, and found many neighborhoods I'd love to live in. I'd pick a house and pretend I lived there just like when I was a poor little girl. Sometimes I'd see a family getting in their car and I'd start crying as I ran by, because I used to have a home and a family.

I started stopping at homes for sale and reading the information on the flyers inside the little box on the For Sale sign. I'd memorize the square footage, if they had a fireplace, hardwood floors, a pool, granite countertops, a view, a three car garage, a wine cellar, a fireplace. If there was an Open House, I'd go inside. I'd play a guessing game of which house I thought would sell first based on its condition and its listed sales price. Sometimes I knew a house would sell faster because it wasn't overpriced. I could tell when an owner had slapped a fresh coat of paint on it to make it look better than it was so they could jack up the price. I learned which real estate companies had the most successful brokers based on the amount of listings they had and how many of their homes sold and how fast.

Then one day I decided to run around Calabasas. I couldn't get in the Oaks, of course, because it's a gated community. I was no longer allowed inside the gates since Mindy turned Carl against me so I ran in the Calabasas Lakes area. The lake is surrounded by attached homes so you can't get to it unless you live there, but you can run on the streets that surround the lake and get a view of the water here and there.

Being in Calabasas territory, I was nervous that I'd see someone I knew so I wore a hat and sunglasses and since I had a bob haircut, I figured that was enough of a disguise. I ran through the streets, reading the real estate signs, and I saw a man in a suit putting flyers in a holder on a sign. I stopped.

"Excuse me. Are you the realtor?" I asked.

He turned to me, took off his sunglasses and my heart did a flip. He was so handsome, I wanted to kiss him. I hadn't wanted to kiss anyone since I saw Tom in Mindy's bathroom with his pants down to his ankles.

He held out his hand and smiled. His teeth were so white, they sparkled. "Yep, but I'm thinking about buying the place. Jake Drake, Prudential Realty."

I wiped my hand on my pants. I'd been running for over an hour, and my body was covered in sweat.

"Candy Katz, unemployed divorcee."

"I think I know you."

"You look familiar too."

"The Oaks. I sold you your home in The Oaks years ago."

"Oh, yeah. I remember."

"Your husband was the one who only cared about the square footage?"

"Yep, that was him. The bigger the better. He just upgraded from these," I gestured to my boobs, "to my best friend's double D's."

He looked embarrassed. "Sorry to hear that. Divorce is hard. You still living in that house?"

"Nope. She is."

"Ouch. That's gotta hurt."

"Yeah, but I did it to myself."

"How?"

"Pre-nup."

"Ah, so that's what I forgot to get when I got

married. My ex-wife is living in my house with her Sicilian lover."

"Ouch. That's gotta hurt." I said, and we both laughed.

"Yep. Everyday when I come home to my tiny apartment."

"Oh, my God. I go home to the same thing. How old is your carpet?"

"Thinking ten, fifteen years."

"I've got you. Mine's over twenty."

"Ouch, brutal." He glanced at his clock. "Oh, I should get going. I'm meeting a client at Starbucks."

"Oh, okay."

"Nice to meet you again, Candy Katz." He said.

I watched him walk towards his Mercedes E Class and bingo, like I was having a light-bulb moment, I thought, maybe I should be a real estate agent.

I ran over to Jack's car just as he started driving away. I had to pick up my speed to catch him, so I was really lucky that I was wearing my running shoes. I tapped on his window.

"Jack! Wait." I yelled and he slowed his car down to a quick stop and rolled down his window. I leaned down to talk to him. "Jack, can I ask you a personal question?"

"Sure."

"Do you have a high school diploma?"

"Of course."

"Oh." I said and I must have looked real sad, because he looked me in the eyes.

"Why do you want to know?"

"I need a job. I'm thinking of becoming a real estate agent, but I don't have a high school diploma."

"Candy, you don't need a high school diploma. All you need is your real estate license."

"Really?"

"Yeah. Any idiot can become a realtor, but you

won't be successful unless you work hard. It's commission only and hundreds of realtors fighting to get every transaction."

"What's a transaction?"

He looked at me as if I wasn't sure if I was serious, but I was.

"Tell you what. Here's my card. Call my office and we'll set up a time for you to come in so we can talk."

I wanted him to tell me to call his office to set up a time we could meet at his crappy apartment and make-out on his disgusting carpet, but figured that would be too forward. I took the card.

"Thanks, Jack. I will call you."

"Good. I look forward to it."

I tucked the card inside my pocket and ran down the street in front of him, hoping he was checking out my shrunken tush and liked what he saw. As he drove by, he honked and waved, so I waved back.

I was so excited. A real estate agent! I never would have thought about being an agent for a career if I wasn't running all over the city, checking out homes for sale that I couldn't afford to buy. I didn't have to be someone's assistant and I didn't have to go back to high school to get my GED, all I had to do was go to real estate school and get my real estate license. I picked up my pace. I couldn't wait to get back home and tell Rose she wasn't a quack and that she really is a psychic.

The minute I got home, I ran up to her door. "Rose. Rose." I yelled as I pounded. "Let me in. Let me in."

Rose opened the door. "Wow, sugar, you got a beam of light shooting out of you today!"

I grabbed her hands. "I know! I know! You were right about making me run all over town. I know what job I'm gonna do now and I don't need my high school diploma to do it."

"Well, sugar girl, spit it."

"I'M GONNA BE A REAL ESTATE AGENT!"
I yelled and jumped up and down.

"All right, sugar, don't jump too high, you're gonna
bust them balloons right out of your shirt!"

"You're not a quack, Rose, like that Randolf guy I
saw. You really are a psychic."

"Uh, huh, I know. Did you think I was full of
crap?"

"Yeah, I kind'a thought so, but if I wasn't running
around looking at homes for sale that I wanted to buy, it
never would have dawned on me to go into real estate,
and I never would have met Jack Drake, the most
handsome real estate agent in the world. In fact, the
most handsome man in the world and he's going to help
me get my start! Can you believe it?"

"Not there yet, sugar, still catchin' up with you."

I grabbed her in a huge hug. "You're my best
friend forever, Rose."

"Hold on now, sugar. Best friends forever, that's a
big deal, you know. Don't just bring people into your
life so easily, sugar, or you get burned. You don't know
me that well. I could be like Mindy and take advantage
of you. Ain't you learned this lesson yet, sugar? You
headin' for a world of trouble, you don't check people
out."

"Oh, my God, you're right. I don't know that
much about you at all except you don't spend money on
furniture, only rugs and pillows, you like to sleep in and
eat, and you're from Jamaica."

"Yes, but you don't know that I read Shakespeare."

"Really?"

"Uh huh. I watch the Martha Stewart Show
because even though I don't got a garden, I like
gardening."

"Wow, who knew?"

"See, sugar, you don't know me that well yet. You
gotta sit with a soul for a long time before you know it.

A woman too trusting of people too soon gets her vagina stolen."

"Um, excuse me."

"The vagina is the heart and soul of a woman. Got to protect it like you protect a baby."

"Wait a minute. Why would I give you my vagina? I'm a heterosexual."

"Oh, sugar, you are a dense one. I ain't talking about your vagina exactly. It's a metaphor."

"What exactly is a metaphor?"

"Sugar, I got to take a break 'cause you're draining the energy out of me. You come back tomorrow and we'll get into it, but I'm increasing my price to two turkey sandwiches on Rye, easy mayo, Swiss cheese, bean sprouts and a salad with tomatoes, cucumber, onions, blue cheese dressing, and a bag of chips, any kind 'cause I like them all. Come back tomorrow, and I'll explain how you got to protect your vagina from strangers." Rose got real serious. She held my by the shoulders and looked in my eyes. "'Cause you don't' learn this lesson sugar, there's no hope for you, even if you become a realtor."

I went home deflated. No hope? Was it that important to protect my vagina? Then I worried about Kelly. If I didn't know how to protect my vagina, how could she since I never taught her. I called her on the phone.

"Mom, can't talk now." She sounded out of breath, and sort of panted like a dog.

"Kelly, this is important."

"Um, like, I'm making out with Chris, so like, hello, can I call you later mom?"

"Oh, sure. Sorry." I said and hung up.

It was probably a good time to tell her to protect her vagina, but she'd been trying to get Chris in a lip-lock for months so I didn't want to ruin the mood.

I took out Jack's business card and called him, but I

got a machine. I left a message, then worried that I should have waited longer than an hour to call. I didn't want to seem desperate, even though I am, but oh, my God, he called me right back.

"Candy, its Jack Drake."

"Oh, ah, hi, Jack, it's Candy." I said, and cringed because that sounded so like high school.

"I know. I'm calling you back."

"Oh, right." My heart was pounding and I kept making this stupid giggling sound.

"I'm glad you called. I wasn't sure if you were serious about real estate or just wanted to date me." He laughed, but I was quiet because I was going to say both, but didn't want to sound slutty, but then he said, "I'm joking."

I laughed as if I knew he was joking. "Yes. I'm serious. When can I come to your office so we can discuss this?" I said, and wanted to add, when can I come in your arms, but again, too slutty I reminded myself. I was trying to become a pro, not a ho.

"Tomorrow at noon I've got some time."

"Sorry. I can't make that. I have an appointment." Even though I wanted to get going on my new career, I really wanted to know how to protect my vagina, so I didn't want to cancel Rose.

"How about three o'clock?"

"Three's good." I said. "Thanks, Jack. I really appreciate this." I said, thinking I sounded so professional. Thank God he couldn't read my mind.

We got off the phone and I could not believe my good fortune. A divorced hunky realtor was helping me get into the biz. I might bag a husband and a career in one shot.

The next day, I made Rose's order just as she told me, because even though there are a lot of things I don't understand, at least I can remember them. I brought the food to Rose and we sat across from each other as she ate it, moaning and groaning and licking her lips. And I may be wrong here, but since I'd been feeding her lunch everyday, she was gaining weight and going in the opposite direction of becoming a medium. I felt bad that I was keeping her from reaching her dream, but I needed my sessions with Rose so I didn't say anything to her.

"Look into the flame." She told me, as she picked turkey out of her teeth, but the flame didn't rise and a wind didn't come into the room and blow it out. "Sugar, you're stagnant." She said, sounding upset.

"Is that bad?"

"No, not yet, but it is if we can't move you on." She spread out her Tarot cards. "Ah, I see. You're focused on that man."

"Not a man, really, well he's a man, but not a man to me in that manly way, he's just so handsome. And I mean, totally hot handsome." I was getting tongue-twisted just talking about Jack.

Rose looked so disappointed in me. "It's a crucial time, sister. You got to listen to me now." She said.

Rose spent the next fifteen minutes explaining that a metaphor is something that represents something else. The vagina is a metaphor for our womanhood, representing what goes in and out of our spirit. Our vagina is a thing all men want. Our vaginas represent our essence, our soul, and if I wasn't more careful with the people I allowed into my metaphoric vagina, my life would go into ruin again. She told me it was my fault that Mindy and Tom betrayed me. They showed me signs for years that they were jerks, but I wasn't protecting my vagina. Then she warned me against having an affair with Jack yet, because he's just a guy I met on the street and could be a handsome devil. It was an intense fifteen minute lecture.

"Can I go home now? I'm real tired." I asked when she stopped talking. I felt winded, like she punched me in the gut. Protecting my vagina went against how I was. I trusted everyone until they screwed me over.

"Go on, sugar. It's a hard lesson you just got."

I went home depressed again. How could it be all my fault that Tom and Mindy were so mean to me? I was wiped out, so I laid down on the couch and accidentally fell asleep. When I woke up, it was 2:42 p.m. I had eighteen minutes to get to the appointment with Jack that would jump start my career. There wasn't time to get myself dolled up, so I threw on a dress and was out the door.

I arrived at Jack's office just in time. Being there got me feeling self-conscious again. Could I really do something like this, work as a real estate agent and wear a bland navy suit with a white button up shirt like the girl working at the reception desk?

"Hi there. I'm Candy Katz. I'm here to see Jack Drake." I said to her in a real peppy voice, because when I'm nervous I smile real big and my voice gets high.

She looked me up and down, real bitch like, and I figured it was probably because she was the bland girl in the office secretly in love with the handsome and newly divorced Jack Drake, but didn't have the courage to tell him.

"In the pit down the hall." She said, real mean, and went back to filing papers in her desk. She seemed so angry that I was almost about to ask her if she was all right, but then she looked at me and in a super nasty way said, "Anything else?"

"No." I told her, while thinking how much I wanted to bitch slap her.

I'd always heard there was competition between women who work in the same office, but I had no idea it was this bad.

I moved down the hall, and passed two women dressed in conservative clothes with hems below their mid-thigh. In Calabasas, we wives always wore short dresses, because we didn't dress for success, we dressed to compete with each other. They looked me up and down, and I started feeling embarrassed about how I was dressed. I was in such a rush, I'd thrown on a white tube top dress I got from Victoria Secret. I didn't think the dress was that revealing. It wasn't even that expensive, but it might have been the shoes I was wearing that threw them off. They were Sam Edelman's cut-out bootie in python material and those boots, with the dress, did sort of make me look like a stripper. I pulled my dress lower, but this made my cleavage show more. It was a no win situation. The dress was all wrong.

I put my shoulders back as I turned from the hallway, into the pit. All eyes turned to me and it got quiet. Staring at me in an open room full of cubicles were about fifty agents which meant a hundred eyeballs directly on me.

Thank God I had my smart looking Jenny McCarthy bob and I'd shrunk back down to a size two from running all over he city for months in search of a career. The men smiled at me, but the female agents started whispering to each other, pointed at me and gave me dirty looks. I wanted to die.

"Candy!" Jack called out from the back of the room just in time to save me.

Jack was on the phone, but he waved me over, which didn't make the women pointing at me happy. They were probably in love with him, just like the receptionist who was rude to me. I walked over to Jack and sat down at the chair in front of his desk in his tiny cubical, out of sight from the other agents. The room went back to buzzing with agents calling people on the phone and asking them if they were interested in selling their house and reporting on the status of their loans. One man was arguing with his wife about an $800 dollar charge she made on their Visa, which I thought was pretty rude. At least Tom never did that to me.

Jack got off the phone, stood up and shook my hand. "Candy, you made it."

"Barely. I took a nap and woke up fifteen minutes ago."

"A nap? You're lucky. I haven't napped since I was three." He said.

Suddenly, I felt so embarrassed. I didn't fit in with these people. They dressed in neutral colors, yelled at their wives for Visa charges and didn't nap. I started thinking about becoming a stripper again.

"Going for the gold, huh, Jack." Some guy shouted from the other side of the room and everyone laughed.

"Gonna cost him a grand per hour." Another guy yelled, and everyone in the room laughed.

"Shut up, Herb, or I'm gonna call your wife and tell her about Vegas." Jack yelled.

"Jack, maybe this was a bad idea. I'm gonna go." I stood up to leave, but Jack leaned forward and put his hand on my arm.

"Candy, wait. They're idiots. Don't let them offend you. I know you're going through a difficult time. Divorce is hard. I know. I've been there. Please, stay."

I sat back down and damn it, got tears in my eyes. Again! If I wanted be anything more than an ex-stripper, divorced street runner, I'd have to learn to stop crying every time my feelings got hurt.

"You're interested in real estate. I'm a real estate agent. What do you want to know?"

Jack was so nice to me, that it made me sort of uncomfortable. I wondered if he was a handsome devil. I crossed my legs to protect my vagina, even though I knew my actual vagina was only a symbol for my womanhood. But the weird thing about Jack was that he didn't notice my body. He seemed he only cared about helping me.

I dabbed my eyes and took a deep breath.

"Where do I start?" I said.

"Real estate school."

Jack told me the fastest way to get started would be to sign-up on Real Estate Express.Com to complete my required 135 hours of college level courses needed before I was able to sign up to take the real estate exam. I was too embarrassed to tell him I didn't have the money for the course or an actual computer to take the online course on, so I left his office with a plan I didn't how I would pull off and a stack of thick real estate study books Jack loaned me. He walked me to my car, carrying my books like we were in school together. It was so cute.

"Call me anytime you have questions." Jack said and shook my hand. I was hoping he would say call me anytime you want to get me naked, but that would be tacky and it was becoming clear that Jack Drake was a classy guy.

"I will." I said and slid into the driver's seat carefully because my skirt was so short and I didn't want to give this classy guy a Britney Spears flash. I was wearing underwear, but they didn't give me much coverage. I chose a tiny pair so I wouldn't have a horrendous VPL.

I went home and flipped through the pages of Principles of Real Estate Practices. God, it was so thick and boring. There were all kinds of codes I had to learn and real estate terms. I had no idea when real estate agents called themselves experts, that they really were required to learn so much stuff. Being a real estate agent always seemed like the easiest job to me. You put on a cute outfit, meet your client at the house you're selling, and give them a guided tour like a trophy girl at a car show. But actually, there were all these rules and laws that had to be understood. Who knew?

I hung my tube top dress in the closet with my other dresses that in the real estate world seem to be considered slut wear, and realized that not only would I need to get my real estate license to be a realtor, I was going to have to get another wardrobe too. I felt overwhelmed, so I decided to go on a run.

I hit the streets and opened my soul to bring in the answer, and I tell you, it wasn't more than forty-five minutes of running that it hit me, literally. I was running past a library when a car pulled into the parking lot just as I was about to cross the driveway. I had to jump back to avoid getting hit. My head slammed down on the Woodland Hills Library sign and I scraped my forehead on a brick wall. The driver was the librarian and she insisted I come inside so she could apply first aide to my cut.

When we walked through the doors, I saw rows of computers they let the public use for free.

"Excuse me. Are those computers free?" I asked.

"Yeah." She said, and when I tried to walk over to a computer, she stopped me. "Ah, lady, you've got blood on your forehead. Don't you want to clean it off in the ladies room?"

"I will in a minute." I said.

People were staring at me, but I didn't care. Two little girls saw me coming towards them and they ran away.

"No, really, there's a line of blood dripping down the side of your face and it's scaring the children."

She grabbed a box of tissues from the librarian desk and handed me the box.   "Thanks." I said while wiping off the blood on my face.

I sat down at the computer and typed in Real Estate Express.Com and bingo, there it was. I didn't have to buy a computer to study on for my test. I could go to the library and use a computer for free.

"Got four watchers." An old woman said next to me.

"What's a watcher? I asked.

"On EBay, dear. I'm selling my granddaughter's Barbie. I feel bad about selling it, but my granddaughter has so many she won't miss it and I need the money.

"Oh, is selling on EBay hard?"

"Easiest thing in the world. People buy crazy things too. Sold my old dentures for fifteen bucks. Probably some creep with a used denture fetish bought them, but you know, if I didn't sell them it would be like putting a five and a ten in the trash."

Bingo! I could sell my clothes on EBay, use the money for real estate school and buying a new wardrobe. I didn't needs Tom's money after all. I found a way to do it on my own.

After that day, I became obsessed with being successful. I picked ten trial items to put on EBay, just a few designer dresses that I was starting to think looked a little young for my age. I was going to be forty five soon and I was going to be a real estate agent soon, so I didn't think I needed zebra and leopard print dresses. I had Henry, since he was such a horn dog for me, take pictures of me modeling them with my head cut off of, and posted them on EBay and it took only three days to sell them.

I signed up for my Real Estate class and began studying online at the library. Whenever I had a question, I called Jack and he would explain it to me in a way I understood. The Federal Fair Housing Act just didn't make sense to me. If someone isn't supposed to be discriminated against for their race, color, religion, sex or national origin, then why could they be discriminated against based on how much money they had?

"Candy, if a person can't afford a house, then they can't have it." He said.

"That's discrimination." I told him. "Maybe the government should make it so all homes are the same size so poor kids wouldn't have to feel embarrassed that they live in a studio apartment with their mom and three of her friends."

Then Jack said the most amazing thing.

"Candy, I'm sorry you had to go through that as a child."

Not once, in all the years I was married to Tom, did he ever say anything like that to me. Jack totally, completely got me, even if I was trying to hide something from him or saying it in code.

I told Rose about my conversation with Jack, but she had no expression whatsoever.

"Rose, did you hear me?"

Nothing. No movement of her lips or a turn of her head and she just stared at me, wide-eyed, but looking blank, like she wasn't thinking of a dang thing.

"ROSE!" I yelled.

She jumped.

"Sugar, don't ever do that. There's another world here you can't see that sometimes I step in. Got the spirits swirling, girl, and talking up a storm. Don't ever interrupt them. Spirits give me more information in seconds than your blasted mouth spits out in an entire hour."

I looked around, but I didn't see anything.

"Well, what you yelling at me about?"

"You told me not to speak."

"I told you not to interrupt. They're not speaking to me now. Go on."

"I forgot what I was going to say."

Rose laughed. "Eh, sugar, girl, you a crack-up. We gonna be good friends for a long time. You too funny to kick out of my life." She bit into the roast beef sandwich with Swiss cheese, mustard, tomatoes, sliced cucumbers and sliced red peppers she'd requested that day for her lunch, and chewed with her mouth open. I wanted to tell her to close her mouth when she ate, but I didn't want to be rude.

"You thinking something right now." She said to me. "Go on, girl, say it."

"No."

"Why?"

"Don't want to be rude."

"I know what you're gonna say, already. I hear you talking in your head. It'll be good for you to say it. Get you that backbone, sugar."

"You should close your mouth when you chew."

"I ain't chewing with my mouth open."

"Yes you do. All the time and it's really gross."

"And if you knew what I was thinking all this time, I've been thinking it since the first sandwich I brought you, so why don't you listen."

Rose stopped chewing, and she looked how Mindy used to look at me if I made her real mad, and I got kind of scared.

"I'm sorry." I said.

Rose threw her sandwich down, literally. It broke apart and went all over two pillows. She charged at me. "Girl, do not apologize to me." She yelled while holding onto the front of my shirt.

"Okay." I said, and got real worried that I was in real danger. I didn't really know that much about Rose, except that she was from Jamaica, her family was on the dole and her father might have died from yucky government cheese.

"Take it back!" She demanded.

"What? The sandwich?"

"No, you idiot. Take back your apology! Take it back now, sugar girl, or I'm gonna whomp you!"

Holy crap! She was gonna whomp me!

"Okay, okay, I take it back!" I started screaming. "I'm not sorry. I'm not sorry for telling you chew with your mouth full. I'm not sorry for being nice to you and everyone else I've ever known! I'M NOT SORRY!" I screamed and pushed her back so hard that she fell down onto the pillows, right on top of her sandwich that was broken apart and it mashed into her. "I'M NOT

SORRY!" I screamed again.

Something came over me. I went mad.

Rose sat up and flicked away the piece of bread off that'd gotten stuck on her arm. She looked like she was going to cry and I felt so bad, and then, oh my gosh, she actually started crying.

"Oh, Rose, don't cry. I'm sorry." I told her, and helped her sit up and flicked two cucumber slices off the side of her face.

"It's almost a miracle." She told me.

"What?"

"You." She said and grabbed me into a big bear hug. "I'm so proud of you. When you first came to me for some backbone, I thought there's no way in hell I'd be able to get this sugar girl to break through, to find your inner power, and when the spirits told me it was time to test you, before you rudely interrupted them, I didn't want to do it. You still seem so fragile to me, but you're not. Candy Cane..."

"How do you know my stage -name?"

"Please. I'm a medium."

"Rose, I'm sorry to tell you this, but you're not a medium, you're an extra-large."

She laughed and slapped her foot. "Damn, I'm good. I'm good. You been wantin' to tell me I'm fat since the first day you came and you finally did. This might be the greatest day of my career. How do you feel, sugar. Got an itch in you?"

"I'm kind'a mad at everyone."

"You doing good, sugar girl. Just go with it. Change on you is swirling around your insides."

After my meeting with Rose, I wanted to lay down, but I needed to study. I had to finish my real estate courses fast so I could register for the State License Exam they were giving in downtown Los Angeles the next month. I had to take Real Estate Principles, Real Estate Practice, and Real Estate Appraisal. I crammed day and night at home, at the library, and in my head when I was running. Henry quizzed me since I'd lost so much weight running he liked what he saw, and twice Jack met me at the library to explain the areas I found particularly hard. With my bob haircut and all the studying I was doing, I not only looked smart, but I think I actually was getting smart.

At least I felt better about myself. Once I understood things like adjustable-rate mortgage, escrow, lender, title and prime rate, I felt I had a good grasp of the business. And not that I'm bragging here, with my memorization abilities, I was able to easily recall the definitions, it was just understanding them that I had a problem with.

Jack was great. He never made me feel stupid or ignorant. He never called me an idiot like Tom did when I didn't understand something after he explained it to me five times. We hung out and talked about our divorces, my background as the only daughter of a hash slinging powder sniffing waitress and his life as the youngest child of a family of six who grew up on a farm in Ohio. He came to Los Angeles to be an actor, but when that didn't work out, he went into real estate. He thinks his life's work will be as a life coach, though, because nothing made him feel better than helping other people.

Rose told me she was getting messages that my vagina was safe with Jack and since he never once tried to feel me up when I wasn't expecting it or kiss me or ask me out on a date, I figured the messages she was getting about my vagina were right. Jack Drake, I had decided, was the perfect man, handsome, kind, employed, single and smart. The only problem with Jack Drake I could see was that he was only interested in helping me with my career. But it was also sort of nice. I'd never had a man interested in me only to talk.

I passed my three online courses and was set to take the test in downtown Los Angeles. I crammed late the night before and on my drive downtown I read Real Estate License Exams For Dummies when I was stopped in traffic. The exam was on 4th Street in downtown Los Angeles and since there was so much traffic, I was able to review three chapters on my way.

I had to pass, especially since Kelly was so proud of me for taking charge of my life. She even took a whole hour out of her busy life to quiz me. She told me word got out that I was becoming a realtor because she told Shoshanna, who told Cherry, who told Bianca, who told her mom Barbie, who told Stacy, who told Mindy, who told Kelly, "Your mom's such an idiot, there's no way she'll pass the real estate exam."

I just laughed when Kelly told me this, because I didn't want her to know how much it bothered me and how scared I was that I was going to fail.

"They all have bets on whether or not you pass." Kelly said.

"How will they know?"

"I told Mindy I'd tell her, because I want to rub it in her face when you pass."

"Wow, then I better pass."

I found my way to the testing center, signed in and was seated in a room with a mixture of people between their twenties, all the way into their 70's. The guy I was sitting next to was named Herb. "I'm here to make sure I don't get scammed." He said. He was a retired carpenter who wanted to invest in fixer-uppers. "Lot'a real estate agents are scammers." I was surprised to hear that, because one of the qualifications to be a realtor was honesty.

The test took two hours to complete, and except for a few mind twisting questions, I understood most of what I was asked. I folded up my written exam, handed it to the clerk and was told to look for the results in the mail. I drove home feeling sort of lonely, but then when I walked from my parking stall into the apartment complex, I saw Jack sitting on the stairs and in his hands was a present.

"Jack, what are you doing here?"

He stood as I approached and oh, my God, the cheap white t-shirt and Levi jeans he was wearing with a pair of work boots made my mouth water. I had no idea men's rugged wear would have such effect on me. Tom always wore Armani or Gucci, but Jack's Fruit of the Loom t-shirt was the best menswear ever.

"Just thought I'd drop a congratulations present off."

I unwrapped the present. It was the cheapest and worst present I'd ever gotten, but I loved it. It was a brand new copy of "Success as a Real Estate Agent for Dummies."

"I'm sure you're gonna pass the exam. Figured you'd need it." He said, and I wanted to kiss him, but didn't.

"Thanks. Do you want to come in?"

"No. Can't. I'm helping build a home for a family."

"Huh?"

"Through Habitat for Humanity. It's not a big deal, just a family that lost their home to a fire, and the dad's unemployed because his job got moved to China."

I love this man. I love him. I love him. I love him.

"Wow, I didn't know you do charity work."

"Well, just this and I raise money to send disadvantaged youths to summer camp every year."

I wanted to ask him to marry me right then. Jack Drake was perfect.

"Okay. Well thanks for this. I appreciate your help." I said and even though there was a lull in the conversation like I had with Katie and Lisa Rinna, this lull felt like even though we weren't saying anything that we were saying a lot.

I saw Henry peek his head out his doorway. "You

all right, pretty lady?"

"Yeah, Henry." I yelled down. "Well, I should go inside."

"Yeah." Jack said and he started walking down the stairs. I wanted to tell him to stay, but my vagina was still in its protection phase. Then he stopped, turned and looked up at me. "You know, Candy, don't ever let anyone put you down. You're a terrific person." He said and walked off.

I couldn't speak. No one had ever made me feel that way before and I hadn't even given him any tail. Was it possible to be this involved with a person without being involved at all?

"Oh, God, sugar girl, that was beautiful what he just said." I heard Rose holler out her window. I hugged my new book tight against my chest. It meant more to me than any diamond Tom ever bought me.

Rose came to her doorway. She was crying and looking larger than ever in her horizontal striped muumuu.

"Rose, don't you know never to wear horizontal stripes? They add ten pounds to your middle."

"Girl, don't matter. I never leave my apartment anyway."

"Get your running shoes on." I told her, and made a mental note to reduce her lunch down to 300 calories tops. "You and me are going running."

"I'm not running nowhere. You crazy, sugar girl?"

"Rose, am I your friend or just your client?" I asked.

She smiled and laughed. "Shit, girl, you my only friend. No one else let's me boss them around like you do."

"Rose, you're my best friend. I care about you two. You need to get outside and you need to lose weight."

"Damn, sugar girl, you got your backbone grown.

That proves it." She said all sassy, but I could tell she was kind of emotional. "Girl used to be afraid of me, now she's bossing me." She mumbled. I looked around for spirits, but didn't see any.

"Well, how 'bout just a walk?"

"Walk on these tired feet?" She said, then laughed. "All right. I'll walk with you once around the block."

"Deal, but next week you go twice."

And so began my daily walks with Rose as I waited for the results of my real estate exam to come in the mail. And the funny thing is, we usually didn't talk about much and I was okay with it. Something was settling down inside me where I didn't feel like I had to always talk about this or that to keep someone interested in me. Something was happening inside me that I'd never felt before. Rose told me my yin and yang weren't battling anymore and I told her I didn't understand what she meant.

"It's called inner peace, sugar. It's what you've been searching for."

CANDY LEARNS HOW NOT TO GET SCREWED AGAIN

CHAPTER TEN

I put my tiny key into the lock and turned. Rose stood next to me, dancing on her feet.

"Open it, girl. I have to pee."

She had to pee for the last block we walked. I told her to go to the bathroom before we left, but she insisted she had a bladder of steel and only went twice a day.

Rose pushed me aside. "I'm going on that tree over there, you don't hurry." She opened my mailbox and inside, there it was, a letter from the State of California addressed to me. It was thin and manila colored, just an ordinary piece of mail that meant the world to me.

"Hurry!" Rose said, dancing about.

"'I can't." I said and refused to take the envelope from her. She jumped up and down and I did feel pretty bad for her. "Just go to the bathroom already, this can wait."

"No! Dreams don't wait sugar. I ain't going anywhere till I know what's in that letter. Don't you make me stand here and pee in my pants, girlfriend."

I ripped open the envelope, and accidentally ripped apart the letter.

"Oh, my god, I've ripped apart my dream!"

Rose pranced side to side as she took the two pieces of the letter inside the envelop and held them together. She started reading out-loud while doing the pee-pee dance. "Candace Lilly Katz… Candace?"

"Candy's my nick-name."

I bent over, put my hands on my knees and started hyperventilating.

"It is my honor to tell you, Candace Lilly Katz, that you have passed the California Real Estate Exam with a score of ninety-two percent!"

"AAAAAAHHHHHHH." I screamed.

Rose threw up the two pieces of paper and ran up the stairs to her apartment screaming the same thing, "AAAAAHHHHHH," until she disappeared into her apartment.

I heard clapping. I turned around and saw Henry standing in his doorway and he was crying.

"Oh, Henry, are you crying because you're so happy I passed the test?"

"I'm happy for you, pretty lady, but it's not why I'm upset."

"What's bothering you?"

"Nothing."

"No. Really. It's something. Tell me."

"Thought you and me were best friends."

That was news to me. I liked Henry, but the title of best friends was something I didn't hand out easily since I learned from Rose to protect my vagina. "Well, sure."

"Then how come you only go on walks with Rose?"

"Henry, you never leave your apartment. You won't even walk one block to get a gallon of vodka."

"So, Rose never left her apartment till you got her huge behind to go around the block"

"I'm sorry. I didn't mean to make you cry."

"I'm not crying." He said, while wiping tears off his face with a tissue and blowing snot out of his nose.

Rose came out of her apartment upstairs and down the walkway, slamming the door and stomping like an elephant. "Lord, oh Lord, oh Lord. That was close. Henry, you hear? We got ourselves a realtor."

"I heard."

Rose picked a rose from the garden and handed it to me.

"Rose, I told you don't pick the roses." Henry yelled.

"Stop your complaining, old fool. It's a special occasions." Rose said and handed the rose to me. "A rose from Rose, sugar girl. Now you remember that letter when you're feeling dumb."

"Thanks. I couldn't have done it if you two didn't help me."

"Got that right, sugar. You met me, you were timid as a fawn." Rose said.

"She met me, she was so naïve I got to look so far down her shirt, could almost see her nipples." Henry whispered to Rose.

"I heard you, Henry."

"Why you got tears coming out your eyes, fool?" Rose asked.

"I'm not crying." Henry said.

"Yes, you are. You got bloodshot eyes and snot. Signs are all there." Rose said.

"Rose, we're going one more time around the block." I told her.

"Not me sister. Got a bad pair of underwear that's riding up today."

"Rose, Henry wants to go with us. Come on."

Rose laughed. "Henry! He never goes nowhere. Ain't that right, Henry, you never go nowhere."

"Oh, forget it. I ain't going." Henry said.

"Don't get your panties in a bunch. You go, whitey, then I'm in. You and me are gonna talk about black people." Rose said to Henry. "He thinks Africa is a country, not a continent." She whispered to me.

"It is?" I said, confused because I thought Africa was a country too.

And so began my walks with Rose and Henry who, if I wasn't mistaken, had a thing for each other. Even though their skin didn't match, they were a perfect fit because they did the same things every day. They stayed home and both lived in the same apartment building. They argued like they were brother and sister, but it was all in fun. He'd laugh when she'd push him on the back and tell him to move along or call him an elephant, and she'd laugh when he called her chocolate milk or psycho psychic. He didn't even get mad at her when she yelled at him for drinking too much. "You're liver's on fire, fool. Stop drinking that poison." And she didn't get mad at him when he told her the calories in a tuna melt after she said she loved them so much. She usually ate three for a one meal.

On our walks, they fell in love, so I didn't feel bad when I took a job working for Jack as his assistant at his real estate office and couldn't be with Rose and Henry as much. Jack could only pay me minimum wage and it was only a temporary position until I learned how to be a real estate agent. I needed experience. That meant answering phones, learning how to use a copy machine, learning how Jack likes his coffee, watching him make cold calls to get a listing, how to run an open house and how to sell a house. I had to build relationships with escrow officers, loan officers, appraisers, photographers, termite inspectors, low-flush toilet installers and home insurance agents. There was so much to learn that the books never taught me.

But I just loved coming to work so I could see Jack. Even though none of the women in the building talked to me, all the guys in the office were real nice to me. They'd answer my questions or hand me a napkin when I was eating my lunch or a tissue if I sneezed.

Then I'd come home and go on a long run. I'd look at the sparkling leaves on the trees, shimmering under the sun and shaking from the breeze. I'd wave to all the neighbors. I'd forget about understanding an escrow account or who our contract mortgage broker was over at Financial Investments and think about Jack. I'd remember how he made me laugh over something stupid, how he didn't laugh at me when I said something stupid and instead would explain it to me slowly and calmly. I'd think about how even though I lived in a horrible apartment in the valley making minimum wage, that I'd never been happier.

I'd forgotten about Mindy and Tom for a little while. Life was sweet until a Tuesday morning when I was faced with my old life again. Jack and I went on an agent bus tour of foreclosed properties. Of all the places in the valley that we could have gone, the bus pulled up at the Oaks. As the bus driver talked to Carl in the security booth, I scrunched down in my seat, even though there was no way Carl could see me in the bus full of real estate agents.

Jack looked at me. "What's wrong?"

"Oh, nothing, just dropped my pen." I pretended to look on the floor as the bus drove on. Jack did too. Then everyone started asking what we were looking for and after Jack told them I dropped my pen, all the other agents started looking on the floor for my pen. I was so focused on pretending to look for my pen, and was feeling really bad when Jack insisted that if I dropped it, it had to be there somewhere, that I wasn't paying attention to the streets we were driving on.

The bus stopped.

I looked up. Holy crap! We were in front of Mindy's house. I looked down the road, and there it was, my old house. I couldn't speak. I couldn't move.

"Candy. You feeling okay?" Jack asked.

I got out of the bus, walked down the sidewalk and stood in front of the six thousand, five hundred foot Tuscan villa that still had elegance from the outside in, a gorgeous entertainer's yard, a pool, a spa, built-in barbeque, a grassy area and beautiful views.

"Candy?" Jack said as he stood next to me.

"I used to live here."

He hung his head down. "I know." He said and that was it. He knew all about the wealthy life I used to have before eating produce grown in my neighbor's backyard and shopping at the dollar store.

"That house in foreclosure, it's Mindy's."

Then I heard the muffled voices of Mindy and Tom yelling inside the house.

The garage door opened.

My eyes opened wide. "Oh, my God. That's Mindy and Tom." I said to Jack.

"I hate you!" Mindy yelled at Tom as he put his briefcase in his trunk. She was still in her pajamas and she hadn't brushed her fake Indian hair so she looked wild and crazy.

Maria was right behind Tom, holding his blazer, and waiting for him to take it so he could go off to work. She looked out at the street and saw me. "Ay yi yi. Mi Candy es aqui."

"Oh, shut up with that Spanish, Maria. You're in Calabasas now. We speak English here. Get it. No espanol. English." Mindy said, just as she turned and saw me standing on the sidewalk with Jack.

Maria rushed out and gave me a hug. "Ay yi yi, Mrs. Candy. "She's a hiho de puta." She whispered in my ear.

Tom walked towards me. "Candy?" He said with a smile on his face. "You look amazing."

"Maria! Go do the dishes!" Mindy yelled. Maria ran off, terrified of getting in trouble. Mindy tried to fix her hair, by pulling it into a pony tail.

Tom was staring at me like he did when we first met and he watched me as I spun on the pole at Boobs and Babes.

"Tom!" Mindy said as she rushed over. He flinched when he heard her voice. "You're going to be late for your meeting. How'd you get in here?" She said to me. "I thought they didn't let your kind through the gates."

"Mindy, knock it off." Tom said.

And I was speechless. I had nothing to say to the man I thought I would love forever.

"Candy, the bus is leaving." Jack said.

"That your boyfriend?" Tom asked.

"It's none of your business, Tom." I said.

"What are you jealous?" Mindy said to Tom and she sounded a tiny bit insecure.

"We work together." Jack said, in a protective way.

"I heard you got your real estate license, Candy Cane." Tom said with that sly smile on his face he always got before we made love.

"Don't call me Candy Cane. My name's Candace." I said to Tom.

"Oh, please, Candy, stop acting so righteous." Mindy said.

"Don't talk to me you… you… backstabbing bitch!"

She tapped on my skull with her charcoal colored acrylic nails. "Nothing up here. Never was, and never will be."

I smacked her hand away. "Don't touch me, you gypsy scum."

"I always knew it'd come to this. I always knew you and me would be enemies." She said.

"How, Mindy? Because you were planning it all along?"

"Of course. If you had more streets smarts, you

would have seen this coming."

"No one, unless they're insane, crazy or a gypsy would have seen this coming." I growled, poking my finger into her chest repeatedly and pretty hard. I didn't hurt her though because my nails were short because I couldn't afford acrylic nails.

"Whoa, whoa, aaaahhhh." Mindy said as she lost her balance and fell back into a rose bush. "Tom! Don't just stand there." Mindy yelled.

Tom had a huge smile on his face, and he was looking at me. I don't even think he knew Mindy had fallen in the bush. Either that, or he just didn't care.

Jack rushed over and helped Mindy out of the rose bush.

"Candy Cane, you're different." Tom said. "And I like it." He whispered in my ear. "If I can help you in any way with your new career, just give me a call. If you need any leads, I know some guys at the club looking for properties."

"You okay?" Jack asked Mindy as he unraveled her Indian hair that was stuck on some rose thorns.

The bus driver honked his horn. All the agents piled back inside the bus.

"We have to go." Jack said to me while holding Mindy back. She was trying to get at my face with her claws, but couldn't reach. And the funny part about it was that I didn't flinch, my heart wasn't racing and I wasn't scared of her at all.

"This is war!" Mindy yelled at me.

"Calm down." Tom said to her.

"But Tommy, look what she did to me." Mindy held out her arm to show him a scratch she got from a rose thorn and then pointed at strands of her hair stuck in the rose bush.

Our real estate bus pulled up. "You coming or staying." The bus driver asked.

"Going. I don't live here anymore." I said to the

driver.

I got on the bus. Jack followed and sat next to me.

"I'm never getting in a fight with you." He said.

"That used to be my house. That used to be my husband. That used to be my best friend. That even used to be my maid. But that's over. I have to move on." I told him, and I had tears in my eyes, again.

"You are, Candy. Look how far you've come."

The bus wound around the streets inside the Oaks gated community. I looked out at the homes I used to consider so fantastic. The bus drove by the playground where Mindy and I first met. I thought back to the first day at the club when we bonded even more as we realized Opi Nail polish was our favorite.

"You can't go back home again."

"I know. Mindy lives there now."

"No, I mean, you know, Thomas Wolfe, you can't go back home again."

"I don't know him. Sounds sort of familiar. Is he one of your friends? Has he called the office?" I asked.

"No. He's a famous writer. It's a metaphor for how things change."

"Oh."

The bus pulled to a stop at the guard gate and inside I saw Carl twiddling his thumbs in between pushing the button to raise the gate.

"Bus driver, give me a second." I yelled. I pushed down the top section of the window and poked my head out. "Carl. Up here. It's Candy Katz." I yelled. He looked out at me and then crouched down. "I need to talk to you. Why don't you talk to me anymore?" I asked.

He poked his head out of the guard gate. "I can't."

"What'd Mindy tell you? Did she say she'd put a gypsy curse on you that'd make your dick shrivel up and fall off if you talked to me?"

Jack stood up. "Candy, this isn't the place for

this."

I looked back at all the realtors and the bus driver. "Do you guys have two minutes?"

"Sure, yeah, no problem." They all answered.

"How'd you know?" Carl yelled up at me.

"I just know. Look, Carl, I want you to know I still consider you my friend."

"Awe, Mrs. Katz, you know you were always my favorite." Carl said.

"And that there actually is a gypsy disease that could make your dick fall off, so if you get symptoms, call me. I know a gypsy who can reverse the spell."

I tossed him my card. He caught it.

"Okay. Thanks, Mrs. Katz. You take care of yourself."

"I will, Carl. Bye."

I poked my head back in the bus and everyone was looking at me with mouths wide open.

"Sorry. We can go now." I said.

The women in our office, who still never gave me the time of day, started laughing at me.

"I wouldn't laugh." Jack said. "Her best friend is a gypsy."

The women stopped laughing. I sat down on the bus seat next to Jack and right then, after standing up to Mindy and Tom, and working out my issues with Carl, I felt ready to get on with my real estate career.

"Jack, I appreciate all your help and training, I do, but I think I'm ready to make more money. How do I actually sell a house?"

"Get a listing and find a buyer."

"Sounds easy." I said.

"Yeah, it does." Jack said. "Sounds real easy, but you'll see."

I knew it wasn't easy. I'd seen Jack at work making three hundred cold calls in a day just to get one listing a month, but I learned about setting goals from Jack, too.

He had a white board above his desk where every month he set new goals for himself. He had columns. Some weeks he'd focus more on finding new listings when his current listings sold. Other weeks he focused on buyers for foreclosed homes. So, just like him, I set up a white board for goals on the wall above my desk, but I had only one goal that month. I wanted to get my first listing, and I knew exactly who I was going to approach first.

Katie worked every Thursday, Friday and Saturday nights at the bar, and while she had slipped me free drinks when I was poor, I hadn't gone back to Chapter 8 since I left there in a blackout with my daughter's eighteen year old ex-boyfriend, but this was business. I put my fire hot body that I got from running all over the city in a pair of jeans and a simple tank top and headed out to Agoura. I drove to Chapter 8 and stood in line with a long line of cougars to have my I.D. checked by the snot-nosed bouncer who recognized me.

"Back again, huh." He said and nodded his head up and down. "Last time you left here you were in bad shape." He added.

"Can I have my license back?" I asked him.

He leaned in close to my face. "Just you remember, you need a long ride home, and I mean a long ride, you just come see me. I'm your man."

"I'm not drinking tonight. I'm here on business." I told him.

He laughed and handed me back my license. "Gerome, we got a hot one in house tonight!" He yelled inside the door.

I walked into the bar. Gerome was dancing high on the D.J. platform. He pointed two fingers at me, spun around in place, and leaned into the microphone. "This next one here's for a wild woman. Come on, girl, give it up for Gerome! Give it up for Aerosmith. Give it up again on the pole!" Love on an Elevator blasted out the speakers. Gerome double pointed at me and at the pole, and then spun around in place.

I went over to the bar where Katie was blending a pitcher of margaritas. "Katie, I have to talk to you!" I yelled over the music.

"I can't hear you." She yelled back at me.

"What?" I yelled back.

She took a cocktail napkin and wrote, parking lot, 10 Mins.

I shook my head yes and went over to the dance floor where a large woman, who had a bit too much to drink, was trying to spin around the pole. It was so horrible to watch. I was sure her husband just dumped her and she was feeling pathetic and was drunker than a skunk. Been there, done that, I thought, and walked outside.

"Not any good male meat in there tonight, huh, you sexy cougar in your tight jeans. You looking for it, I just know, that's why you should take me. I'm your boy toy, right here." The bouncer said.

"How old are you?" I asked him.

"Twenty-three, but I could be younger if you want. I know you cougars like 'em young."

I leaned in close, bending over so my cleavage showed. "Young man, if you don't stop sexually harassing the women who come in this bar, I'm going to sue you." I said and he looked terrified. I walked off to my car, laughing. Having backbone was hilarious some times.

Five minutes later, Katie came outside. She lit a cigarette as she walked over to my car.

"Oh, my God. You smoke?" I said.

"Not for twelve years, but I started again. It was either smoke and die of cancer in twenty years or commit suicide and die now. I'm taking the twenty years."

"Your husband still out of work?"

"Yep. We're two months behind on our mortgage.

I don't know what we're going to do."

"Katie, let me sell your home. You may have heard, I'm a real estate agent now. Although I haven't sold a house yet, if you give me a shot, I promise to find a buyer for your house and sell it before you go into foreclosure."

I had only five minutes to convince Katie that it was a good idea, because she was on a short break. The next day, Katie talked with her husband, Ajit, who asked that I come over and explain how I was going to find a buyer for their house in only six weeks. I asked Jack to come along as backup.

Ajit was Indian, not Native American, but from India and didn't understand much English. Katie married him only six years before. After dating him for three months, she knew he was the man for her when she learned he made $300,000 a year. He was the West Coast Senior Financial Analyst for an Indian based company. When they let him go, he didn't have connections in the area and couldn't find another job. At first I was worried that Katie was just going to leave him high and dry, like Mindy would have done to Barry if he didn't croak first. It turned out she really loved him. At our meeting, they kept kissing. It made Jack and me uncomfortable. I almost told them to go upstairs to a room, but I didn't want to lose the listing.

The house was located in a gated community on the other side of the Calabasas Country Club. It had nice architectural details, although nothing compared to the type of homes you get in the Oaks. They purchased it for $2,185,000 four years before, but housing prices had fallen and with the loss of Ajit's job as a financial planner, they were already $23,000 behind in payments with no turn around in site. Foreclosure and financial ruin was right around the corner, unless I could sell their house within six weeks. They almost owed what the house was worth, but if I could sell it at market value, they'd have a hundred thousand to put in their pocket.

"I've overcome worse odds." I explained to Ajit, throwing in my life story. Stripper, Sweet N' Low addicted mom, dumped by Tom (which he heard about anyway), dumped by Mindy (who he hated since she dumped Katie). I explained that I knew the area better than anyone because I'd driven every street in Calabasas and I knew the people in the area. Ajit was still on the fence until I got down on my knees, begged, and agreed to reduce my commission to 1% which could be given to me in payment installments.

We filled out the paper work that committed me as their agent for six months. In two days, I achieved my goal so when we went back to the office, I erased my white board and put up my next goal which was to sell Katie's house. Jack and I went over all the usual forms of selling. I promised him a .25% of my 1% commission as incentive for his help, but he refused. He said this one would be free and that in the future we could team up on listings. I almost thought he was going to say that we could team up, you know, sexually, but still, Jack didn't seem to have sex with me on his mind.

I scheduled Tuesday and Friday broker opens and an open house on Sunday. I was sure, with the excellent shape Katie's house was in that I'd find a buyer within weeks, even though Jack warned me selling a home usually took four to six months.

"Jack, I don't have four to six months." I told him.

"Look Candy, you got a listing right after getting your license. Not many realtors are so lucky."

"Jack, I have to sell this house. It's my goal for the month and I'm two weeks into the month."

Jack laughed. "Goals are good to set, Candy, but you're not always going to hit your target numbers. It's just the nature of the business."

"You don't understand. I have to sell this house, just so I know I'm worth something."

"Selling this house isn't going to make you know that." He pointed to my heart. "It comes from in here,

Candy. It doesn't matter what anyone else thinks about you, only thing that matters is what you think about yourself."

That evening, on my walk with Henry and Rose, the two lovebirds who were so happy with each other that it made me want to vomit, I didn't want to talk, not because I was doing the whole inner peace thing and not because I was at one with myself. I was irritable.

"You're bad vibes are scratching up my energy. What's gone and shut your mouth girl. Got to be something wrong with you, 'cause you ain't talking." Rose said.

"Just work stuff. That's all."

"Tell me. I used to be in sales. Sold Encyclopedias door to door for ten years." Henry said.

"You walked door to door for ten years?" I asked.

"Why you think I've been staying home since buying the apartment building? Got tired of walkin'."

"I have to sell Katie's house, but aside from a crazy guy who walked around her house with muddy shoes and was unemployed, no one's put in an offer."

"Sales is a tricky business. If you can't get them to come in the front door, then get them in the back door." Henry said.

"So I should have my open houses start in the backyard?" I asked.

Henry and Rose both stared at me like I was nuts.

"It's like that protecting your vagina thing I've been trying to explain to you, sugar. It's a metaphor. What whitey's saying is if things ain't working out, switch it up. Find your own groove. Do it different. Sell that house however you can."

"Well, I could throw a party in the backyard and then take people on tour of the house after they've had a few drinks. Maybe they'd want to buy the house if they're drunk."

Rose and Henry just looked at me again.

"Stupid idea?" I asked.

"Actually, not a bad idea at all. I once did shots with a lonely old man who was on the fence about buying the entire Britannica selection from A-Z. He only wanted A-N, but who buys an incomplete set of Encyclopedia."

"Seems weird." I told him.

"But he had his budget and didn't want to go over, so I pulled out a stash of Cuervo Gold I kept in a flask inside my jacket, 'cause when you're walking door to door, sometimes you get thirsty, and when he saw that, he told me he'd buy the whole alphabet if I'd just give him the rest that was in the flask. I didn't know at the time he was an alcoholic who'd been sober for eight years or I wouldn't have given it to him, but he bought the entire collection.

"I do throw a fabulous party. I make sure there's Chanel Eau De Toilet spray's in the bathroom and all the drinks have those cute umbrellas."

I went home determined to become an event planning real estate agent. I had to get people to Katie's backyard so I could get them in the backdoor and make a sale. I paced inside my apartment, I swear, for two hours at least, focusing my attention on the problem. I had just one goal to complete, sell Katie's house, and I was going to use all the power in my one brain to do it. I decided to treat this like I did Barry's funeral. I gave myself only three days to come up with the solution and I decided all parts had to be in place by Sunday, the next open house, which was where I would find my buyer.

In real estate, Jack taught me that the first rule is location, location, location, and in event planning, the first rule is organization, organization, organization. I had the location, now it was time to get organized. First order of business, make a list.

Candy's Open House Action Plan

1. Theme.
2. Budget.
3. Food and Drinks.
4. Entertainment.

I needed to throw a party that would bring in separated or recently divorced men with money who don't have a house because their wives were smart enough not to sign a pre-nup like me. I learned about target buyers from Jack. He said, don't go after someone who doesn't want your business. Just walk away, because no matter how hard you try to sell them, it's not going to work. If it's not business they want, you've got no business getting in their business.

Then it hit me. The theme at my event open house would be "open." We'd have an open house for sale that people could tour at their leisure, we'd have an open bar, and we'd have open women dancing on tables and on poles in the living room and master bedroom. I'd give the client an all access pass to the house by drawing them in to have a good time, because nothing attracted single men more to a location than attractive women. It was a brilliant plan.

I talked to Katie and Ajit about my idea. We agreed to pool a small budget together for the open house event and I promised to return their investment if the house didn't sell. Katie would do the bartending, Rose agreed to do table readings and narrow down the men who were serious about buying a house with her psychic abilities, and Henry agreed to be a party host, guiding the clients to the open house party in the backyard.

Now my only problem was I needed to find five reliable strippers who were willing to dance in the light of day outside in the backyard. I planned for them to wear bathing suits with little cute skirts, because little skirts are just so damn cute. I went down to The Double D, and sat at the bar in the back, because I didn't want to be close to the stage. I ordered a Diet

Coke and stayed there for an hour watching ten different girls perform so I could see who had the charisma I was looking for at my open house. I was willing to pay each girl a $500 flat rate for three hours and I was sure some of the men who came through would slip them some cash.

I snuck back into the dressing room, pushed my way through a rack of boas and scarves and hats and found the women.

"Hi girls. I'm Candy. I've been out of the business for a while, but I used to be a stripper. Actually, Candy Cane was my stage name and I used to have a real popular act where I licked a large oversized candy cane and I..." I looked around at the women, and I could tell they were getting a little bored with me. "Anyway, that's not why I'm here. I'm a real estate agent now, and I'm having an open house for this house I'm trying to sell... It's my first listing and the owners are about to go completely bankrupt and lose the house in foreclosure..." I looked around again. Most of the women looked bored, some even went back to putting on their makeup and nipple tassels. "Well, that's not important either..."

"Honey, what you looking for? One of us to sleep with the buyer?"

"Oh, God no. Nothing like that. No. No. Not at all. I need five dancers from 2 to 5 on Sunday willing to dance, and only dance, at the open house. I'm paying a $500 flat rate, but it's in an expensive neighborhood so I'm pretty sure some of the men coming through will slip you some cash on the side." I placed a stack of my cards on a makeup table. "Here's my card. Give me a call if you're interested."

The women were silent for a moment, then they all rushed over to grab my card and a few got knocked down to the ground. I felt sort of bad, but you know, strippers will be strippers. I once knocked over another dancer just to get the fuchsia boa on the costume rack before her because fuchsia is my favorite color.

Next on my plan was to take Tom up on his offer to put me in touch with recently divorced Calabasas men with a lot of money. I gave him a call at his office.

"Candy Cane, you called."

"Yeah, that's why I'm on the phone."

"Still my silly girl." He said with a laugh.

I had an urge to cuss him out, but since I was calling on business and wanted his cooperation, I laughed too.

"I'm calling about business. You said you would help me. I'm having an open house on Sunday and I need men with money to come through. I'm having a backyard party. There'll be dancers and a bar. It should be a lot of fun."

"Oooahh, and sexy." He said.

"Whatever." I heard myself saying.

Whatever!

How was I going to get Tom to help me by saying whatever? I just couldn't help it. He sounded like such a creep.

"What'd you say?" Tom asked.

"It's better." I answered. "Sexy is better for a party."

"Yeah, yeah, Candy Cane, sexy is always better."

I'm going to barf all over this phone, I thought. It's not a great moment when you realize the man you spent twenty years with is a total creep. Really, it's not. It does make you want to barf.

Tom agreed to meet me at the Calabasas Country Club for breakfast the next morning so we could go over the names of men he knew who were in the market for a home. And then he added, "Oh, and don't tell anyone about this. Mindy's got spies all around. I'm risking a lot for you, Candy, by agreeing to do this."

"I understand, Tom." I said, thinking that maybe that gypsy disease Rose was telling me about was actually a metaphor and that Tom's dick wasn't actually going to shrivel up and fall off, but that his manhood was going to disappear by being with such a skunk woman like Mindy.

My next item was to make professional postcards at Kinkos announcing our open house. Then I walked around the Commons and handed them out to any lonely depressed looking man wearing brand name casual wear, because they were more likely to have more money. I made the card look like a backstage pass at a concert. It said, all access pass on it and open house. It listed all the property information and cute drawings of girls dancing that sort of looked like stick figures, but they had more on the top of their body than should be allowed. I also hung out in the parking lot of the Calabasas Tennis and Swim Center and put the cards on the windshields of expensive cars.

Jack was impressed, but also a little confused about my plan. He said no realtor he'd ever known had thrown an open house like this. "Candy, you are an original." He said to me as I answered another call from a stripper who wanted to work the party. Turns out, there were a lot of strippers who wanted to work the party. I was getting calls from girls who worked in clubs all over the valley, not just at The Double D. I had already picked my five girls, but I told the other women that I would keep their number and call them if another job came along. So far, I had a list of seventy-eight strippers willing to work an open house.

The worst part, though, were the comments and looks I got from the women at the office. None of them talked to me, even though I wore suits in muted tones with skirts that went nearly all the way down to the middle of my thigh. Three of them were always in a group looking at me. I couldn't hear what they were saying, but I knew they were talking about me. I just ignored them and went on doing my work. I had my goal which was sell Katie's house and I was going to do it my way. I just hoped that this open house brought me in a buyer, because if it didn't I'd be totally embarrassed.

I met Tom for breakfast at the Calabasas Country Club at 6:00 a.m. He was wearing golf casual wear. I used to think he looked so handsome in these clothes, but when he stood up in his lime green Le Coste polo shirt, plaid pants and white golf shoes, his look just wasn't working for me anymore. After seeing Jack in his Fruit of the Loom T-shirt and his Levi jeans and his muddy scuffed up work boots, designer casual wear wasn't my thing.

"Candy Cane." He said to me so sweetly and stood there with his arms open.

This is business, I kept thinking. Smile for the jerk. Smile for the sale.

"Hi Tom." I said and sat down, skipping right past his arms I used to run into. "Thanks for doing this. I really need your help." I pulled out my notepad from my briefcase. "I want to get straight to work, because I know you have a standing tee time at 6:30 and I don't want to waste your time."

He sat down, smiling from ear to ear. "Well, look at you, my little stripper is a business woman."

Oh, he so did not just say that. Don't kill him. Look down at your paper until you can look up with a smile.

"That's me." I said.

"It sure is, Candy Cane, and it's so attractive. I never knew you had this side in you."

"Yep, well, it was and now it's out." I handed him a stack of the postcards. "This is the information on the open house."

Tom picked up the postcard and started laughing. "Well, there is a little stripper left in you after all." He said.

Don't throw your drink on him. Close the deal. Get the contact names. Keep it together.

"Yes, I guess there is." I said with a smile. "If you could put those postcards in the men's locker room, I'd appreciate it."

"Candy Cane, I'll do it for you if you have a drink with me tonight."

OH, MY GOD!

"We had so much together. I miss us." He said.

"We're over Tom. You've got Mindy now, remember?"

"I know. I don't want to lose her, she's so feisty and I love it, but Candy, I gotta say, you really work for me now."

"Wait, how long wasn't I working for you when we were married?"

"It's not important."

"It is important to me. How long?"

"Just a few years."

"Really. I had no idea. How many years?"

"Like ten or fifteen. You know, when we stopped fighting all the time, our marriage, it just got boring."

The golden years, he's talking about all the years I thought he was so happy because we were getting along great and didn't fight. The years I was so happy and the reason why I wanted to recommit myself to Tom for the rest of my life.

"You were such a rug. No matter what I said or did to you, you just took it. How could a man be interested in that? Honestly, it's why I was so attracted to Mindy. We fight all the time, but it's passionate. It really turns me on." He said.

I didn't want to look up. I had tears in my eyes, and damn it, I was not going to cry in front of this enormous asshole. Get it together. You're a business woman now, Candy, I thought to myself. Close the deal.

I looked up.

"You're right. How could you stay interested in

235

me? I completely agree. Now, are you going to give me the contact information of the men you know that are looking for a house or did you get me here just to flirt with me, because let me tell you Tom, there is no way in hell I would ever be with you again. I'm not nice anymore. You know what I want. You either give it to me or I leave."

"God, Candy, I love this new side of you." He said with a laugh. "I'll give it to you, since you want it." He added just because he could and just because he was a creep.

Tom gave me a list of ten club members who had in the last year gotten separated or divorced from their wives and one guy who was looking for a house for his family. I agreed to keep it quiet where I got the numbers from if he would agree to stop coming on to me.

After Tom went to play golf, I went to the parking lot and put postcards on all the expensive looking cars, then drove back to the office, sat at my desk, put my head down, and cried.

"Candy, what's wrong?" Jack asked.

"It's nothing. I'm just gonna step outside a minute."

I walked outside sat on a planter in the courtyard and watched cars zoom by.

And then there was Jack. He came out to check on me, but he didn't say a word. He just sat next to me on the planter, silent, and it didn't feel uncomfortable. In fact, it felt real comfortable having him there.

"My whole life I've been a joke and didn't even realize it." I said.

"Don't you think you're being hard on yourself?"

"No. I'm being honest with myself." I said, and Jack didn't say anything back to me at all, he just sat there next to me as I cried. "I'm fighting back."

Then I got real angry and real determined. I went back in the office and called all the men Tom gave me contact numbers for. I explained to each of them that Tom gave me their personal cell phone numbers and insisted that they come by the open house, not only to check out this hot property, but also have a good time. I burned my bridge with Tom and felt great about it, because after this open house, I was never going to whore myself again by going to such a scumbag for help, even if he is the father of my daughter.

I met with the five dancers in the conference room at the office and had them bring three conservative outfits of little skirts and tank tops so I could approve one of them for the open house. I heard one of the women in the office say, "This is what happens when a stripper gets her license." And you know what, I ignored her. I was sick in tired of getting upset about people putting me down. I was going to throw an awesome open house, I was going to sell Katie's house and I was going to become the most successful real estate agent in Calabasas, California.

I purchased snack food at Smart and Final. I had information packets put together with brochures of the house, my cards, the sell sheet, information about the neighborhood, including a breakdown of their neighbors that Katie and I put together on her computer. I felt a little bad about this, but I learned from Jack that who you're living next to is as important as location. You might have a great house in a great location, but if you have a sucky group of neighbors, you'll never want to come home.

By the time we opened the backdoor to Katie's house at 2:00 p.m. on Sunday, the dancers were on their tables, music was playing, the blenders at the open bar were spinning, Rose was at the sign-in table and Henry was at the front of the house to direct the flow of potential buyers to the back of the house. I had on a sexy Calvin Klein, simple yet elegantly delicious black dress that said I was a woman to be taken seriously, but also a woman you might consider taking sexually because sex sells. The dress, paired with my smart and sophisticated bob hairstyle, I was ready to give the tours. Jack was my tour guide backup if I was busy with a potential buyer, but he was weird that day. He wouldn't stop looking at me, like how I looked at him when he was dressed in a t-shirt and jeans.

"Candy, you look amazing." He said.

"Oh, this dress. It's off the rack."

"Nervous?" He asked.

"Terrified."

"If someone asks you a question you're not sure of, just bring me over. I'll be standing close by."

God, I love this man.

"I will. Thanks, Jack."

I stood at the side gate ready to welcome buyers. I had plastered the neighborhood for a five mile radius with open house signs, flags, and balloons. Kelly was supposed to help me, but when I called her, she snapped at me. "Mom, like come on, it's Sunday. You didn't actually think I would get up at six in the morning to put signs up. I thought you were joking."

I was disappointed, but Rose told me to shake it off and get my mojo up because today I had no time to deal with it. She got Henry out of bed early and both of them helped me paste the streets with signs.

I looked down at my watch. It was 2:00. If no one showed, I'd be the laughing stock of the real estate office. I remained poised and in position, with my brochure packets ready. If stripping taught me anything, it was that you have to put up a front, a shell, so that even if you're scared or nervous or your arm pits are dripping with sweat, keep your shoulders back and your chin up. When I danced, sometimes I just took off my shirt sooner in the act than I meant too, because I'd rather them see my tatas with tassels than my sweat circles.

"Keep that chin up, sugar girl." Rose said to me.

I stood there for twenty-five minutes waiting and I thought I was going to have a heart attack. Then our first potential buyer parked his black Mercedes 550 in the driveway and came inside.

"Hello, sir, I'm Candy Katz. Follow me and we'll set you up with a drink. We have entertainment for you to enjoy right after I give you a tour of this lovely, and extremely reasonably priced home. We start taking offers at 6:00. My card's in the packet. Just give me a call and I'll be happy to help you make this beautiful home yours. If you play golf, this home is located only one mile from the Calabasas Country Club…"

I went on and on as I gave him a tour of the house. After, I sat down with him and had a drink while he watched the dancers and Henry brought over a plate of cheese and crackers for us. And can you believe it, he called two of his friends to come over. Soon I had a yard full of drunk businessmen who all probably made $200,000 or more a year, drinking and slipping the girls twenties into their bras.

When the men signed in, Rose held up a finger to me to tell me if the soul coming in was really a potential buyer or just a guy looking for a fun time on a Sunday afternoon. One finger meant the guy was a serious buyer, two fingers meant he wasn't. Jack and I would stick to the one finger guys, escort them through the house, find them a seat and make sure they had a drink in their hand at all times.

And any real estate agents that came in, Jack and I made sure to make them at home, because even if they didn't come in with a buyer, they might know someone who wanted that house and we wanted to make sure they were happy.

The Open House was a huge success. The girls made a fortune in tips and we had a huge pool of potential buyers. Jack and I headed to the office to field any offers when the bidding opened at 6:00. Rose and Henry stayed back to help Katie and Ajit with three stragglers who didn't want to leave.

In the office, Jack heard my cell phone ring. I looked down. It was Kelly.

"Aren't you going to get it?" He asked.

"Kelly, are you okay?" I said into the phone. She said yes and started talking about something and I cut her off. "I can't talk right now. I'm in the office. I'll call you later." I said and hung up. Kelly called me ten more times and each time I ignored her call.

At the office, Jack and I stared at the telephone. At 6:07 it rang.

"Prudential realty, this is Candy Katz and Jack Drake speaking." I answered the phone on speaker.

"Ah, Candy, this is Bob Beauford. I met you today at the open house."

"Yes, Bob I remember. You wore the black Gucci suit with the slip on shoes, grey socks, and white button up shirt." Jack looked at me as if I was nuts. "I memorized their name with their outfit so I could remember who they were." I whispered to Jack who just smiled. My cell rang again. It was Kelly. I pushed the ignore button again. "Are you interested in putting an offer in on the house?" I asked.

"Well, not exactly. I was wondering if you'd want to out to dinner sometime."

We had seven calls, and all of them were men asking me out on a date. Jack thought it was hilarious. I didn't. I had a goal. I needed to sell the house or I would be a laughing stock. Katie kept calling me and I kept pushing the ignore button.

"Do you want to answer that?" Jack asked.
"It's my daughter. I'll call her later." I said.

Almost an hour went buy, and not one offer came in. Then the phone rang. A realtor for the first gentleman that came to the open house called, and offered twenty thousand below our asking price. Jack and I called Katie and Ajit, who agreed to accept the offer. I'd jacked up the price anyway. At the selling price of 1,929,000, Katie and Ajit had nearly a two hundred thousand dollar profit they could start their new life with. We called the realtor back and set to meet the next morning at 10 a.m. to sign the paperwork.

Jack pulled out a bottle of sparkling apple cider he kept in his drawer for such occasions and poured us each a glass. Then when I calculated that my commission from the sale was going to be 48,225, I thought I was going to have a heart attack.

"To you, Candy. You did it." He said. "Congratulations."

I held up my glass. "We did it." I told him.

We clanked our glasses and it was one of those fabulous moments when everything in the world is right and you're with the man of your dreams and you think he's going to pull you into a passionate embrace and kiss you deep and hard while bending you over backwards. But that didn't happen. Jack backed away, just as I leaned in to kiss him, so I backed away.

"That's embarrassing."

"Candy, I don't think it's the right time, you know, for you and me." He said.

"Why?" I asked.

"You're an amazing woman, but you're on a path of self-discovery right now and I don't want to get in the way of your growth. I don't think being in a relationship is a good thing for you right now."

"Oh." I said. "This is so embarrassing." I picked up my coat and purse.

"Candy… I… I'm just looking out for you." He said.

"Thanks. I appreciate that, I think."

"I'll see you tomorrow at 10."

"Yeah." I said, and started walking to the elevator.

Get in the way of my growth? Is this guy for real?

Path of self-discovery? This has got to be a joke. I looked around the office for a camera crew, thinking maybe I was getting punked, but no one was around.

I pushed the button on the elevator. "Jack!" The elevator doors opened. I put my hand out to keep it open. "How long do you think this path of self-discovery will take me?"

"No telling. Months. Years."

"Years? Really?" I said. "Cause that's a long time. It's like months and months, you know?"

"I know." He said and took off a chain around his neck that had a pendant on it as he walked over to me. "Here, I want you to have this." He said, and put it around my neck. I looked down at it. It was the cheapest piece of jewelry I'd ever seen, like 10K gold if even that, and it had words engraved on it. "It helped me cope with my divorce and when I was putting my life back together."

I picked up the pendant, and read it. "Remember that not getting what you want is sometimes a wonderful stroke of luck."

Yeah, right, I thought, what I want is for you to give me a big fat wet one, not this silly necklace.

"Thanks. I guess." I said.

"It's a quote by the Dalai Lama."

"Are we gonna just stand here all night?" I heard a voice say. I looked in the elevator and saw the building janitor.

"Oh, sorry." I said.

I got on the elevator, thinking, oh, my, God, the Dalai Lama is sending me messages now. This is too cool. I'd forgotten all about kissing Jack. I'd forgotten all about having sold a house. I remembered what that crazy Randolf said to me, that I was going to be respected like the Dalai Lama.

"See ya tomorrow, Candy."

"See ya tomorrow." I said back, because I couldn't

think of my own words so I used his.

The elevator doors closed.

"Have a good day?" The janitor asked me.

I looked at him and took a moment to think about his question. "Finally." I said and smiled.

I thought about going on and on about all that I'd been through, my horrible childhood, my years as a stripper, my horrible ex-husband and my horrible ex-best friend and my horrible apartment, and how I just sold my first house, but instead I was quiet because that inner peace feeling had come back and I was okay with being silent.

CANDY'S COMING UNSCREWED

CHAPTER ELEVEN

I pulled into my car port in the back alley of my apartment and looked around for a burglar or rapist before getting out holding my baseball bat. Even though Henry installed motion sensitive overhead lights, he said I should carry a baseball bat to and from my car because a carport is always a good spot for crime.

I walked into the hallway leading to the courtyard and I saw a shadow of a person hovering at the end. I raised my bat, ready to clobber the lurker.

"Stay back! I'm warning you. I've got a bat."

My heart was pounding and I thought I was going to have a panic attack as the person came towards me.

"Mom! Why didn't you answer my calls?" Kelly yelled at me. I almost just clobbered my daughter. She was crying.

"I did. Three of them. You said you were okay and I told you I would call you tomorrow."

"How could you just call me tomorrow, Mom, like God, I'm like, your daughter."

"And how could you not help me put up the signs for my open house, Kelly, I'm like, your mother?" I said and walked into the courtyard. Kelly followed me.

"Oh, my God, you're so all about you." She yelled

at me.

"Kelly, you told me you would help me out. It was a big day for me."

"It was early, Mom, and I can't handle early. God, like what's the big deal?" Kelly snapped.

"The big deal is that it was a big deal to me." I told her.

"Well it's a big deal that you take my calls. I mean, do you know how embarrassing it is to have to come this far into the valley?" Kelly said.

"Candy, you raised a brat!" The little old lady in apartment three yelled out her window.

"Shut up, Granny. This is none of your business." Kelly yelled back.

"She needs some tough love." The guy from apartment eight yelled out.

"F-off, jerk." Kelly yelled up at him.

I was so shocked. I could not believe that this was my daughter.

"Kelly Matilda Katz! Do not talk to people that way."

I realized my daughter was a brat and it was my fault because I was never around her when she was little. I was too busy getting my nails done, playing tennis and going to Neiman Marcus with Mindy.

"Be tough with that girl, sugar. Don't let her push you around." Rose yelled down at me. She and Henry were standing on the second floor landing.

"Who is she again?" Henry asked Rose.

"That's Kelly, Candy's daughter." Rose said.

"Kelly, go home and don't call me until you're ready to apologize." I said and walked up the stairs to Rose and Henry. "We sold the house!" I said to them and we all hugged.

"Congratulations, pretty lady." Henry said.

"Mom!" Kelly screamed and started jumping up and down. It was her version of a temper tantrum while standing up. I'd seen many of them during her teenage years. They last about fifteen minutes. "Mom! Mom! Mom!" She yelled again and again.

"Sugar, don't you go down there." Rose whispered to me. "Tough loves only way that girl's gonna respect you."

"God, I'm sorry." Kelly said with an attitude as she came up the stairs. I said nothing. "Well, like God, isn't that good enough?" She added.

I looked over at Rose, because I was kind of thinking it was enough, but Rose shook her head side to side.

"Actually it's not." I grabbed Kelly's arm. "Come with me." I told her, and walked her over to the little old lady in apartment three who refused to open her door and had Kelly apologize through her open window. Then I took her over to apartment eight and had her apologize to the guy who lived there, and I was shocked to see he was only four feet tall. Who knew?

Rose was right about the tough love approach. Once I stood up to my daughter, Kelly never spoke to me like I was a dog again and she even started coming around the apartment more. One night, while having dinner with me and Rose, Kelly opened up about her fear of being in love, because after she had to dump Chris when she realized he was just like Brad, it brought her so much pain and suffering. And even though I was sitting right there, she told Rose that her parent's marriage was a joke and that she grew up with a mom more interested in shopping than her and a rich and good-looking dad who was never home. They bonded, and after that night, Kelly started seeing Rose once a week for therapy sessions.

Meanwhile, I was quickly on my way to being the top selling agent real estate agent in Calabasas. My themed open houses were a smash and my system of getting to my target buyer worked every time. One house I sold had a lap pool, so I focused on potential buyers in the area and across the nation who had a history of swimming competitively in high school and college. Another listing I got had a two bedroom tree house in the backyard, so I held a George of the Jungle open house for families and focused on selling the tree house to the kids. I knew if the kids wanted the tree house, they would beg their parents to buy it. Another house had a wine cellar stocked with vintage wine because the owner died of cirrhosis of the liver before he could drink all the bottles. I made the open house a wine tasting event and found potential clients at high-end liquor stores and wineries.

I made a name for myself in Calabasas as the can-do realtor and soon every single woman who got the house in the divorce settlement used me as their listing agent.

I sold Tatonka's house in two weeks. She had installed an enormous smoking pipe in her back patio, along with a sweat cave to cleanse away evil spirits. I targeted Native American casino owners and politicians to come to the event and a few rich businessmen rumored to be pot-heads.

I even sold Samantha the dominatrix's house. After standing by her man and his man pump, he left her when he realized he was gay. Her house flew off the market after I had my network of strippers put out the word to their wealthy clients that there was a dominatrix dungeon.

I was the talk of the town. Kelly even overheard Mindy telling Stacy that she was thinking about getting her real estate license because if an idiot like me can sell homes, so could she. Even Lisa Rinna cornered me when I was at the Commons to sell one of her three houses that she just didn't need anymore.

I'd reach the pinnacle of my career in a year and had money, lots of money, so I went shopping. I bought the latest designer jeans and reconnected with my personal shopper at Nordstroms. I went to Zen Spa, had massages and got my hair and nails done. I put my name on the waiting list at the Calabasas Tennis and Swim Club for a membership, even though the wait was two years. I remodeled the inside of my apartment with new furniture and carpet.

I was on my way to getting my life back like it was before, but then I had a crisis, and I'm not talking a mid-life crisis, I had a shallow crisis. I was in a Nordstroms dressing room, trying on the newest 7 Jeans by Seven, which is a confusing brand name, when I heard her voice.

"Get me this in black." Mindy said.

"We don't have it in black." I heard my personal shopper, who apparently was still Mindy's personal shopper, say.

"Get me this in black now or get yourself a new job. I've had a bad day and I want what I want now or I will personally see to it that you shrivel up and disappear in the wind like dust."

That did it. I snapped. I slammed open my dressing room stall wearing only my bra and underwear, but I didn't care because I was a runner now and even though I was over forty, I looked damn good.

"Leave her alone, Mindy." I said in a low, but super fierce and threatening tone.

Mindy turned and OMG, and I mean OMG times twenty, she smiled at me.

"Candy, oh my gosh, what are the odds of you and me in here together?" She said, and I'm not kidding you, SHE WAS NICE! She turned to the personal shopper and said, "I'm sorry. I have a migraine. I didn't mean to be a bitch."

I could not believe it. The universe had flipped. Mindy Klein was putting on a nice act just for me.

"Candy, I think it's time you and I bury the hatchet."

"Um, Mindy, are you kidding me?"

"Come on, we used to be best friends. Remember how we used to come here and shop together. This is like old times."

"You fucked my husband. You took my house, my swing, my maid. You stole my life."

"Ah, come on. You should thank me. I did you a favor. Look at you now. You're a real estate agent. If I didn't ruin your life, you wouldn't have found your true calling. We should be friends again. I'll go into real estate with you. Oh, Candy, we'll have so much fun. It'll be just like the old days. Together we can become the top real estate team in Calabasas and just think how popular we'd be if we did. Everyone would be talking about us."

"Mindy, I'm already the top real estate agent in Calabasas."

"Just think where you'd be if you teamed up with me? You could be the top real estate agent in the country."

The words "true calling" kept ringing in my ears. I loved real estate, but it wasn't my true calling. I thought back to Angelina Jolie walking in Namibia, the crazy woman in Beverly Hills who didn't have shoes, the gang members who couldn't afford lunch and the eulogy I gave at Barry's funeral.

"Mindy, stay away from me or I'll have Rose put a gypsy curse on you."

"You're so stupid. A gypsy curse is only for men."

"Don't call me stupid. My name is Candy." I grabbed my purse and walked out of the dressing room, real dramatic. When I hit the shopping floor, everyone turned and looked at me, helping me realize that I forgot to put on my clothes. I turned around immediately and rushed back into the dressing room where Mindy stood laughing at me with a sneer. I went inside my dressing room, slammed the door, and got dressed quickly before rushing out as fast as I could.

I drove home with a car so full of shopping bags

that I had to hold one of them outside the window and use side streets instead of the freeway so I could drive slowly. When I got home, I ordered a delivery of a gallon of vodka and a gallon of sweet and sour mix from the liquor store around the corner, sat on the floor with all my shopping bags, got real drunk and called Jack.

"Jack. It's Candy." I blubbered into the phone.

"You all right? You're slurring your words."

"No." I started crying. "I'm not all right. I'm really, really, really, really, really shallow again. Oh, my God, how could this happen to me, again?"

"Candy, are you home?"

"Yes, alone with bags of designer clothes I spent $23,000 dollars on today and… and... and…" I started crying really hard again. "I don't even want them now!"

"Stay put. Don't drive. I'm coming over."

When Jack got to my apartment, I was watching a Save the Children pledge show surrounded by expensive clothes that could have fed those children for years. I let him in, then tripped over a Nordstrom's shopping bag and fell to the ground.

"Easy there." Jack said as he lifted me up and helped me walk to the couch.

"Can I make you a drink?" I asked him in between hiccups.

"No thanks."

"Good because I'm out of vodka." I lifted up the empty gallon so he could see.

"Did you drink all of that?" Jack asked.

"I wish. Only half. The rest I spilled."

"Oh, that explains the smell in here." Jack said.

I looked over at a little boy on the TV running around in shorts, bare feet and a big belly. He looked straight into the camera with his gorgeous brown eyes and I started crying.

"Candy, what's wrong?"

"He's hungry." I said and pointed to the TV.

"Okay."

"I have to get out of here, Jack."

"Where do you need to go?" He asked.

And I started crying so hard again so that the word came out in long drawn out parts, "Aaaaaaa. Frick. Ca…ca….ca."

"Did you say Africa?" I heard him ask, but his voice sounded distant and far away, and the room started spinning. I couldn't keep my eyes open, so I was real surprised the next morning when I woke up in bed with a bitch of a hangover and walked into my kitchen to get coffee and saw Jack.

"AAAAHHHHHH!" I screamed.

"Good morning." Jack said as he handed me a cup of coffee.

And then I realized, if I finally made love to the man of my dreams the night before, that I didn't remember any of it. I didn't remember our first kiss. I didn't remember what he looked like naked, which I'd been hoping to see since the day I saw him in the Levi jeans. What a nightmare!

"Did we?"

"No, we did not. You passed out, so I put you in bed. You were snoring and making this really horrible sound so I was afraid to leave you alone. I didn't want you to choke on your own vomit."

"You're not the first guy to say that to me." I said, and then cringed. That was something I should have said to myself with my inner voice.

"Are you still planning to go to Aaaaaaa…frick… ca…ca….ca?"

"What did you just say?"

"Remember. Aaaaaa. Frick. Ca…ca…ca?" Jack said again while laughing.

"Oh, Africa. I thought you were losing it for a minute, but you're just making fun of me, right."

"You catch on fast."

251

"I'm going to Africa just as soon as my hangover's gone."

"Because if you're serious, I have a friend helping a few orphanages in Namibia. I'm sure he'd love help."

"Did you say Namibia?"

"Yes."

"OMG!"

"Okay, whatever that means."

I explained to Jack how unbelievable it was since it was the video of Angelina Jolie in Namibia that got me so confused and wanting to feed starving children back when Mindy and I were BFF's and I was still with Tom. I laid it all out for him, how Pretty Woman was my favorite movie and how it stared Richard Gere and how Randolf, the spiritualist I thought was nuts said I would be respected like the Dalai Lama and how Richard Gere and the Dalai Lama were like BFF's and how he gave me the charm that had the quote from the Dalia Lama on it and how now he was telling me he had a friend doing work with orphans in Namibia!

"You put it into the universe." Jack said. "Doesn't surprise me a bit." Obviously, Jack had read The Secret. "You'd have to cover your travel cost."

"I'm in." I said and that was it. My next goal was set.

Jack left. I showered, drank another pot of coffee and headed to the mall to return all the clothes I bought.

"Is there a reason you're returning all $23,000 of new clothes you bought last night?" The rude manager asked me, as if I was a horrible person.

"I'm sorry. Really I am." And I was because I know the sales team works part on commission. "But I need this money to go to Africa to help orphans."

"Yeah, right." The manager said. "That's a new one."

After the mall, I went to the office and called Lisa

Rinna. I explained that I was taking a leave of absence to go to Africa and couldn't sell her house right away.

"Oh, this is so exciting. You're going to Africa." Lisa said. "Anyone who's anyone does work in Africa. You're such a fashionista, Candy. You know, Harry and I are celebrities and getting involved in a charity that helps suffering children would be great for our pubic image."

"Did you say pubic image?" I asked.

"Oh I did. I'm so embarrassed. I meant public image."

We had a laugh at that and she said she could wait for me to return. The house she was selling was a rental and this way she could give the tenants a few more months' notice before she kicked them out onto the street.

When I got off the phone, I erased my white board and wrote one word on it.

AFFRICA!

I sat back and read it over and over again, and I was in this real happy place until Chad, a gay agent who was always rude to me because I didn't want him to be my gay husband, walked by and said, "There's only one f in Africa."

"I know that." I said to him, but as soon as he walked away, I quickly rewrote Africa on my board and from that moment on, I set out to achieve that goal. I got my passport, shots, shopped for khaki wear, and of course, a bandana like Angelina Jolie wore in Namibia.

Within one week, I was hugging Kelly, Rose and Henry goodbye as I got into Jack's car and we drove to the LAX International Airport. We hit traffic of course, which is so L.A., so by the time we got to LAX we had to run inside the airport and I checked in just in time. Passengers were already boarding the plane, so we raced to the gate and got there just as they were announcing last call to board British Airways Flight 0278. This wasn't leaving me any time for a romantic goodbye kiss from Jack. I'd been hoping to get one ever since he offered to take me to the airport, but there we were without any time.

Then Jack leaned in close to me. I thought this was going to be the big moment between us, our big whopper of a first kiss, but he looked at me sort of odd and said, "Candy Katz."

"Yes." I said and swallowed so hard that I heard a loud gulp in my head.

"You're always a surprise."

"Is that good?"

"Yes. Very good." He said with a smile and then, if you can believe it, he walked away.

"Jack!" I called out. "Don't forget…." He looked back at me. "Don't forget…" I said again and it was right then I realized I totally completely loved this man who had never even felt me up or kissed me or inappropriately slapped me on my ass as I walked by him.

"Don't forget what?"

"I forget." I yelled back, but I lied. I didn't forget. I just didn't have the courage to say what I wanted to say.

"See, you're always a surprise, Candy Katz!" He yelled and then waved one last time before disappearing in the crowd.

"Don't forget that I love you." I whispered to myself.

"Miss, it's time to board." A flight attendant said to me.

I turned around. The place was empty. Everyone was already on the plane. I was about to miss my flight to my true calling. I rushed inside and started a 36 hour flight that took me directly to Windhoak, the capital city of Namibia, after a change of flights in London at the Heathrow airport.

Jack's friend, Frank, was meeting me. We had

emailed each other about my visit. He told me to look for the biggest black man I could find wearing a Hawaiian print shirt. I explained that I was only able to stay for three weeks, because I had to get back for Kelly's high school graduation and that I needed to sell more houses because I was a getting divorced from a hundred percent asshole who cheated on me with my best friend and hardly gives me enough money to live on. Then I emailed an apology for cussing since he was a church worker, so I figured that offended him. Frank emailed me back that even Christians curse from time to time and that it sounds like my ex is a hundred percent asshole. Right then, I knew I was going to love hanging out with Frank in Africa.

After forty hours of grueling travel, my plane touched down at the Windhoek International Airport which is half an hour from the city. When I peeled my butt off the seat, my legs were wobbly and my head hurt. I had a traveling hangover.

As I got off the plane, I looked around. The airport was in the middle of a wide flat area that looked like the dessert surrounding Las Vegas, but this wasn't Las Vegas, I was finally in Africa. Oh, my God! I was so excited, even though I was exhausted from sitting in a plane and irritable because I'd hardly slept.

I headed into the small airport lounge and standing in a bright red and white Hawaiian shirt was Frank, a three hundred pound man smiling ear to ear and holding a sign that said "Looking for Candy Katz."

"Candy." He said to me and gave me a big hug. He was so soft and cuddly, it was like sinking into the waterbed my mom had in the 70's.

"How'd you know it was me?" I asked. He let go of me and took my bags.

"Jack emailed me that you were the prettiest girl in the world."

Oh, my God. Oh, my God. Oh, my God.

"Jack said that? Really, he said that?" I asked as we

255

walked through the airport.

"Uh, huh. Said you got him in a pickle? Hasn't been the same since the day he met you running on the street."

"He's never said anything to me about being in a pickle."

"Oh, no, maybe it was a secret. Pretend I never said a word, but just between you and me, Jack's got it grooving for you."

Unbelievable! Now that I was half a world away, I finally knew that Jack had feelings for me.

After getting my luggage, we headed outside into Frank's beat up white van and he drove me into Windhoek where I was staying the night in a hotel to shower and rest after the traveling.

"Get some rest tonight, 'cause starting tomorrow, you're gonna be busy twenty-four hours a day." Frank said.

"I'm kinda nervous."

"Don't be. Just kids. Same everywhere you go in the world."

We drove into Windhoek a half hour later, but it was nothing like I'd imagined. I was thinking it would be full of shacks and shoeless kids running all over the streets and goats and chickens and dogs and cats running around like an Animals Gone Wild video, but it was nothing like that. It was a city with tall buildings. It was clean, and hardly anyone walked the streets.

"I was expecting Africa to be a little dirtier." I told Frank.

"It doesn't all look like this." He told me. "You'll see tomorrow."

Tomorrow he was taking me to the township of Katatura, a half an hour outside of Windhoek, where the orphanage was.

"Where are all the people?"

"This country's been hit real hard by AIDS. Most

of the kids at the orphanage, their parents died of AIDS."

"Oh, my God." I told him. "Oh, I'm sorry, I shouldn't say God like that in front of you since you're a church worker."

"It's okay, Candy. God's not keeping a close tab on stuff like that. He's more interested in other things that you do with your life."

"Thank, God." I said and Frank laughed.

"Candy, you're a funny girl. Kids are gonna love you. People ever call you Candy Cane?"

"It was my stage name when I was a stripper."

"You were a stripper?"

"When I was younger. I never hit the big time and played in Vegas or you know, got into making porn films. I got married and had a kid instead."

"You took a better path." Frank said and laughed.

"Yeah, if you're gonna have sex all the time it might as well be with your spouse."

"That's what I hear. Wouldn't know though, I'm a priest."

I spit the swig of Evian water I was drinking out the window and luckily the window was down.

"You're a priest?" I asked.

"Yep."

"So, you're like, Father Frank."

"That's what they call me."

"And I'm talking to you about stripping and porn films and sex."

"Uh, huh."

"I just might be going to hell." I said and held my forehead in my hand.

Father Frank just laughed. "Don't be so hard on yourself, Candy. You've got too good of a heart to go to hell."

We pulled up to the Hotel Furstenhof, which was like a five start hotel. What in the heck was going on in

Africa? This was so not what I expected. Where was my shack? This hotel was so awesome, I'd go there for a spa day anytime.

Frank stayed with me as I checked in, and as we walked to my room, he gave me a lot of warnings. "Stay in the hotel. The streets have a lot of criminals who will try to rob you. No one has any money here, so they're looking for a woman like you to take advantage of. Don't take a taxi. Taxi drivers will drive you off and rob you. Some men might put a knife to your neck and take your purse." Father Frank said.

"Jeez, it's like I'm going into South Central L.A." I said.

"No. It's much worse. I'll be back later tomorrow morning. I have to go back to Katatura tonight."

"You will come back?" I asked him as a hotel worker opened my hotel room door and placed my bags inside. I was feeling a little scared after all his warnings. I didn't want to become one of those tourists you never see again.

He just laughed. "Kids know all about you coming tomorrow. Can't wait to meet woman they're sure is gonna be as sweet as her name. "

"Oh. That is so sweet. Did they really say that or are you just pulling my leg."

"You tell me tomorrow, when you see their happy faces. Now get a lot of sleep. You're going to need it."

After Father Frank left, I took a nice long bubble bath in my five star hotel room designed by a designer and thought about how wonderful it was that Jack Drake was in a pickle over me. Why didn't he just come out with it? Why'd he keep it a secret for so long? My personal growth thing was on its way. I was in Africa, after all. It could have been interrupted for a few nights of raw passionate sex with him before I left.

After my bubble bath, room service delivered my dinner and I ate it on my balcony that overlooked a beautiful pool and I could see the skyline of the city.

None of those late night TV shows ever showed this part of Africa. I didn't even think they knew how to build skyscrapers, but here they were, right outside my hotel balcony. The city of Windhoek was so nice, that I was starting to wonder if I should be back in Van Nuys helping hungry people there instead of Africa.

Satisfied with my delicious dinner, I hit the sack thinking about Jack. Because I was so exhausted, I was out in seconds so it seemed like only a few hours since he left when Father Frank knocked on my door the next morning. I opened the door and standing there with him was an adorable little boy.

"Good morning, Candy. This is Kandali."

The little boy had big brown eyes and seemed scared of me, so I bent down to speak to him.

"Kandali, it's nice to meet you. How old are you?" I asked.

"Five." Kandali said with the sweetest little voice and at that moment I fell in love with him. Kandali stood behind Father Frank, holding his pant legs. I reached into my bag where I had hard candies I'd stolen on the airplane, but it's not really stealing when you spend over four thousand dollars for a round trip airline ticket.

"Kandali, my name is Candy." I told him and handed him the mint.

His face lit up. He took the candy out of my hand and in the sweetest little voice I've ever heard he said, "Father Frank, Kandali know Candy lady." And giggled.

Father Frank and I laughed. "Ready to go?"

I was ready to go. I'd slept twelve hours and had forgotten the long grueling plane ride.

I checked out of the hotel and as we drove to Katatura with Kandali sitting between us on the front seat of the van not taking his eyes off me, Father Frank talked and talked about what I was getting myself into.

"Katatura's a shantytown, one of the poorest

townships in the country so you need to brace yourself." Father Frank said, and I didn't see him laughing so much this morning. "You'll be doing a homestay with Tuhafeni. She's lives next door to the orphanage and houses our volunteers. She's an older woman. She has one son who went off to be a fisherman on the coast and her two daughters both died from sickness when they were young. She makes her living by selling boiled goats head out of a pot.

"Boiled goats head sound disgusting."

"It's good." He said, "And the tongue's the best."

When we pulled into the township, my eyes began to tear up. I thought I was poor living in a one bedroom bug infested apartment in the Valley, but this was ridiculous. I looked around and saw metal and wood shacks, and dirty kids running around in the streets barefoot. We drove through dusty unpaved streets. People were selling clothes, shoes, and food. One man was getting his head shaved in a chair out on the street underneath a sign selling a head shave. I was definitely a long way from Zen Spa.

We headed down a road where a group of men and women were dancing in the street to music that sort of sounded like reggae mixed with dance music. They were blocking the road and Father Frank drove straight towards them, almost as if he didn't see them, and I got real nervous.

"Is that a gang?" I asked.

"No, no. It's a shebeen. It's like a bar someone's set up in their house for the day. Lots of fun."

The group of people started waving to Father Frank and calling out his name as they separated to make room for our van to drive through. Father Frank slowed to a near stop in the middle of them, to shout hellos and shake a few hands. The people were dressed in colorful clothes which was good because all stylist will tell you that if you're depressed, and who wouldn't be if they lived here, wearing color will boost your mood. They were dancing and having fun. I kind of wanted to jump out of the car and join them, but instead I stuck my head out of the window and waved. Some men started whistling at me.

"Candy lady crazy." Kandali said to Father Frank and laughed.

And as we drove through the group, and I looked out at the crowd, something dawned on me. I was not only the only white person in Katatura, I was the only white women with bleached blonde hair and a breast augmentation.

"How come I'm the only white person here?" I asked.

"Whites don't come here. They're too afraid. Katatura's got a reputation of being dangerous."

"Really? Am I in danger?"

"No, just don't go on any shebeens by yourself." Father Frank said and laughed.

Everyone here laughed, and I just didn't get it. Life was looking pretty miserable to me in Katatura so what was there to be happy about?

We drove on to the orphanage which was just a shack that'd been extended to have three rooms. Father Frank told me it was an unofficial orphanage. Dakarai, the house mom, got tired of seeing stray kids walking on the streets and took them in. As we neared the orphanage, Father Frank honked his horn and out of the shack came a beautiful woman and four little girls, and then from all around the neighborhood children ran towards us. We pulled to a stop. As I got out of the van, the children touched my hair and the skin on my arms. The woman walked up to me and took me into a great big hug.

"I am Dakarai." She said.

"Oh, hello. I'm Candy Katz." I said.

I felt overwhelmed, and needed to take a deep breath, but Dakarai was still giving me a long tight hug.

"Welcome." Dakarai said, and gestured for me to come inside.

I followed her into her home and a group of children came with us. She pointed to a ratty chair in the corner. "Sit, please." Dakarai said.

I sat down. The children lined up in front of me in order from youngest to oldest. Dakarai pointed at each one and said their name. "These are the children. Rach, Zina, Nailah, Femi, Saidah, Paulo, Femi, Kesa, Sukutai, and Kandali." All the children were smiling and happy. Only two, Katatura and Zina, had shoes to wear. The kids were all between three and twelve years old.

"Hello." I said to the children.

"Hello." They said back together. "Welcome."

"They practiced your greeting all morning." Dakarai said in her beautiful accented voice. She was a large and beautiful woman, with a peaceful looking face.

After the greeting, Dakarai told the children to go outside and play. They listened to her right away. I don't think once Kelly listened to me the first time I asked her to do something.

Dakarai showed me the three rooms of her home. She only had room for six children, but couldn't turn away the three that came to her doorstep. One was Kandali's mother who was dying of AIDS and had no family to care for him and the other two came to her asking for food. With the help of Father Frank and his church, she'd been able to feed and clothe them, and made it a priority to school them in the day as much as she could. I asked her where her husband was and she told me she did not know. He went out one night and never returned. That was eight years ago and since then, she's dedicated herself to helping children because she got tired of seeing them walking the streets homeless and hungry.

After Dakarai showed me the house and explained that she needed help cooking, bathing the children, making meals, getting fresh water, and giving them hugs and kisses, Father Frank walked me next door to the place I was to do a homestay. There are no hotels in Katatura, so if you have to sleep there, you have to sleep in someone's house. I was doing a home stay with Tuhafeni, an older woman who was missing many teeth, but still, when she smiled, she was beautiful.

"I'll be going now." Father Frank told me after I got settled at Tuhafeni's house.

"You can't leave me here alone. I thought you were staying with me. I… I… think I'm going to have a heart attack. I don't know these people."

"Candy, I live on the other side of Katatura. There are many orphanages like this that I help. You'll be fine. I'll check in once a week, and if you need me sooner, have Dakarai send a boy to get me."

He gave me a super big bear hug, and oh, my God, he left! After telling me to be careful in Katatura because of the crime, he left me, the only white person, alone in the middle of the shantytown with a woman missing her teeth and a house full of children with only one woman in charge. I almost peed in my pants.

Tuhafeni showed me my tiny room that had a clean bed and one small table to set my clothes on. She was boiling a goat's head and offered me the tongue because it is the best part, but I told her I was still full from breakfast. She laughed and told me soon I'd eat the tongue, the ears and the brain when I got hungry enough. I laughed and told her I didn't think so.

After settling in with Tuhafeni, I began working for Dakarai. In the morning I'd help her feed and dress the children and give them reading lessons. I cleaned the house. I scrubbed clothes in buckets full of brown soapy water. I helped prepare meals. But most important, I sat and played with the children and gave them a hug when they fell and helped referee when they would get into fights. Kandali always stayed near me, asking me questions about America, helping me remember the children's names and setting up a meal.

"You be my momma, Candy Cane?" He said to me one day.

"Oh, Kandali." I was just about to tell him that I couldn't be his momma, but just couldn't. Instead I gave him a big hug.

"Momma Candy Cane." He called me and smiled.

I tickled him in his tummy.

"Momma Candy Cane." I said in agreement.

The days flew by because there was not a minute to spare. Never in my life had I worked so hard, even when I practiced six hours a day to achieve the longest spin on the pole, followed up with a flip into the splits down on the floor. I couldn't imagine working this hard every day for years like Dakarai.

"It is my life now." She told me one evening as we sat outside after a long day listing to the laughter and music coming from a shebeen down the road. Tuhafeni had just left with a pot of goat's head to sell there and gave us each a piece of tongue on her way. I had gotten hungry since I came, and just like she said, I now ate the tongue and the ears, and even tried the brain.

"She is my angel." Dakarai said about Tuhafeni after she walked on to the shebeen. "She's old and cannot work hard, but she helps me feed the children."

She went on and on about how wonderful Tuhafeni was to her. How she listened to her cry at night when she thought she couldn't take the pressure anymore. And she said Father Frank was a saint. If he didn't bring her supplies and help get the four of the nine children who were HIV positive the proper medical care, the children would not survive.

That night was the first of many nights where Dakarai and I had sat outside, looking up at the stars and talking. I told her my life story, all about my daughter, my failed marriage, how I had it all and it wasn't enough.

"My people have a saying." Dakarai said. "Only the strong survive."

I thought back to my enormous house in the Oaks, my Nordstroms shopping trips, my days lounging by the pool at the club and tried to figure out what she was meant. I wasn't strong. I was the biggest wimp in Calabasas. So wimpy that Mindy was able to kick my butt out the city, out of my marriage and out of my house in the Oaks.

"I don't know about that Dakarai." I said and started crying. "I'm just a big wimpy fool sometimes. Everyone bosses me around. I'm always the one to get picked on. I'm not strong at all." And there I was pouring out my feelings, and you know what she did, she started laughing at me. "It's not funny." I told her.

"You don't see yourself." She told me and would not stop laughing. "Candy, you need to have fun. You've been working too hard. Let's go to the shebeen." She told me.

"What about the children?"

"I'll have Joseph watch them."

Joseph was an older man who lived three shacks down. He had a crush on Dakarai, but she told me he was too old for her. He was only 52, but Namibian's don't live to get real old because life is so hard.

We walked by his shack. She pounded on his door. "Joseph! Come watch the babies." She yelled and walked on. I followed her, nervous.

"You sure he's there?"

"He's there." And I looked back behind us and Joseph came out of his shack and walked down to Dakarai's, and sat in a ratty chair she had outside her front door.

"Do you have a boyfriend?" She asked.

"No, not really, but there's this guy I'm in love with and when I get back home, I think I'm gonna tell him.

"Good. Life is short." She said, and she was right. Life was short. Here I was over forty and in Namibian years that wasn't good. I decided right then, that when I came back home, I was going to tell Jack exactly how I felt about him.

We reached the shebeen which was three streets over. It was easy to find. We just followed the sound of reggae music and laughter booming out of the house. Inside people were dancing. There was a bar at one end where we got beers and found Tuhafeni selling her goat's head out of her pot. There was a jukebox on the wall and there were toddlers and kids dancing there too. The people all stared at me and at first I was scared, but Dakarai introduced me as the angel Father Frank brought to help her with the children. I was treated with respect after this. We had beer and danced for hours. No one cared how they looked or how they acted, only about having a good time.

I took a break and sat down at a table in the corner of the room where Tuhafeni was selling meat from her pot of boiled goat's head. Together we watched Dakarai dance with a man who twirled her around.

"Do you know what Dakarai means?" She yelled at me across the table.

"No." I yelled back.

"Happiness." Tuhafeni said, then took her pot and left.

Happiness. That was what the people in Katatura had, even though they didn't have much of anything else.

Two days after that night, I stood outside Dakarai's home with the children, Tuhafeni and Dakarai, and watched Father Frank's dirty white van rush up the road, leaving a trail of dust behind him. I was all choked up about going and every second was about to cry. I bent down and gave Kandali a big hug goodbye.

"I'll think of you all the time."

"Nobody thinks of us after they leave." Kandali said.

"Kandali, I'll never stop thinking of you." I told him and that wasn't a lie, because for the rest of my life,

I would never stop thinking about them. "I'll send a message to Father Frank to give to you so you know."

"What will it be?"

"You'll see? It will remind you of me."

"Momma Candy Cane."

"That's right. Momma Candy Cane."

Father Frank honked his horn and came to a stop. I picked up my bag, gave Dakarai another hug goodbye, and I could see tears in her eyes which made me tear up.

"Only the strong survive." She said and I shook my head yes.

All the children were screaming Father Frank, Father Frank, and swarming around him as he got out of his van passing out pieces of red licorice. I gave Tuhafeni and the other children hugs goodbye, and soon we drove off. I cried all the way to the airport.

"Thinkin' you're in a pickle there, girl." Father Frank said and tapped me warmly on my shoulder. I laughed for a second, because I was in a pickle. I already missed my new friends, and I'd just left them ten minutes ago.

At the airport, Father Frank gave me a big hug. "Been nice meeting you, Candy."

"You too. Oh, I promised Kandali I'd send him something, so watch for my package okay?" I told him.

"You got it, Candy. Now go on home to Jack. I'm gonna email him that if he doesn't get out of his pickle, I'm gonna leave the priesthood and snap you up for myself."

The plane ride home was as exhausting as the plane ride there. By the time I reached LAX, I thought my head was going to explode. I'd developed a head cold, and that mixed with the pressure inside my head made my head feel like it was going to split apart. Rose was supposed to pick me up from the airport, but when I came inside the terminal, she wasn't there. I checked my watch. Our plane was on time. I couldn't believe no one was there to meet me.

Then in the distance, I saw him.

JACK!

Walking towards me, and oh, my, God, he was wearing Levi Jeans with a white t-shirt and work boots.

I wanted to eat him up right then and there!

"Jack? What are you doing here?" I said, in my stuffed up voice.

"Rose's having car problems." He gave me a hug. "Welcome home."

I love being in your arms. Kiss me, Jack. Kiss me now, for the love of God.

"Aaaachoo!" I sneezed real loud and blew my nose in a tissue.

"You don't sound too good." Jack said and backed away.

Damn it! This man is never going to kiss me.

"Sorry. I have a head cold." I admitted. Jack picked up my carry-on bag and the muscles on his tanned arm bulged and I wanted to die, he was so handsome.

When we made it home, Rose, Henry and Kelly were waiting there with a welcome home party set up in my apartment. It was so sweet. We had the best time as I told them about Katatura, the people I met, the children, Dakarai and staying with Tuhafeni. I told them about the poverty, but also the happiness. And how everyone looks out for each other and about my special friendship with Kandali, the little boy who stole my heart. Then I started crying and couldn't stop. I told them I was sorry for ruining their great party, and they all told me not to be silly and that I was sick and must be exhausted so I should get some rest, especially since the next day was Kelly's graduation.

I did what they said, I took a long shower and went straight to bed and didn't wake up for twelve hours, but when I did, I was still depressed. I almost couldn't handle how terrible I felt having left Dakarai alone with all those children. I felt ridiculous thinking this way, because what on earth was I going to do, move to a slum in Africa? But I missed them all, I did, and I couldn't stop thinking about Kandali and how sure he was that I would forget him. That was impossible. He was unforgettable.

I got dressed and went to a warehouse store. I bought a case of extra-large candy canes and went to a postal office and had them sent by Federal Express to Father Frank for the children. Inside the package, I put a note that said "Love Momma Candy Cane" then rushed back home to get ready for the graduation. I was going to see Tom and Mindy and all the Calabasas mom's so I had to look good.

Two hours later, Rose, Henry and I drove to the Calabasas High school to watch Kelly get her diploma. It was a gorgeous Southern California day and I was wearing a cute, off the rack dress that I didn't even know the brand name off, if you can believe it. I'd gone from living and dying by brand names, but after going to Africa it seemed sort of silly to be worried about such a thing.

We sat down in the bleachers. I was nervous about the ceremony, because I'd actually never been to a high school graduation before. This was a big deal. Kelly would be the first in a line of women from my side of the family to actually get their high school diploma.

"Thanks for coming with me." I said to Rose, while blowing my nose and sneezing three times. Of all the days to not want to have a head cold, this was it. My daughter was graduating high school and I was about to be seen in public for the first time next to my ex-husband and my ex-best friend. What a nightmare.

"It's what best friends are for." Rose said. "Besides, got to see my girl get the certif. Ain't never been to one of these high school graduations."

"Me either."

269

I looked over at the gate to the field and there they were, Tom and Mindy, dressed in the perfect matching outfit that I was sure Mindy coordinated. Tom had on, if you can believe this, the suit he wore for our recommitment ceremony with a light periwinkle button up shirt that was the same color as Mindy's dress. They looked stupid, I thought, and regretted all the times she made me color coordinate my tennis outfit with hers. Tom and Mindy climbed up the bleachers and I tried not to look at them, but OMG, they sat on the end of our row. Then, if you can believe this, Mindy leaned forward and scowled at me.

"That sister's got it in for us." Rose said.

"Just ignore her, pretty lady." Henry told me, but I couldn't help it, I leaned forward and scowled back at Mindy. Everyone in the stands were watching us since in Calabasas, the breakup of my marriage was as talked about as the breakup of Brad Pitt and Jennifer Anniston.

Lines of graduating students walked onto the field and I saw Kelly. I waved. "Kelly! Over here!" I yelled, and she looked up at me in the stands and for a minute I thought she was going to roll her eyes and look away and that I'd be real embarrassed in front of Tom and Mindy. But when she saw me, she smiled the biggest smile I've ever seen on my daughter's face, she waved and jumped up and down.

"Hi Mom! Hi Rose! Hi Henry!" She yelled to us. She kept looking up at me, smiling and waving, like she was super happy I was there.

"Rose?" I said.

"What?"

"I think my daughter loves me."

"Oh, hell, sugar girl, your daughter thinks you're the cat's meow. Now I'm not supposed to tell you this 'cause my sessions with Kelly are confidential, but let's face it, I'm not a real therapist so I'm not going to lose my license by telling you, but do you know what your daughter said to me when you were in Africa?"

"No."

"She told me that one day she wants to be just like you."

"She did?" My voice cracked. I was about to start crying, again.

"She did, Sugar. Now don't cry yet, you got to look good, honey. You're in a war right now." She eyed Mindy and Tom down on the other side of the bleacher. "That gypsy's still got it in for you."

I looked over. Tom was checking me out, and I saw Mindy smack him on the knee to get him to turn away.

The ceremony began and after a few speeches by the Valedictorians, they announced the special guest speaker, who turned out to be Anthony Robbins, the motivational speaker. I overheard two women in the bleacher in front of us say that Brad's father paid a fortune to have him speak at Brad's graduation. Anthony Robbins was so inspiring. His speech to the graduates was about what would make an extraordinary life, making five million dollars or being a good parent. He talked about figuring out what that is for you and then going for it. It seemed like Anthony Robbins was speaking directly to me. It was at that moment I remembered Kandali telling me that I would forget him.

"Rose." I whispered, then sneezed.

"Quiet, girl, this guy's good."

"Rose!" I said louder. The women in front of us turned around.

"What, sugar girl, can't you see I'm payin' attention?" Rose said, real loud.

"Keep it down, you too." Henry added, but Henry's never been one to talk quietly, even when he means too, so everyone turned around and looked at us, including Mindy was looking at me with her horrible scowling face. I had had enough. I just couldn't help myself. I stuck my tongue at her and everyone in the

271

stands, including Tom, cracked up.

"I'm going to start a charity to help the children of Katatura." I said with such confidence that I kind of wondered if it was me speaking.

"Sugar, that's coming from that flame I saw the first day I read you. Knew back then you were something special." Rose said and she reached over and hugged me real tight.

After the ceremony, I rushed down onto the field and gave Kelly a huge hug. "Kelly Bean, I'm so proud of you.' I told her.

"Thanks, Mom."

Brad walked by us. "Hey, Mrs. Katz."

"Hey, Brad."

"Lookin' good." Brad said, and lifted his Ray Ban shades and eyed me up and down, before walking off with a smirk on his face.

In the distance, I saw Mindy and Tom walking towards us, so I wanted to get out of there fast. "You're father and Mindy's coming. I'm going to get out of here so there's not a scene." I gave her a hug and said quietly in her ear so I didn't embarrass her. "Kelly. I love you."

I let go of her and started walking away when she yelled, "Mom!"

I turned. "What?"

"I love you, too." She said with a smile, and I almost had a heart attack. It was just about the best moment of my life. Then I turned around and things got even better. Coming right towards me was my knight in non-brand casual wear.

"Jack? What are you doing here?" I asked. He was holding a bouquet of roses. "Are those for me?"

"Um, no, for Kelly, actually, but you can have one, I guess." He said and pulled a rose out and handed it to me, and then handed Kelly the flowers.

"Thanks." I said.

"Candy, I have something to tell you and it can't

wait anymore." He looked real nervous.

Oh, my God. Oh, my God. Oh, my God!

"I love you." He said.

Yes! He loves me! He really, really loves me!

"Jack, how do you know if you love me? We haven't slept together. In fact, you've never even kissed me."

"Well then…." He said, and took me in his arms and kissed me long and hard right there in the middle of the field. I dropped my handbag, I dropped my rose, and if there weren't hundreds of people standing around cheering us on, I would have dropped my drawers.

The kiss ended. He stepped back. I was floating on air and could hardly move.

"Oh, please. I'm gonna be sick." I heard Mindy say off to the side.

I looked over at her. I was about to tell her to shove it in her nose, but this was Kelly's day and I didn't want to run it, so I just smiled and flipped her off.

CANDY LIVES SUPER-DUPER HAPPILY EVER AFTER THANKS TO GETTING SUPER-DUPER SCREWED BY TOM AND MINDY

CHAPTER TWELVE

Oh, my God, oh, my God. I can't believe this is actually happening to me. I'm on Oprah's Next Chapter. In all my life, I never thought I would be interviewed by Oprah.

As I listened to the opening, I realize I should have gone pee a second time when I had the chance.

"She went from rags to riches and then lost it all. Then she single handedly raised ten million dollars in one year to help feed starving children in Africa through her Candy Cane Food for Freedom Organization. She's made the cover of Time magazine, the cover of Playboy, and she's here with us today. Candy Katz."

The audience is clapping. For me!

"Welcome. Welcome." Oprah said.

"Thank you. Thank you."

"Let's just start with the cover of Time Magazine."

Oprah gestured to the back wall. I turned around and there I was, on a cover of Time Magazine in my blonde bob haircut on huge wall screen and with that bob, I looked so damn smart.

"Oh, my God." I said, and the crowd laughed and clapped.

"So, how did this all happen?" Oprah asked.

"Well, I was a wealthy housewife and my husband cheated with my best friend." The audience gasped. "I know. It was awful. I had no idea they were having an affair and I found them together on the day of my ex-best friend's husband's funeral. "

"No!" Oprah said.

"Yes!" I answered.

"Oh, no, it doesn't get any lower than that."

"I know." I said. "And suddenly I found myself broke and struggling to put my life back together after a terrible divorce where she got everything of mine."

"How'd that happen?"

"I signed a pre-nup."

"Oh."

"I was young. I didn't read it."

"Oh, girlfriends, let's all read the contracts before we sign them."

"But I look back on all that now and I'm grateful."

"You are?"

"Yeah, because even though I had a big beautiful house, the maid, the Mercedes, that I still have by the way 'cause I'm not giving up that car and it's paid for, and closets full of designer clothes and shoes, and all the time in the world to go shopping and play tennis and lounge by the pool, except for my wonderful daughter, Kelly, my life was empty. I was really, really, and I mean like really super shallow. I started thinking, I've lived half my life and I haven't done anything to help feed starving children."

"So you were called to start this organization, kind of like a priest gets a calling to go into the ministry?"

"I guess. I never really thought about it. Just one

275

day I started thinking there's got to be more to life than just shopping, and I got the urge to feed children. Go figure."

"Time magazine lists you as one of America's 100 most influential people this year. What do you think about that?"

"Amazing. I mean, I'm just doing what I love to do, and getting the cover of Time Magazine, while I'm excited about it, it's not why I do what I do."

"Your organization, Candy Cane Food for Freedom has in one year managed to raise twenty million dollars. How did you do that?"

"Well, five of that came from Hugh Heffner."

"You mean your spread in Playboy? I was going to get to that next, but turn around girlfriend." I turned around and there I was again on the back wall, on the cover of Playboy Magazine posing in a skimpy striped jumper and licking a candy cane.

"Yeah, they got a hold of me after the Time Magazine article and I agreed to do it since the money would go to good use. I mean, being an ex-stripper, I used to take my clothes off for five dollars so this was a no-brainer."

"So tell me about that? Being a stripper?"

"I was a stripper for years before I got married. My mother was a drug addict all during my childhood, so I needed to find a way to make money fast so I wouldn't starve. Candy Cane was my stage name. I had this act where I licked candy canes and put them in between…. Well, I won't go into details." I said and laughed.

"Yes, we can fill in the blanks." Oprah said. "Do you think that's what's behind your drive to help others?"

"Yeah, I guess because I've been there. I've had days where there's no food in the house and no money to buy any. I'm not that smart. I don't have a high school diploma and a lot of times I don't understand what people say to me, but I do know that if you set a goal and do everything in your power to reach that goal, that the universe will make it happen. I'm living proof that when life throws you salt, you can turn it into sugar."

"My producers and Candy put together a video so you can see how Candy Cane Food for Freedom gathers and distributes food."

On the wall behind us, they played the video of me in our food warehouse in Van Nuys.

"Hi everyone. I'm here in our warehouse that's located in Van Nuys, California. Standing next to me is my warehouse manager, Henry, and my shipping manager Carlo and behind us are all our warehouse workers."

You could see Carlo's gang members that I hired and some of the strippers that worked at my open houses, including some of the women from the real estate office who used to hate me, but now all want to be my friend. They were all wearing pink t-shirts that say Candy Cane Food for Freedom, even the guys, so they all were color coordinated.

I picked Van Nuys for our warehouse, because the rent was so much cheaper than anywhere in the valley and was close to an airport. Then I searched for Carlo and his disadvantaged gang members and asked them to work for Henry. They did since I bought them lunch one day when they were all really hungry.

"This is where all our food donations come in. First we sort the items into different bins." I walked over to the sorting area to show the large bins labeled dry goods and canned goods and candy canes. "This one here is for candy canes. People all over the world send in a few candy canes with their food donations because we like the children in Katatura to have a little sweet treat here and there. The kids just love it. Once the food is sorted, it's placed on a conveyor belt and moved to the packing and shipping area where it is boxed up, put on a van and driven to the Van Nuys airport that's right around the corner."

In the video, I hop inside the van and drive with the boxes over to the Van Nuys airport to the airplane loading dock.

"Here at the Van Nuys airport, it's immediately loaded on a plane for Windhoek, Africa."

The video then cuts to me at the unloading station at the Windhoek airport.

"Hi everyone. Now I'm at the Windhoek International Airport in Namibia. Here the boxes are unloaded into vans and driven to our distribution center in Katatura, a shantytown a half an hour out of the city where people are so poor, they live in shacks and thousands of orphaned children whose parents have died from AIDS are struggling to survive."

The video shows me driving up in a van to our distribution center in Katatura.

"Here the boxes are unloaded, unpacked and distributed by our workers to hundreds of people each day. "

On the video, there is a long line of people waiting to be handed a bag of food.

"Now I'd like to introduce you to a woman whose name, Dakarai , which stands for happiness. "

The cameras follow me as I walk down the road to Dakarai's home, and a large group of kids follows me.

"A widow, Dakarai got tired of seeing so many homeless children wondering the streets, so she started taking them in one at a time, not knowing how she was going to feed or clothe them, but with the help of Father Frank, a priest dedicated to helping the needy here in Katatura, for years she managed. When I first came to Katatura, I worked for Dakarai in her home, helping to feed, bathe and teach the children reading and writing. I was so inspired by her that I came back to America and knew I had to do something to help her."

I stop in front of a large building named "The Candy Cane Orphanage."

"So I came home and started Candy Cane Food for Freedom, and with the proceeds, built this orphanage which Dakarai runs today."

Dakarai and Father Frank and Tuhafani are standing in front of the orphanage with Kandali.

"This is Dakarai, Father Frank and this is the Candy Cane Orphanage. This is Kandali, the little boy who told me everyone forgets about them after they leave Katatura, and was my inspiration for Candy Cane Food for Freedom." Me and everyone in the video yelled goodbye and waved.

The video ended. The camera went back to Oprah.

"Fantastic. So I understand, you went out to strip clubs all across America and asked strippers to donate to your organization?"

"I did. Strippers, housewives…"

"And you've started a trend of women doing their own nails and donating the money they would have spent on a manicure to help feed the hungry?"

"Yes. I just asked for their help and tried to make it as painless as possible. I explained, that if they just took the money they used to get their acrylic nails done and donated that, they could feed five children a year. So women have been doing their nails themselves, plucking their eyebrows instead of going to the salon and getting them professionally waxed, then donating that money. Women have been wearing their hair in a short bob like mine instead of getting hair extensions and then donating that money. It's been amazing."

After the commercial break, Oprah had my spiritual advisors Rose and Randolf on to explain how I had come to them after my divorce looking for spiritual guidance and that they saw something in me, a fire of sorts that made them know, that I was going to do something amazing with my life.

"Did you suspect any of this?" Oprah asked me.

"No. I was just trying to figure out a way to get out of my cockroach infested apartment. I had no idea when Randolf said that I would be respected like that Dalai Lama that this was in the cards.

"Well, we have a friend of the Dalai Lama who heard you were coming on the show and wanted to say hello."

And then, if you can believe it, calling in on the phone was Richard Gere. Yikes! He read all about my story in Playboy Magazine and how Pretty Woman was my favorite movie and how Randolf told me I would be respected like the Dalai Lama if I kept it real, and how at the time, I'd never even heard of the Dalai Lama and how funny he thought that was. He wanted, he told me, to thank me personally for helping others. I honestly could hardly talk.

"Oh, my God. Thank you. Is this a dream?" I asked Oprah.

It wasn't a dream. This had actually become my life. I was respected. I was no longer shallow, and most importantly, I was really, really, super-duper happy.

After the show, money and food started pouring in and I opened a wing of the charity that gave food to hungry kids in America after Carlo's suggested I should feed some of the hungry children in Van Nuys. I worked six months out of the year in real estate, and pledged thirty percent of all my earnings to be given to my organization.

Jack and I got married in city hall and Kelly was my Maid of Honor. She opted not to get a breast augmentation after her graduation and instead enrolled in the Peace Corps and took off to Eastern Europe to work as a young development volunteer.

I moved into Jack's small house on the Calabasas Lake, settled into my new life and on some days, while lounging on the deck and looking at the lake and the ducks floating around, I'd even forget about how Mindy always called me an idiot or that Tom never looked me in the eye when I talked to him.

I got an email from Katie, who moved her family to

India with the profit she made from the sale of her house that she heard from Tatonka, who heard from Hunter, who heard from Charlotte, who heard from Samantha that Tom and Mindy were having problems, but I didn't care anymore. I was just so happy that the two of them were out of my life. I was thinking this very thing when I heard that voice.

"Candy!"

It was Mindy!

And she was calling my name!

I sat up, lifted my cheap sunglasses and looked out in the water. Mindy was rowing a small fishing boat towards our deck.

"Candy, I need to talk to you!" She yelled, and stood up in the boat, but then lost her balance and the boat tipped over into the water. "Aaaahhhh! So gross." She screamed.

I watched her flop around in the filthy water. She tried getting back in the boat over and over, but couldn't. I started laughing and couldn't stop. She swam over and climbed onto my deck, out of breath and panting.

"Mindy? What are you doing here?"

"Tom left me for a Mexican."

"You mean Mexican-American?"

"No. I mean Mexican. He went to Mexico and is living with a wealthy Mexican businesswoman he's been sleeping with. He's been skimming from his company and it's gone under. He took all his money and headed to Mexico for the Mexican and left me. I'm ruined. You've won. I mean, look at you. Who would have thought an idiot like you would make something of yourself?"

"I know. I still don't believe it some days." I said and then realized she got me again. She just called me stupid and I was still too stupid to catch it. "And don't call me an idiot." I added once I realized it.

"Whatever." Mindy said. "It doesn't matter anymore. Nothing matters. My life is over, again. Now I'm going to have to find some sucker to manipulate so I can take his money. It's exhausting."

"Yeah, I bet." I said, because you know, it really did take a lot of effort to be sneaky. You had act like you liked someone when you didn't, sleep with men who looked like Fred Flintstone and smelled like salami. I kind of felt bad for Mindy a little.

"Hey, Mindy, I'm curious. How'd you manage to turn everyone against me?"

"I used a voodoo doll and a gypsy spell. Then I just did the normal female things, like talking behind your back. That seemed to work the best. It was really pretty easy to screw you over so bad, but hey, look at you now. Maybe I was the best thing that ever happened to you."

"You know, Mindy, with your brains you could do some good in the world if you wanted to."

"I know, but I really don't want to."

And then the most miraculous thing happened. There was a gap in our conversation. Me and Mindy never had gaps in our conversations. It wasn't one of those inner peace feelings between us, it was one of those, well there's nothing more to say things between us. Right then I just knew it was time to kick her to the curb.

"Well, anyway, you have to get out of my life, so go on, get back on your boat and row back to wherever it is that you came from."

"Ah, seriously?

"Seriously."

"I've got nowhere to go. Tom sold the house right out from under me."

"Go stay with one of your friends."

"I don't have any friends anymore. They all cut their hair into bobs and took off their acrylic nails to be just like you. They all hate me."

"Mindy, we can't be friends again."

"Look, Candy, I know I screwed you over pretty bad, but I'm really sorry. I'm asking you for a favor here. You help people all over the world and you won't help an old friend. This is not gonna look good when I go to Entertainment Tonight and tell them how the real Candy Katz won't even help a friend in need."

Damn she was good! For a tiny moment, I felt confused about what to do. Then I put my shoulders back and lifted my chin.

"Mindy, not only are you a gypsy whore, a backstabber, and not nice, I think you're really, really shallow. I can't hang out with someone like you anymore. Not only is it bad for my karma, but I find you kind of boring now. But you know, if you ever want to turn your life around, I can hire you for $25 dollars an hour in my warehouse packing boxes of food, but you'll have to take off your hair extensions. I have a policy of no Indian hair extensions in my organization. I think it'd be good for you to see how it feels to help other people."

"Bite your tongue, Candy. I'd rather find some vulnerable ugly schmuck with money and marry him."

"Well, okay, good luck with that." I said and she just stood there quiet for two minutes at least. I was waiting for her to get back in the water and swim away, but she wasn't.

"So, okay, you have to leave."

"You mean now?" Mindy asked.

"Yeah. Go. Get back in your boat and row back to wherever it is that you came from."

"Candy, you haven't seen the last of me." She hissed in my face.

I thought back to when she could make me pee in my pants with just a mean look, but this time I felt nothing. I wasn't afraid, I wasn't worried and most importantly, she didn't scare even one drop of pee out of me. But then, just as she was about to get back into the water to swim to her boat and row away, I had a change of heart.

"You know, Mindy, if you want to go out my side gate instead of getting back in that dirty water, that'd be okay. In fact, here, you can have this towel."

She snapped the towel I held up out of my hands and oh, my God, she had tears in her eyes. Mindy Klein was about to cry, and all I could think of to say to her was...

"Bye-bye."

ABOUT THE AUTHOR

Rae Weiser lives in Los Angeles. This is her second work of fiction, but her first stab at comedy. She hopes she has not fallen on her sword because that would hurt, like really super-duper hurt.

CPSIA information can be obtained
at www.ICGtesting.com
Printed in the USA
FSHW01n0752170518
48357FS